the summer we danced

THE DESTIN DIARIES

HOPE HOLLOWAY

AND

CECELIA SCOTT

The Summer We Danced

The Destin Diaries – Book 2

Hope Holloway & Cecelia Scott

Copyright © 2025 Hope Holloway

The Destin Diaries

May 30, 1990

It's summer again!!

Excuse this messy handwriting, diary. I'm in the van because—happy news alert—we are on our way back to Destin!! I'm so excited I could scream. But I don't have to make any noise because buttpain Crista has been doing enough of that since we left Atlanta. If whining was an Olympic sport, my little sister would get a gold medal.

At least I didn't have to go all the way back to "steerage"—which is what Dad calls the third row. (Not sure anyone could steer from back there but, okay, Dad.)

Eli and his friend Peter (♥) are back there with their noses stuck into their Game Boys playing Super Mario Land. (Why do they care so much about plumbers in overalls?) They should pay attention to real life because we are going back to the summer house on Gulf Shore Drive, and that means I'm finally going to see Kate and Tessa Wylie again!

Mom said Aunt Jo Ellen and Uncle Artie (who, reminder, diary, they aren't our "real" aunt and uncle, but Mom and Dad's friends from college—Go Dawgs!) left Ithaca yesterday and spent last night in Virginia. They should get to Destin right after we do! I cannot wait!!!

This is our second summer in a row, but this year is going to be totally different! Like me, Kate and Tessa (the opposite twins) are THIRTEEN now! We're teenagers!

I wonder if the Wylie girls have changed. They sent us a Christmas card with a picture of them in snow up to their knees! I hope they are exactly the same. Except I hope Tessa didn't get any prettier—she was already like a supermodel last year. And Kate is still the smartest girl in the world—she won her STATE science fair. Oh, and she got glasses which she hates but I think they're cute.

Anyway, I cannot wait to swim and sunbathe and dance to our song—"Walkin' on Sunshine"! Woohoo!

That little house will be crowded, like last year. Four girls in one room (Crista wailing because she has to sleep in a sleeping bag until one of us takes pity and lets her in a bed). The "rents" each have a room, and Eli and Peter sleep on a bunk bed in that sunroom in the back.

The boys are sixteen, and they can drive this year! I can just see it now...cruising down 98, windows open, wind in my hair, sitting next to Peter!

It should be so mu—

Ugh. I had to cover this up fast because Crista dropped her stupid stuffed bunny and

Peter got out of his seatbelt to get it for her. Which meant HE COULD HAVE SEEN THIS DIARY. Disaster Alert!!

I wouldn't want him to know I have a teeny tiny microscopic crush on him. But I'm thirteen now! Maybe he'll notice me.

I have to go—Crista is DEMANDING I play a card game with her, but after this, I'll be done constantly entertaining a seven-year-old. We are two hours from the beach, the sun, my best friends, and the most epic summer of our lives! What will happen this year? I get so excited thinking about it. I'll share here, natch!

Destin awaits!

Vivien, now a teenager!!!

Chapter One
Crista

Present Day

As she made the turn onto Gulf Shore Drive, Crista's headlights illuminated the long stone drive first, then landed on three stories of white stucco, teal shutters, and decorative railings.

The new Destin beach house stood proud and stunning, a far cry from the ramshackle summer cottage of their childhood. Well-placed sconces lit the architectural masterpiece so it gleamed against the night sky, a beacon of new hopes and old memories.

And Crista Merritt sat, once again, on the outside... looking in.

For one thing, their mother kept the fact that she owned the property a secret for thirty years, in typical Maggie Lawson fashion. Then, only Crista's older brother, Eli, knew about it, charged with taking down the old house, then designing and building this behemoth on the beach.

Next, her older sister, Vivien, had been recruited to decorate and stage the place, so the two of them moved in for a month. And the final insult? They'd had so much fun the past four weeks that they wanted to ditch the plans to sell it—which would have made Crista, Vivien, and Eli all a small fortune—and keep this house in the family forever.

While this unfolded last month, Crista was stuck in Atlanta, struggling with her daughter, bickering with her husband, and getting told what to do by her mother. Including being sent on this fun little errand—driving five and a half grueling hours to inform her siblings that they'd been unknowingly fraternizing with the enemy.

And that, Maggie had insisted, had to end.

She turned off the engine and took a deep breath, giving herself the pep talk she needed to hear more often lately: *Don't lose it, Crista. Don't blow in there like an emotional hurricane and fling this terrible news in their faces.*

She knew she'd long ago been pegged a "drama queen" by her family, but she'd mostly outgrown her penchant for overreacting. But lately, she'd slipped into her old ways. That could happen again, considering how tense she was—and this news *was* dramatic.

Would her brother and sister understand that what she was about to tell them changed everything about their father's death? Like *it didn't have to happen!* And would they understand that they could not, under any circumstances, ever talk to anyone with the last name Wylie again?

She stepped out into the night air, but the soothing effect of the Gulf breeze couldn't calm the storm inside her. She was here to deliver a message that would shatter any illusions about the so-called "friends" that Vivien and Eli had reunited with over the past month.

A whiff of saltwater and jasmine wafted memories over her. She had been just a kid—a child, really—when they'd spent seven summers here. Back then, the old Summer House had been noisy, cramped, and chaotic, filled with too many people and not enough space. But it had been magical all the same.

She'd idolized her older siblings and their friends, even if they barely noticed her.

Crista slammed the car door, heading toward stairs that led up to the entrance, stopping mid step when the front light bathed her in yellow and she heard the click of the lock inside.

In the open doorway, she saw the silhouette of her ever-reliable, ever-steady older brother. Eli's salt-and-pepper hair was tousled, his smile warm at first, faltering as he got a good look at her.

She always wore her emotions all over her face, and tonight was no different.

"Crista?" His voice was a mix of surprise and concern.

"What? Did you say Crista?" Out of sight, her sister Vivien's voice rose, tinged with excitement.

"Yes!" Eli pulled the door even wider, and she stepped inside, the air-conditioned coolness biting at her flushed skin.

"I have to talk to you," she said, her voice tight and breathless, her head a little light in anticipation. "I have to talk to both of you. It's really important."

"I'm right here." Vivien appeared in the entryway and darted toward her, arms outstretched, her face lighting up. "What a wonderful surprise! I can't believe it!"

But Crista held up her hands, stopping her sister in her tracks. "What you are not going to believe is what Mama told me this morning."

She stepped past them, her sneakers squeaking on pristine hardwood floors as she tossed her handbag onto the entry table. The house was breathtaking, but Crista barely noticed. She was too consumed by the revelation that had upended everything she thought she knew.

As she came around a corner, Crista froze at the sight of Eli's son. Her thirty-year-old nephew was standing near the kitchen island, a dish towel slung over his shoulder, his expression calm but curious.

"*Jonah?* What are you doing here?" she asked, shocked to see him for the first time in years.

"Hi, Aunt Crista," Jonah said easily, shaking back long hair that made him look like he should be in a rock band, not the kitchen. "I'm living here now."

"Me, too!"

Crista turned and blinked at Lacey. Vivien's daughter was here? The young woman practically bounded toward her. "It's great to have you here! Did you bring Nolie?"

Crista hardly heard her niece's bubbly enthusiasm. Her gaze darted between Jonah and Lacey, her mind reeling.

"All of you are here? The whole..." She shook her head, unable to finish the thought. "Never mind. That shouldn't surprise me. What is it about this town that makes me the family pariah?"

"No!" Vivien exclaimed, stepping closer. "We're so happy—"

"You won't be," Crista interjected, knowing she had to get it all out before the niceties and small talk. "When I tell you what I drove five hours and fifteen minutes to say to your faces, you will not be happy. You might abandon the idea of keeping this house, and you will, I assure you, never lay eyes on anyone with the last name of Wylie ever again."

Eli drew back, his brow furrowing. "What?"

"Didn't you say you'd seen them?" she asked. "The Wylies? That they'd been here? You have no idea what that family did to us, Eli."

"Crista, stop," Eli said firmly, lifting his hands as if to quiet her. "Whatever you are about to—"

"You need to know this," she insisted. "You need to know that if it weren't for Arthur Wylie, our father would still be alive. He would never have gone to jail, only to die alone in his cell."

The words spilled out of her like a flood, unstoppable and raw, followed by a stunned silence and every eye on her.

"It's true," she continued. "Some ethics professor, huh? Our dear 'Uncle Artie' totally stabbed his best friend in the back, and we would still have a father if it weren't for that snake. Now, do you want to talk to anyone named Wylie?"

"This can't be true," Eli said, his voice only a rough whisper.

"Oh, it's true. Mama told me today," Crista said, finally catching her breath. "It's why she doesn't want to come here and why they never talked after that. But when I told her you said you'd seen those Wylie girls, she exploded. She called them the devil's daughters."

"Excuse me?" The voice came from the landing, cold and sharp.

Crista whipped around, her heart plummeting as her worst fear materialized before her. Thirty long years might have passed, but that tall blonde with the movie star face and blazing amber eyes could only be...

"Are you...who I think you are?" Crista asked, hoping she was wrong.

The other woman took one step forward, her hands trembling but her voice strong. "I'm the woman who's going to kill you if you speak one more word against my father."

The heat rose to Crista's face as she stared at the daughter of the man who had ruined their family. The woman whose presence in this house was a slap in the face to everyone who missed Roger Lawson.

"Tessa," Crista whispered, struggling to get the name out. "I...I can't talk to you. I'm sorry, but I think you should leave. I don't...you shouldn't be here. You need to leave this minute."

Before Tessa could respond, Jonah stepped forward, his voice calm, but his grip on her arm firm. "And you need to chill the hell out, Aunt Crista."

Crista jerked her arm away. "I will not chill. I can't be in the same room as a Wylie."

"Will you please be reasonable, Crista?" Eli interjected, his voice tight with frustration.

"Reasonable?" Crista spat, turning on her brother. "Her father basically killed our father!"

"He did not!" Tessa shouted, shooting forward, but Jonah moved between them, his broad shoulders blocking her path. "He did no such thing!"

Tension snapped like a taut rubber band as Crista crossed her arms and glared at Tessa, getting a golden-eyed scowl in return.

"I have the facts," Crista said, keeping her voice as level as she could. "And you probably know it's true! Why would you come here?"

Tessa closed her eyes, her lips trembling. Crista struggled to steady herself, a pang of guilt flickering briefly before her anger swallowed it whole.

"I'm sorry but..." Crista took a slow, deep breath. "You are not welcome here."

Lacey stepped forward, her face flushed as she hugged Tessa. *I hugged* her! "She is so welcome here."

"Lacey!" Crista exclaimed, her voice rising in disbelief. "Did you hear what I said?"

"The whole beach heard you," Lacey shot back. "But that doesn't make it true."

"It's not..." Tessa's voice cracked. "It can't be. He'd never... My father didn't have a disloyal bone in his body."

Crista's eyes narrowed, the bitterness rising in her

throat. "Really? Well, that's not what I heard this morning."

Tessa's face crumpled, and she pressed her fingers to her temples, as if trying to block out the words. "He's not here to defend himself," she murmured. "He's dead, and you can't talk about him like this! He's dead!" She looked like she might buckle if Lacey hadn't been holding her.

Crista closed her eyes. "I'm sorry for you," she whispered. "Sadly, we know how hard it is to lose your father. But, under the circumstances, I think it's best if you leave our house."

"Crista!" Vivien's voice was as sharp as her scowl. "You don't even know this woman. You're just doing what you always do—parroting Maggie."

Crista grunted with frustration. Yes, she was here doing her mother's dirty work. But their father went to prison and died there because of Artie Wylie. That changed everything. Didn't they see that?

Looking around at their expressions of disapproval aimed at her, it appeared they did not.

"Believe me, I don't want to—I don't," she insisted. "I know you all think I'm Maggie two-point-oh, but it's not true. This is not a rumor or gossip or a memory. This is a fact. He was the reason Dad went to jail, where he died."

White as a ghost, Tessa held up a shaky finger and pointed at Crista. "You have no idea what you're talking about. My father was a paragon of virtue and integrity. No finer man ever lived. And yours?" She gave a bitter, humorless laugh. "A common criminal convicted of fraud, embezzlement, and theft."

Crista gasped and looked at Eli, waiting for him to rise to their father's defense, but he just flinched, his jaw tightening, his eyes closing as though he'd taken a punch to the face.

Tessa looked at him, too, her face softening slightly. "I'm sorry, Eli. I know that hurts you. But…" She shook her head, taking a step back. "Never mind. I don't want to do this. I don't… I can't…" She turned on her heel and strode toward the back of the house. "You win. The Lawsons win. I'll leave now."

"Tessa!" Lacey called, running after her. The sound of her footsteps echoed down the hall, leaving the rest of them standing in awkward silence.

Vivien turned to Crista, her expression both disappointed and weary.

Jonah's face looked pale, his lips pressed into a thin line.

And Eli? Crista couldn't stand to look at her big brother. The sadness in his eyes was unbearable.

Silent, Eli stepped out onto a dimly lit deck, disappearing from sight. Crista's shoulders slumped, the fire that had driven her here slowly cooling into ash. She hadn't meant to hurt him. Or Jonah. Or Vivien. But what choice did she have? They needed to know the truth.

Plus, she'd given her word to her mother she'd tell them and get them to agree never to speak to a Wylie again.

Vivien followed Eli outside, and Crista remained in the living room, her arms crossed over her chest as she tried to come down from the adrenaline rush. She glanced toward the hallway where Tessa and Lacey had disappeared, her stomach churning with a mix of guilt and anger.

What if Maggie had been wrong? What if it wasn't as simple as Artie Wylie betraying Roger?

Her fingers tightened on her arms, her nails digging into her skin. A flash of her daughter and husband danced through her head, a reminder that the perfect life she'd built back in Atlanta felt like it was hanging by a thread. Her sudden bouts of temper like this were certainly not helping her rocky marriage or Nolie's challenges in school.

Slightly calmer, she looked out toward the deck, where Eli and Vivien were deep in conversation, their heads close. Like every other moment she'd spent in Destin, they were keeping her out of the inner circle, having lives and friends and conversations she was too young and too distant to enjoy.

And what had she done to change that? Forget drama queen. She'd come in like the Grand Empress of Theatrics, proving that some things never change.

"Aunt Crista." Jonah put a light arm around her, his hazel eyes looking clear and warm. "Can I get you something to eat or drink?"

She smiled up at her handsome nephew, who she hadn't seen in way too long. On a sigh, she dropped her head on his strong shoulder. As fast as it came on, the fight left her body.

"Yeah, I'll have a great big bowl of damage control."

He chuckled and gave her a squeeze. "Around here we call that a gin and tonic. Coming right up."

Chapter Two

Eli

Standing against the railing next to his sister, Eli closed his eyes as Vivien delivered a whispered pep talk about how he was the architect to build bridges between the families.

All he could hear in his head was...

You will never lay eyes on anyone with the last name of Wylie ever again!

Crista's histrionics aside, he knew who'd really issued that decree. He didn't know why—Crista hadn't actually explained anything other than sweeping accusations with no specifics. Did it matter? Only one person in this family had the power to tell all of them what to do, when to do it, and what the price would be for disobeying.

When Maggie Lawson told her grown children what to do, they usually did it.

But never in his life had so much been at stake. He'd either lose his mother...or Kate Wylie, the woman he'd only just realized he loved.

"Hey."

They both turned at the sound of Crista's voice. She stepped outside onto the deck, the lights in the house silhouetting her narrow figure. Her hair was weirdly wild

—she normally managed to tame her dark curls into smooth submission. Her shoulders seemed a little slumped, as if the fight had gone out of them, or maybe they were just pressed by the weight of her job tonight. She seemed even more petite than usual, and very, very sad.

At ten years her senior, Eli had often felt like both brother and father figure to his perfectionist little sister. Especially tonight, despite how her arrival had damaged the lovely peace they'd spent a month happily building at the Summer House.

Poor kid. It wasn't easy being Maggie's messenger.

"Come on out, Cris," he said, taking a step forward. "Let's start over with a nice family hello."

She smiled and lifted a red Solo cup. "Jonah's version of a greeting. It's strong and I'm dizzy enough. Want it?"

He shook his head and led her to the grouping of furniture around a coffee table. "Have a seat."

Before she did, Vivien came closer, the two of them regarding each other in silence.

Crista blew out a breath, caving first. "Hurricane Crista, cat five, has arrived."

Vivien smiled at the ice-breaker. "Hey, it's Florida. We get hurricanes here." With that, she put her arms around Crista and closed her eyes. "Sit down and tell us everything, okay? Without..."

"Raising my voice?" Crista suggested with a wry self-deprecating laugh. "I'll try, but it's...upsetting. I'm really upset and when I saw her..." She huffed out a breath. "Yeah."

Vivien reached for a throw blanket on the back of the sofa and Eli touched the wall switch to turn on the fire feature built into the coffee table.

Crista sat down on the sofa and took a sip, then quickly set the cup down. "Look, I'm sorry for...that. I was stunned to see her, is all. But..." She bit her lip and looked over the dancing flames into Eli's eyes. "I stand by my position. We cannot fraternize with that family."

Fraternize? Eli almost laughed. Should he tell her that he'd fallen so hard for Kate Wylie he couldn't see straight? That he planned to get her down here from Ithaca this summer with her two kids? That Tessa and Lacey had started an event planning business together and they'd basically been one big happy family for almost five weeks?

God forbid.

No. The God he loved would never forbid that. But his mother would.

He opted to start on slightly more neutral territory— the house. He made a vague gesture around them. "So what do you think of the Summer House, twenty-first century version?"

"It's nice." She gave an easy laugh. "Understatement alert, and I'm not known for those."

Eli smiled. "It's fine, Cris. We know you're upset. We just don't quite understand why."

"Well, this house is a work of art," she said. "I mean, wow, what a flip. I can't believe it's the same place we came and stayed as kids."

"Just the same piece of land," Eli said. "Although we

saved a few things from the original place, like the front door, which has been repurposed as the pantry door. And some ancient window glass. What else?" he asked Vivien.

"My diaries," she said. "Those are a good time."

Crista rolled her eyes. "I can only imagine." She air-quoted, "'Crista had a meltdown.'"

Vivien snorted. "That's in there."

Crista smiled, but her expression grew pained as it became obvious that they had to stop the small talk and get down to the business of why she was here.

"This is very serious, you guys." She closed her eyes. "I'm sorry, but Artic Wylie is responsible for Dad's death."

"How?" Eli demanded. "Do you realize you haven't told us yet?"

She nodded, taking another sip, but the booze made her shudder so she put the cup down and slid it away. "I couldn't tell you while she—"

"Tell us now," Vivien interrupted with an impatient look.

"Artie Wylie turned Dad in to the police," she said softly.

Eli stared at her, quite literally unable to breathe. He couldn't have heard that right.

"He discovered...something, I don't know what. And he went straight to the cops and because of him, because of his gross disloyalty to his best friend, the police launched an investigation that sent our father to prison. And prison, we all know, caused him to have a fatal heart attack. So, Artie is responsible for our father's death."

Eli shook his head. "How? When? Why didn't we know this?"

"My answer to all your questions is a fat, I don't know," Crista said. "I have just told you the sum total of what Mama would share with me. You know how she is."

Vivien grunted. "Information is power, and she wants it all."

Crista angled her head in concession. "But she wanted us to know that much, especially after you said... *they'd* been here."

"They?" Eli scoffed, ire rising at the word. "*They* have names. Kate and Tessa Wylie."

"Is Kate here, too?" Crista asked on a gasp.

"No, but she was," Vivien said, sneaking a look at Eli.

"So now it's just"—Crista jutted her chin—"her."

"Yes, just Tessa," Eli replied. "For now."

"Well, she needs to leave. There's no debating this, Eli. Mama would have a cow."

He managed not to roll his eyes, having not called Maggie anything but "Mom" or her first name since he was twelve. But to Crista, she was "Mama."

Honestly, it didn't matter how they referred to her— she called the shots in the Lawson family.

As for a debate? There'd be plenty of debate when the truth came out. And he'd have to tell his mother eventually, wouldn't he? He wasn't going to hide his feelings for Kate. This whole household already knew he and Kate were on the brink of...something.

Something that could disappear as fast as it had happened under the weight of a revelation like this.

What if it were true? Could he love Kate if her father played a role in Dad's arrest?

Yes, but it would introduce one incredibly ugly complication.

"Why don't you tell us every single thing Mom said," Vivien suggested to Crista. "Because this narrative doesn't fit anything we know."

"It's not a *narrative*," Crista shot back. "It's a fact that I suppose you could look up in police investigation files."

Eli shared another look with Vivien, knowing she was thinking exactly what he was—they could contact Peter McCarthy, their friend and a detective in Pensacola. Maybe he could look up those files.

"What did she say, Crista?" Eli pressed. "Exactly, word for word."

"It was the typical conversation with Maggie Lawson," she said with a shrug.

"In other words, she told you what to think," Vivien said dryly.

"Pretty much," Crista muttered, the comment surprising. Had he ever heard Crista utter an unkind word about their mother? "But Mama has strong feelings about things," she added, as if she felt guilty even for implying anything negative about Maggie. "Some people do, you know. I appreciate that you hate conflict, Viv, but sometimes conflict is necessary."

Eli looked from one sister to the other, who'd always been different on the subject of conflict.

Vivien hated it and usually capitulated, a pacifier in most situations, though she'd been working on her backbone this past month. But Crista seemed to thrive on conflict, along with a crippling need to have everything as perfect as she could make it.

All of which made him wonder just how hunky-dory it really was living with Maggie.

"Come on, Cris," Vivien urged. "Time, dates, details? We need to know."

Crista inhaled slowly, gathering her thoughts. "We were on our way to the airport for her big month-long trip to Europe with her gardening club. I told her that you two had called me to see what I thought about the possibility of keeping this house instead of selling it. And I told her that I thought that was something worth considering," Crista added. "Because I do."

She did? Eli felt his brow raise. He hadn't been expecting that.

Vivien reacted, too. "I'm glad you do, Crista," she said. "It's an incredible place—"

Crista held up her hand. "But it was given to us by our mother for the sole purpose of selling it for a profit to make up for what we went through with Dad," she reminded them.

What they went through? A familiar disgust hit Eli in the chest at the thought of the decisions his father had made, the crimes he'd committed, and the shame he'd brought to the family name.

But somehow, his mother—wily and secretive as she was—had managed to squirrel away the beach cottage that Dad bought only a month before he was arrested, hiding the asset in a trust. For thirty years, she'd rented it out through an attorney, accumulating a considerable amount.

She'd used that money to hire Eli as the architect of this house, cleverly waiting until the statute of limitations on Dad's crimes had passed. The law said that the house, or the profit from its sale, belonged to Roger's three children, since their father had died while serving his sentence.

"Is she opposed to us keeping it?" Eli asked.

Crista shrugged. "Surprisingly, no. At first, she was a little taken aback because she knows that kind of financial windfall would be amazing for all of us."

True. No one could argue that the cash from selling this place, even split three ways, would be a boon to all of their lives.

"She reminded me that under the weird loophole that her attorney found, we are legally permitted to sell and keep the profit, on or after the thirty-year anniversary of his death. Likewise, we are also permitted to keep the house. It's our choice."

Eli and Vivien shared a look, liking this news. They both fully expected Maggie to balk at the idea of keeping the house, but maybe she had recognized that it was their house to do with as they wanted.

"But then," Crista continued, falling back as if the story was just too much, "the ground shook when I mentioned you'd been in touch with the Wylies. I made a game-time decision not to tell her they'd been here because...well, I could read the room. Or, in this case, the car. At the mention of the Wylies, she flipped out."

"Eesh," Vivien muttered. "Never fun."

"No, it wasn't." Crista's eyes shuttered. "She ordered me to tell you in no uncertain terms that we—none of us, all of us—are never, ever to speak to anyone from that family ever again. This is not negotiable. She said that our father would never have gone to prison if Artie hadn't ratted on Dad to the police. Because of that tip—from a Cornell Law ethics professor, no less—they launched an investigation and the rest, as you know, is sad history."

A sad and sickening history that had become etched in Eli's life and heart.

"A history," Crista continued, "that could have been avoided if Artie Wylie had kept his mouth shut and looked the other way, at least according to our mother."

"Did she say how or why Artie would turn him in?" Vivien asked.

Crista shook her head. "She just said that he did, and that's what ended their friendship and our summers in Destin with the Wylie family. She said that Artie Wylie was a 'pompous goody two shoes'—that's a quote—who somehow sniffed out that Dad was, um...doing some untoward things."

Eli shifted in his seat and cast his gaze down. After thirty years, he still physically loathed the subject of Dad's crimes. It hurt him body, soul, and spirit. And it had made him determined to be the polar opposite of his father, even though he had followed in his professional footsteps and become an architect.

"I know Artie taught ethics, so he should have known it was wrong to ruin all those lives," Crista said, coming forward to look hard at them. "There's such a thing as loyalty to your friends, you know. That's ethical, too."

"That's why we're defending Tessa," Vivien said. "She's become a friend. So has Kate."

Crista grunted with visible disgust, and Eli fought the urge to respond. Not yet. He couldn't tell her yet. But he would, eventually.

"That won't go over well with Mama," she said. "In fact...I'd rather she never found that out. The Wylie family is...our mortal enemy. If it weren't for them, Dad would be alive today."

"Quit saying that, Crista." Eli's words came out harsher than he meant them to, but he was sick of hearing a phrase that surely came straight from Maggie's lips. "There's got to be more to the story. If it's true, there's got to be a reason for Artie to make that decision."

"Who cares what his rationale was?" Crista volleyed back. "I don't need to know why he stabbed his best friend in the back. But I do know this—Mama made it clear that we are not to have anything to do with that family. Period, end of story. What difference does it make? They've been out of our lives for thirty years and they can stay that way."

Eli winced and Vivien shot him a look that Crista definitely noticed.

"Why did you even get in touch with them?" she asked, fixing her gaze on Vivien.

"I wanted to talk to Kate," Vivien said. "Finding out Mom still owned this property made me want to reconnect with two of my childhood best friends."

"But you knew we don't talk to them," Crista said.

"I knew our parents had a falling out, and no one had any idea why until you came in here tonight. Not them, not us." Vivien inched closer. "We had great memories of those seven summers. We honestly wanted to recreate them, and this past month? We have."

"Well, how nice for you," Crista said coolly. "My memories of those summers weren't as spectacular."

"Oh, Crista." Vivien made a face. "I hate that."

"Whatever," she said, flicking off the sympathy. "I loved it here, too, but I was lonely a lot of the time. And at the end of those summers? You two were both in college, Dad went to jail, and Mama and I had to move into an apartment. She was never home because she had to work at that dentist's office, remember?"

Eli sighed. "You know what, Cris? That's a valid gripe. You were alone a lot those summers and as teenagers, we never really went out of our way to include a kid so much younger. And you're right. During the worst of the legal wrangling, we were away at college and it was a lot easier for us to separate from Dad's arrest. Then you ended up living with Mom, and she had to work."

"I'm still living with Mom," she said, a weirdly droll note in her voice as she lifted the cup again, but didn't drink.

"And that's okay, isn't it?" Vivien asked, obviously hearing it, too.

"Oh, sure, it's..." She tipped the cup from side to side,

then put it down. "Is this truth serum? I've hardly had a drop but definitely feel it."

Eli leaned closer. "Is everything all right with you?"

For a second, she looked like she might cry—no surprise, this was Crista the Crier. But it was the pain in her expression that got him. The deep, real pain that wasn't just being annoyed by their mother.

"Crista?" He reached his hand out, but she drew back.

"Nothing's going on," she said, crossing her arms. "Nothing at all."

Whoa, it might be worse than he realized. Of course she'd keep quiet about problems—she'd inherited that trait, or learned it, from Maggie. Add to it that having the appearance of a perfect life was very, very important to her, and...yeah.

His little sister had problems.

"Maybe you could spend some time here," Vivien suggested, no doubt picking up all the same things. "This summer? When Nolie's out of school?"

She shook her head. "No, we'll have other things to do this summer," she said vaguely, again giving the impression there was more she wasn't saying.

"Can you stay a few days?" Eli asked. "Destin's so good for the soul and we can keep talking." Not only did he think that might help her, but he also had to break the news to her about Kate.

"My soul is fine," she said lightly, then smiled. "Maybe not as fine as yours, Eli, but then, I don't go to church like you."

"But I do want to keep the dialogue open," he said, not willing to give up. "Please think about it."

She closed her eyes. "I'm not thinking about anything until both of you promise there will never be anyone named Wylie in this house again."

Was she serious? Eli grunted softly and closed his eyes.

"You can't promise that?"

He ran a hand through his hair, a band of pressure around his chest as he rooted around for the right words.

"Look, Cris," he said. "We completely understand and respect that there's a tough history here, especially for our mother. We love her, too, and would never want to upset her. But she's not always right about everything. There could be much more to the story or even another side to the story. Or it could be a regret that Artie took to his grave."

He almost told her that he and Kate had gone to visit old family friends in search of answers about the falling out, and they'd given conflicting—and ridiculous—stories about the couples having affairs with each other. But what if there was truth to that?

She'd flip out. Eli, Kate, Tessa, and Vivien had all agreed that allegation was simply preposterous.

"Honestly, Tessa and Kate didn't even know our father had died," Vivien told her. "Furthermore, they knew he went to jail but never once in the time we've been together has anyone ever said anything about Artie telling the police."

"Not a word," Eli agreed. "And people's memories

get foggy, especially as they get older. Mom's seventy-eight..." He made a face and held up a hand as if he expected an argument. "I know you two are very close, but..."

Crista's shoulders sagged. "Not quite like we used to be," she admitted under her breath.

He knew it. "What do you mean? You and Mom are best friends. I mean, she lives with you, and you named your daughter after her."

"I did and I would do it again," she said. "I love Mama more than anything. But things...have been really hard recently." Her voice cracked slightly, tears threatening.

Vivien leaned in, touching Crista's arm. "Hey. You want to talk about it?"

"No, I'm just...emotional lately. More than, you know, usual." She managed a quick laugh at herself, which touched Eli.

"You want to know something?" she asked after a moment. "The times you two did include me during those Destin summers? It was pure heaven. And I've been wanting some of that inclusion. I knew you were down here having fun and I...wasn't."

"But now you are," Eli said. "So stay."

She shook her head. "I can't. Anthony can't handle Nolie alone that long. She's got... a lot going on in school."

"It feels like you're the one with a lot going on, hun," Vivien said, putting an arm around her little sister. "No wonder you encouraged Maggie to go to the Netherlands."

Crista gave a guilty laugh. "Maybe a little."

"Well, she's gone for a while," Eli said. "Could you bring Nolie down? She's only in second grade. Could she miss a few weeks of school?"

"Please, she'd love nothing more, but..." She tipped her head toward the house. "Will *she* still be here?"

"Yes." Eli and Vivien answered in perfect sibling unity, the response instantly getting a rise from Crista.

"Why?" she demanded, sitting up like she might have to rocket to her feet again to make her point. "She's not family. She doesn't belong in our house!"

"She's our friend," Vivien said. "And Lacey's working for her."

Crista eyes widened. "What exactly has been going on in this house for the past month?"

Eli shifted in his seat, not ready to get into anything more right now. "Just think about it tonight, Cris."

"I have to get a hotel."

"Are you crazy?" Vivien asked. "This place is huge. I'll move Lacey back in with me," she added under her breath to Eli. "Crista can have Ka—the spare room."

Crista instantly stood up and froze, then dropped right back down. "Either I had more of that drink than I realized or I'm just wiped out. I'll go back tomorrow."

"I'll put clean sheets on the bed," Vivien said, standing.

"And I'll get your bags," Eli said. "Assuming you have them."

"One, an overnight bag."

"Good. Then you'll at least stay tonight." He leaned over and kissed her on the head. "And longer, if we're lucky."

She looked up at him, more of that sadness in her expression.

"Because it's more fun with you, Crista," he added.

She rolled her eyes. "Liar. It's just like it always was. Y'all are one little unit and I'm on the outside looking in."

"But this time we'll let you drink at the bonfires with the big kids."

"Depends on who the kids are," she said. "Because the price to get into the ever-elusive Big Kid Club might be my relationship with my mother."

No one knew that better than Eli.

Oh, Maggie. Why did she make everything so difficult?

Chapter Three
Tessa

Tessa flung another blouse into her open suitcase, the fabric barely landing inside before Lacey snapped it back out.

"What are you doing?" Lacey demanded, grasping the garment with two hands and pressing it to her chest like the top was Tessa herself. "You don't need to leave, Tessa."

Tessa pivoted into the closet, scooped an armful of hanging clothes, and tossed them on the bed. "Lacey, you're sweet, and I get that you don't want me to go. But what your Aunt Crista just accused my father of is completely unacceptable."

"First of all, she's the family drama llama and doesn't even deny it," Lacey said. "Second, how could your dad be responsible for my grandfather's death? He died in prison of a heart attack. Your father had nothing to do with it."

Tessa's throat grew so tight, she couldn't respond. Forcing herself not to replay the words, she slid a dress from its hanger with trembling fingers.

"Tessa, even I know the family's history," Lacey said. "My grandparents and your parents never spoke again after that last summer. There was a hurricane and this house—or what it used to be—got wrecked. No one except Uncle Eli even knew until a month ago that my Grandma Maggie owned it."

"There was a reason for that falling out," Tessa said.

"But my grandfather didn't die until a long time later. They had a fight, is all. People do." Lacey dropped on the bed and put a hand on the suitcase. "You can't leave."

The true ache in her voice touched Tessa, and echoed exactly how she felt. "Well, I sure can't stay."

"Aunt Crista's just trying to get her way, which, nine times out of ten, is Grandma Maggie's way. She does anything my grandmother tells her—it drives my mom crazy sometimes. And Crista's always looking for attention. Classic baby of the family, you know?"

Well, she certainly got attention tonight.

"There has to be some foundation for what she said," Tessa said, gnawing at her lip. "Maybe he testified against Roger and that's why she thinks he's responsible." She thought about that for a moment. "He was a legal ethics professor. He'd be a powerful witness."

"Would he do that?"

"I don't know," she said honestly. "He would only do the right thing—that's what drove him in life." *Unlike Roger,* she thought bitterly, unwilling to say it out loud to Lacey. She couldn't help the crimes her grandfather had committed.

"Even if he did testify against him, it's ancient history," Lacey said.

"Not to Crista."

"Remember who you're dealing with." Lacey looked skyward.

Tessa let out a dry laugh, though it did little to ease the ache in her chest. "Yeah, I can remember more than a few of her meltdowns from when she was little."

"See? It's just the way she is, although she has been a lot better since Nolie was born. This was over the top, even for her. Listen, I can't stand it if you leave, Tessa." Lacey's voice cracked. "We're starting a business. You're so much fun. You can't..."

Tessa zipped the suitcase with a sharp tug. "Maybe I'll stay around town, if she goes back to Atlanta. I'll find something to rent." Even as she said the words, she knew she wouldn't.

This was it. This was her end to Destin. It was time to run. She knew the feeling like she knew her name, like she knew breathing.

When the going gets tough, Tessa gets going...to her father.

Because that's where she always ran—to the arms and strong shoulders of the one person who truly believed in her.

But he was gone. And she had no one to turn to, really. Although judging by the look of pure love on Lacey's face, she could turn to her.

"I can't imagine how much it hurt you to have his name smeared," Lacey said, proving that look was genuine.

Somehow, this young woman—about half her age— deeply understood Tessa even after only knowing each other for a month. Or she wanted to, and that was touching, too.

"Hurt beyond description," Tessa said, taking a step toward the bathroom to pack her cosmetics.

"But if you leave, Tess, it's like you're saying you agree."

She froze. *Oh.* She hadn't really thought of it that way.

"Right?" Lacey said, hope lifting her voice when Tessa didn't move. "Stay tonight. Stay in your room, right here. I'll sleep down here if you want—I'm sure I'm getting booted out of Kate's room and back in with my mom."

Tessa smiled. "It did become Kate's room pretty fast," she said. "And this..." She looked around the guest room, one of the smaller bedrooms in this monstrous house and devoid of any furniture but a bed, a cheap temporary nightstand she'd bought, and a chair she'd found at Target.

Vivien was going to make this a pink room—Tessa had insisted—when she got around to staging the extra bedrooms. But even without a professional's touch, this little space felt like home.

Every morning, Tessa woke up feeling slightly more healed than she had the day before. She'd get her coffee, and feel her grief one ounce lighter than the day before. She'd step out on the deck, look at the sky, and know Dad was up there, watching out for her.

Well, he hadn't seen this coming. Unless...there was some truth to the accusations.

She turned and looked at Lacey. "What if he *is* somehow responsible for Roger going to prison? Directly or tangentially?"

Lacey angled her head and gave an "are you serious" scoff. "Tess, my grandfather, may he rest in peace but probably doesn't, committed a slew of white-collar crimes. No one is responsible for Roger going to prison except Roger. He was greedy, selfish, and believed himself to be above the law."

Tessa nodded, having had this conversation around the bonfire with Eli, who carried a lot of pain from his father's bad decisions.

"And there was nothing and no one my father hated more," Tessa said, "than someone who thought they were above the law."

The air in the room seemed to still as Tessa's mind flooded with memories of her father. His warm smile, his patient guidance, the endless hours they'd spent learning and loving each other whether it was over a textbook or on a fishing boat.

Artie Wylie wasn't just her father; he was her hero, the person who'd made her feel like she could do anything. He'd swooped in on more than one occasion and helped her out of her darkest places.

Losing him seven months ago was the single hardest thing she'd ever had to bear. But she had been healing—slowly and steadily.

Staying and listening to that wild-eyed woman rant lies about him would take her back to square one. And if Eli and Vivien thought their sister was right, then...

"No," she said, shaking her head. "I can't be here anymore, Lacey. I just can't."

"Tessa, drag your beautiful brain back to the fantastic event you managed today."

She gave a dry laugh. "Was that party today? It feels like a lifetime ago."

"Today, this very morning, you were ready to quit when Garrett's wife appeared and rocked your boat."

"Yeah, well, I didn't." She pointed at Lacey. "You're only good for one pep talk a day, young friend."

"Well, it's almost midnight, so I'm counting this as tomorrow." Lacey stood. "Don't run, Tessa Wylie."

Tessa stood stone still, closing her eyes, hearing the words, remembering all the times she'd chosen the easy way out.

"You can't just run away when things get difficult," Lacey pressed. "You know he'd hate that."

She didn't have to ask who *he* was. She smiled and looked at Lacey, placing her palm on the young woman's cheek, a splash of old feelings bubbling up.

"Where'd you come from, sweet girl? How'd you get to know me so well?"

Lacey put her hand over Tessa's. "What are you so scared of?" she whispered.

Tessa turned away and grabbed the edge of the open suitcase. "I... I don't know." She knew it was a lie, but, oh, it was late, and she was way too wiped out for a shrink session.

Plus, if she dug too deep, she'd get to...things she

didn't talk about. And Lacey, for reasons she'd never understood, had a way of pulling the truth out of Tessa.

"Yes, you do know," Lacey said. "And if you don't want to tell me, fine. But you have to be honest with yourself."

Tessa swallowed hard, feeling the old, familiar shame rise in her throat. She'd spent years running—not just from situations, but from herself. From the mistakes she'd made, the things she couldn't fix, the decisions—one in particular—that had broken her in ways no one could see.

But she always had her standard explanation at the ready.

"You know I've always felt a little...not smart," she said on a laugh.

"Dyslexia," Lacey said.

"I struggled to read. I battled my eyes and brain that refused to work like other people's. I got by on my looks and when people start to see through that?" She shrugged. "I take off."

"Tessa, none of that is at the heart of this issue. You have as much right to be here as Crista, who is probably leaving in the morning, if she hasn't already. Plus, I can't plan that Bat Mitzvah alone."

"Yes, you can. Anyway, there's plenty of time."

Lacey stepped closer and placed strong hands on Tessa's shoulders, looking her right in the eyes.

"How about this? I don't *want* to," Lacey said. "I want to do this with you! You're my mentor, my boss, my new auntie, my second mom—and if you tell my first one, she probably would agree."

Tessa tried to laugh, but her throat and heart betrayed her and it came out like a sob. Lacey had no idea what she was saying or how it touched her. Folded her. Darn near broke her in two.

"I'm not kidding," Lacey powered on. "You are the first person who helped me see my real future. Showed me a business and a path that feels right and real. You did that, in one month. Imagine where we'll be in a year. Unstoppable! You did that!"

Tessa just sighed, searching the young, dear face in front of her—the baby blue eyes, the sweet complexion, the wide and easy smile of a twenty-four year-old.

"Please don't leave," Lacey begged. "I need you."

Tessa sank onto the edge of the bed, letting out a noisy sigh.

"That's funny," she whispered, looking up at Lacey. "Because apparently I need you, too."

Lacey smiled, sitting next to her. "Then stay."

"Tonight," she finally said. "But I need to think about this, Lacey. I need to figure out what's best."

Lacey exhaled, relief washing over her face. "Okay. That's all I ask. Just think about it."

Lacey reached over and hugged her tightly. Tessa closed her eyes, letting the embrace ground her.

She was truly like a daughter...like a child she'd never had.

Tessa closed her eyes and squeezed Lacey a little tighter.

The next morning, Tessa sat at the dining table, a steaming cup of coffee next to her open laptop. The house was quiet, the first light of dawn glimmering on the Gulf, the sky pink toward the east.

She tore her gaze from the beautiful view to one that was ugly, strained, and wiggling.

Yes, today was a wiggly day on the computer, which might have been a function of the light. She highlighted the text and changed the font to Arial, which was always easier.

Her fingers hovered over the keyboard as she started writing a step-by-step guide for planning the Bat Mitzvah in case she decided to leave. But every time she tried to focus, her mind drifted back to the night before.

From the weight of Crista's accusations to the balm of Lacey's proclamations to her own dark night of bad dreams, Tessa had yet to make a decision about what to do.

She squinted and waited for the voices in her head and the visual noise on the screen to quiet so she could read. But the screen wasn't cooperating, so she picked up her pen and decided to go the old-fashioned way. She wrote down the words "understand mother's vision for Naomi's Bat Mitzvah" in large but neat writing.

Before she started point one, she heard footsteps upstairs. Was Eli up, or Vivien? Or...

Oh, boy. Here we go.

Crista came down slowly, wearing white pajamas with long pants and sleeves—wildly wintery and fancier than the sleep pants and T-shirts the other residents of the Summer House usually favored. Her hair was pulled back into a tight ponytail. Did she sleep like that? It looked uncomfortable. As she reached the landing, her sharp dark gaze landed on Tessa, and she froze.

The two of them just looked at each other, silence stretching out a few too many heartbeats.

"Don't shoot till you see the whites of my eyes," Tessa said, squinting at her. "And after last night? You might just see red around mine."

Crista didn't smile, but Tessa could have sworn her tight jaw loosened a bit.

"I'm unarmed," Crista said dryly. "Unless there's no coffee; then there might be a problem."

Ah, so an actual human resided under all that precision. Tessa pointed to the kitchen. "Pot's made. Knock yourself out."

She hesitated, visibly trying to make a decision, but clearly the need for caffeine won over all her principles.

Silent, she walked to the kitchen, found a cup, filled it, tore exactly one sheet from the paper towel holder, wiped a drop Tessa hadn't actually seen fall, then opened the fridge and repeated the entire thing with creamer.

She folded the paper towel and tucked it under the holder, presumably for the next wayward droplet.

Through the whole process, there was nothing but awkward silence.

Standing in the kitchen, Crista stared out at the water, slowly bringing the cup to her lips for her first taste. As she sipped, she closed her eyes and let out a nearly imperceptible moan.

"You always liked coffee," Tessa mused, suddenly transported a few decades in the past.

Crista turned and looked at her, a question in her eyes. Because Tessa had dared converse, or because of the odd comment?

"I remember that when you were little," Tessa said, "maybe eight or nine? You wanted coffee like the grownups and your mother wouldn't let you have it."

"But yours did," Crista said through her teeth, as though speaking pained her but the memory was too strong to ignore.

Tessa didn't reply as she waited to see what direction this conversation would take.

"When my mother would go out for her morning walk on the beach, Aunt Jo Ellen would give me half coffee, half milk, and way too much sugar." Crista let out a soft sigh. "I always liked your mother."

Tessa blinked, certainly not expecting that admission or...civility.

"I think she understood that I didn't have a friend like all the big kids, and she taught me how to play solitaire," Crista continued. "She called it Beat the Devil."

"To this day, still her favorite card game."

Crista took another sip, then put a hand on her stomach as if the coffee wasn't sitting well.

"Is she okay?" she asked after a few seconds. "Your mother, I mean."

"Not really." Tessa put down her pen and leaned back, eyeing the other woman mostly because she had no idea when she might turn into Xena: Warrior Princess and whip out her sword.

"Is she sick?" Crista asked.

"She's, um, heartbroken." She swallowed, knowing the rest of the story could cause trouble. "My father died very suddenly of rapidly growing pancreatic cancer seven months ago," she said. "Turbo cancer, they called it."

Crista made a face. "Oof."

"One day he was fine, had a doctor's appointment, and five weeks later, he was gone." She took a shaky breath. "It's been difficult for her. For all of us."

Crista just nodded, then lowered the cup and took a breath to speak.

Tessa held up her hand. "Listen, don't say anything bad about my father. Take up your beef with Eli and Vivien, but I worshipped that man. And I'm still mourning his death."

Crista looked down at her coffee, her face softening. "I already said what had to be said," she whispered, turning to the kitchen. "And I think I'd rather have tea."

"There's a selection in the pantry," Tessa said. "You'll have to heat the water with the microwave."

While Crista busied herself with a change in beverage, the silence stretched again, but this time it wasn't as heavy. She came back with the same cup—washed and dried—the string from a tea bag dangling over the side.

Tessa expected her to go outside or upstairs, but she stood near the dining table, checking out the obvious signs that it was being used as an office.

"I heard something about you and Lacey starting a business," she said. "Is this where you work?"

"Eli uses the office down the hall, so we set up here. We clean it up before dinner most nights."

"What do you do, exactly?"

"Event planning," Tessa told her, surprised she'd showed even that much interest. "And we have an actual client who wants us to plan a Bat Mitzvah. I'm making a list for Lacey in case I, well, because you want me to leave."

Her eyes shuttered. "It's what my mother wants and I...I can see her point."

Tessa looked away, her gaze falling on the document that really seemed wiggly now. "It's a shame, all of it."

"No kidding," Crista scoffed, taking a few steps closer to the table, her gaze landing on Tessa's short list. "What does that mean, 'understand the mother's vision'?"

"Exactly what it says," Tessa replied. "Before I plan an event I want to know what the client sees when she closes her eyes and imagines she's walking into the room the moment the party starts. The colors, the textures, what Lacey would call 'the vibe.'"

"Mmm. That sounds like a fun job." A whisper of a wistful smile pulled. "You were always fun."

"I do place a high value on a good time," Tessa confessed. "Life's too much of a struggle to not have fun."

Crista searched her face, an intensity in her espresso eyes.

"I can't imagine you struggling over anything," she

said. "I mean, look at you. Always the prettiest girl for miles and the center of attention."

Tessa managed a wry smile. "Oh, I struggled."

"Eli had such a crush on you."

She chuckled. "I've heard. Well, now he's..." She caught herself, instinctively guessing that Eli might have kept his budding romance with Kate from his younger sister. Anyway, the relationship was too new to even classify it as anything but friendship. "He's over that," she said instead. "And trust me, people do struggle on the inside even if you don't see it on the outside. I'm sure you know that."

Crista took a sip, her expression dubious.

"I mean, look at this mess." Tessa gestured to her notes. "The awkward writing of a dyslexic."

Crista almost spit her tea as she blurted, "What?"

"Oh, I never made a big deal out of it," Tessa said quickly. "But yeah. The words, they wiggle."

"You're dyslexic? How do you function?"

"Quite well. It's not a death sentence," she replied with a quick laugh. "It's just a challenge to manage, but I do fine most of the time."

Crista just stared at her, so hard Tessa could practically see the wheels turning in her head. Then she set the mug on the table, pulled out the chair across from Tessa, and sat down.

And no one could have been more surprised than Tessa.

"How did you know?" she asked. "And when? How

old were you? How did it manifest itself? When did you learn to read? Did you have to be held back or—"

"*Whoa.*" Tessa held up her hand at the onslaught of questions. "Where did this all come from?"

"I just...I'm curious and I want to..." She blew out a breath, closing her eyes. "I think my daughter might be dyslexic."

"*Ohhh.*" Now it made sense. "Okay. Well, like I said, not a death sentence. Just a roadblock."

She snorted. "Feels like way more than a roadblock to a seven-year-old."

"Oh, yeah. Rough year. Second grade?" Tessa made a face. "Maybe the toughest year of all, if I'm being honest. But now? There are so many programs, even technology that can help her. The tricks of the trade, my—" She was going to say "my father called them" but caught herself. "I call them," she said instead.

"What are they? How do you find them? Where do parents go?"

"Relax. She'll learn to manage."

Crista looked like she didn't know how to relax as she leaned closer. "It's a mess, though. My husband wants to teach her morning, noon, and night. Always forcing her to read, making her power through."

"That'll only make her hate reading—and him." Her own father had exhibited the patience of a saint when Tessa was seven, determined to help as only he could—by making it fun.

"I'm afraid she already hates to read," Crista said. "And my mother refuses to believe that anything is wrong. 'She's a child! Let her play! She's perfect!' It's driven a wedge between Anthony and my mother, which is..."

"Not nice for you, I'd imagine."

She grunted. "You have no idea."

"No, I don't, but I absolutely promise you she'll figure it out," Tessa assured her. "But second grade is this weird time when the good readers and the not-so-great readers really get separated and that kind of stigmatizes and categorizes them for the rest of elementary school."

"Yes!" Her eyes flashed. "You know that?"

Tessa rolled her eyes. "My twin sister was a miniature Mensa candidate, and I could hardly see Spot run. Yeah, I know."

"It's downright discriminatory!" Crista exclaimed. "And I might have to hold Nolie back and have her repeat second grade."

Tessa winced. "That's tough. But it might be best for her, I don't know. What does your husband want to do?"

"Summer school. Private tutors. Timed reading exercises. Whatever it takes to get that child into third grade in the fall. Certainly no play time, no summer dance classes, no fun camps. And no lollygagging in the garden with her grandmother, who says the tests are wrong and Nolie is purely perfect."

Tessa inched back, mostly from the vehemence as Crista blew out her personal storm.

"With all due respect, Crista, *you're* her mother. Maggie's the grandmother, and, well, does she really get an opinion on... No. Never mind. I remember the woman."

"Maggie doesn't just get an opinion, she rules the roost." She muttered the words, but Tessa heard.

"*Your* roost?" Tessa lifted a brow.

Crista looked like she regretted the comment, covering with a sip of tea.

"Whatever," she said after setting the mug down and turning the handle to a precise forty-five degrees. "I need to get Nolie help, and figure out what to do this summer."

"Maybe I can help you," Tessa said, the words out before she really had time to think about whether or not that was a great idea.

"How?"

Tessa shrugged, carried back years to another dining room table, another little girl who went to war with words.

And Artie Wylie had dropped in like an angel to help her.

Wouldn't her father want her to pay that forward, no matter what Nolie's grandmother had said about him? Wasn't that the ethical and right thing to do?

"I could, um, teach her some things I've learned over the years—changing the font on a computer, using different backgrounds, memorizing certain words by their first letter, and even using colored highlighters. I know dozens of writing and reading tricks. Give me three weeks with the kid and I'll have her working at grade level. Or close."

Crista's whole face lit up, then instantly fell, like

she'd thrown a wet rag at the wall which slid down to the floor. "I...I...I don't know about that."

"Right." Tessa smiled. "We forgot I'm Public Enemy Number One."

Her expression softened. "It's a complicated situation."

"Clearly. And if Maggie got wind of it? Yikes."

Crista closed her eyes and stood slowly, sliding the chair behind her. "I'm going to take a walk before I get back in the car and drive to Atlanta."

Tessa nodded, then leaned forward to add, "I'm not your only option, of course. I'm sure there are tons of specialists and tutors who could help you at home."

"There are," she said, taking her cup into the kitchen and rinsing it, using that folded paper towel to dry the edges of the sink. "I just haven't found the right one yet."

She walked back to the stairs, pausing at the bottom before she turned and looked at Tessa.

"Thank you," she said softly. "For the offer to help and the encouragement. It's nice to know you've conquered the situation."

As she disappeared to the second floor, Tessa fell back in her chair and stared at the screen. Only this time she didn't see the wavy words. She saw Crista's face and a flicker of hope in her eyes. And she saw her dear father, who would probably be very proud of his daughter for that offer.

Even with him gone, she wanted to honor his memory.

June 6, 1990

We almost had fun last night. Almost. We built a bonfire on the beach and had everything to make s'mores, but someone melted...and it didn't go on a graham cracker. Why does Crista have to ruin every good thing? I know she's only seven and I feel sorry for her because she just doesn't have a pal like all the rest of us do, but is that my fault?

Anyway, our parents went out with the Cavallaris and we were going to have so much fun on the beach at night, but Crista had a freak-out. When Mom called from the restaurant pay phone to check on us, Crista screamed so loud I thought Mom and Dad would send an ambulance. She told Mom we ignored her and she saw a monster in the water (can you believe that?) and Mom made me stay in the house with her. It ruined everything!

When she finally fell asleep (at the very END of Honey, I Shrunk the Kids), I went down on the beach and they were all laughing so hard. Tessa, Kate, and Eli and You Know Who. (Peter!) To be fair, the boys weren't really paying much attention since they brought Game Boys down there, but I felt like Crista must feel all the time —kinda lonely. It made me think I should be nicer to her—but not so nice I miss the bonfires for crying out loud.

Anyway, Tessa got a little mini boombox for her birthday and of course she made a mix tape, so we danced to "our song" ("Walkin' on Sunshine"—ooh yeah!) and I heard a song for the first time called "Nothing Compares 2 U." I loved it so much! Someday I want to slow dance with Peter to that song.

Vivien

Chapter Four
Vivien

Vivien closed the notebook and dropped it on top of the others in the bright pink plastic box next to her bed, a sigh on her lips. She was always amused and amazed when she took a moment to read one of her diary entries from the summers they'd spent here as kids. She was glad the old Lisa Frank notebooks had survived the weather and years at the original beach house, and grateful that Eli had saved them when he demo'd the place.

She was still working her way through the second journal—too much of a steady diet of pink Flair pen wasn't good for the soul. It was truly enlightening to realize that more than thirty years had passed since she'd written those words, and to be honest? Some things hadn't changed.

Crista was the family disrupter, and Vivien still battled guilt for not being nicer to her little sister.

"Hey, you mind if I shower?" Lacey stepped out of the ensuite, still in her pajamas. She added a crooked smile. "Since somehow we've become roommates again."

"Just for one night, Lace," she said. "Crista will go

back to Atlanta today and you can have that bedroom again."

"It's all right," Lacey said. "I like bunking with you, Mom. I'm weirdly attached to you that way."

"Like Crista and Maggie," she mused under her breath.

Lacey frowned. "I don't think their relationship is as healthy as ours. For one thing, has Aunt Crista ever disagreed with Grandma Maggie? God knows you and I have had different opinions."

"I think there's more disagreement with Crista and Maggie than we realize." As she spoke, Vivien walked toward the wall of French doors that led out to a third-floor balcony and looked down at the beach.

The Gulf was so turquoise today it was almost green, and the sand literally as white as snow. Sun sparkled on the water all the way to the horizon, a vista that Vivien felt like she could stare at forever.

"Did Crista tell you that?" Lacey asked, coming over as if the view drew her closer, too. But Lacey's gaze was locked on Vivien, with concern in eyes nearly as blue as the sky above them. "Are you okay, Mom?"

Vivien lifted a shoulder. "We got whacked by Hurricane Crista last night. It always gets me here." She tapped her solar plexus. "A mix of anger and guilt. I was always the one stuck taking care of her if Mom wasn't around. And I got furious. Then I would fold with guilt because she was the odd man out—all the time, not just those summers. It's hard being that much younger than your siblings."

"I guess," Lacey said, looking past her toward the water. "I'm an only, so—oh." She jutted her chin. "There she is."

Vivien peered to the end of the brand-new boardwalk that ran as an elevated forty-foot walkway from their lower level, over the dunes, to the beach.

Crista sat by herself at the very end, looking out toward the water.

"Oh." Vivien whimpered. "See? I can taste her sadness from here. And I love her. All her dramatics are just a way to get the attention she craved as a kid."

Lacey lifted a dubious brow. "She's married and has a daughter and is forty-three years old. She doesn't need to stir up controversy to get attention."

"She hasn't for a long time, but..." Vivien sighed and listened to her heart. "I'm going to talk to her." She gave Lacey a kiss on the cheek. "You shower and enjoy some privacy."

Wondering what mood Crista would be in, Vivien stopped in the kitchen and poured two cups of coffee, fixing one to Crista's exact preferences, and headed down the stairs to the lower level and the boardwalk.

The April sun warmed her arms, and a soft breeze lifted her hair as she made her way across the wooden planks. Crista sat unmoving on the top step to the sand.

Her posture, usually upright and impeccable, was slouched, her shoulders heavy with the weight of her thoughts.

Vivien knew few people as well as she knew Crista. Of course, her sister, younger by seven years, was not an enigma. She wore her emotions on display, constantly strived for perfection, and was driven by a deep and abiding loyalty to their mother.

A shrink could probably figure out the "why's" of all those things—a late-in-life baby who'd become like an only child at twelve years old to a single mother. Crista was most definitely a product of an unconventional and sometimes sad upbringing.

She was the most like Maggie, too, despite her dark coloring that favored the Lawson side of the family. In some ways, she was the smartest of the three of them, with grades that put Eli and Vivien's to shame.

But then, she was far more studious and never missed a class or assignment in her life, and getting the top grade in school mattered so much to her.

Now, in life, being perceived as "perfect" was still important to Crista, something that was evident to Vivien when she'd helped decorate Crista and Anthony's house. Everything in order, everything just so. It was a difficult way to live.

Vivien cleared her throat softly.

"Oh." Crista whipped around, surreptitiously swiping under her eyes.

Poor thing. Nothing about this situation was...perfect.

With a lifetime of being the middle-child peacemaker spurring her on, Vivien slowed her step, gauging the situation.

"Can I interrupt your alone time? I come bearing coffee—one sugar, one and a half tablespoons of heavy cream, one ice cube."

Crista's shoulders moved in a laugh. "Impressive, Viv. You are granted permission to enter my bubble."

Vivien handed her the cup and lowered herself carefully to the top step, balancing her own coffee. "What's happening in this bubble?" she asked.

"I was just admiring the colors of Destin, actually. I think whoever invented 'seafoam green' must have been to Destin. And the sand? It literally looks like sugar. They're still my favorite colors and, honestly, no other beach I've ever seen quite captures them."

"Totally agree. I've tried to incorporate that palette in the décor." Vivien took a sip, settling in next to her sister. "I had a panic attack thinking you'd left."

Crista shot her a look. "Do you get them?"

"Panic attacks?" She frowned. "Not really."

"Well, I've had a few. Not fun."

"Oh, girl." Vivien draped an arm over Crista's shoulders, noticing how thin they felt. "I wish you'd listen to your older siblings and stay here for a while. If nothing else, Jonah's cooking will fatten you up."

She smiled. "Jonah. Now there's someone I hadn't expected to see here."

"None of us did. He's got some issues and Eli's helping him out."

"He's always had issues," she said, setting the untouched coffee to the side. "Ever since Melissa died and he...changed."

Vivien nodded, remembering the confident, athletic superstar Eli's son had been at fifteen. He'd been utterly destroyed by the loss of his mother, a TV news personality who was killed in a private plane crash.

The entire family had been gutted, but no one worse than that teenage boy, who was now nearly thirty and still fighting the demons of his loss.

"Well, get this." Vivien leaned into her. "He's got a girlfriend named Carly in California...and she's eight months pregnant."

Crista gasped. "Seriously? Does Mama know?"

"Why is Maggie your first thought?" Vivien asked, not able to hold back the question. She braced for blowback from Crista.

But she just shrugged and turned toward the water. "I wish she wasn't," she admitted. "Sometimes I'm suffocated by her."

Sometimes? But Vivien tamped down the thought and brushed some sand off the wood planks.

"No, Maggie doesn't know she's going to be a great-grandmother."

Crista smiled. "She'll flip. She's tough on us, but she's always had a soft spot for her grands. I can only imagine her with a 'great-grand.' And Jonah? How's he feeling about being a father?"

"Terrified, I'd imagine. His girlfriend has sort of booted him with a demand he get his life together. He's trying to get into a local culinary arts program, since it turns out he's a whiz in the kitchen. Which beats being the drifter he's been for most of his twenties."

Crista nodded, gnawing at her lower lip, staring

straight ahead. "That's cool. He's a good guy, just lost and had a tough break."

They sat quietly for a few moments, the sound of gulls and the surf filling the air.

"So, you thinking about Eli's offer for you to stay here for a while?" Vivien finally asked. "We would absolutely love it, Cris."

"I'm thinking about a lot of things," she said.

"Is being around Tessa really that upsetting?" Vivien asked gently, trying to ease into the conversation. "I mean, she's not evil. Maybe if you would just—"

"It's not just that," Crista interrupted, finally turning to face her. "It's not Tessa. It's...everything."

Vivien waited for an explanation, but her sister turned back to the water with a sigh. "My life is a hot mess," she whispered.

"What? Your life? What could possibly be a 'hot mess' in Crista Merritt's world?" Vivien asked.

Crista snorted.

"Seriously," Vivien pressed on. "You have a gorgeous house, a devoted husband, a precious daughter. And Maggie might be a challenge, but you two have always had a freakishly close relationship and, honestly, no one handles her as well as you do. I mean, I'd die if she lived with me."

Slowly, Crista turned and gave a shockingly direct look. "It ain't easy, Viv."

Vivien blew out a breath. "Well, if there's anything I can do..."

"Just understand that there's a lot going on, which is probably why I turned into a raving shrew last night."

"A lot with Maggie...or other things?" she asked gently.

Crista sighed heavily, rubbing her temples. "Nolie is having...some issues. And things with Mom are tense because of it. And Anthony and I have been fighting a lot about it, and it's a big ugly mess."

"Nolie?" Vivien's concern deepened, thinking of her precious seven-year-old niece. "What kind of issues?"

Crista hesitated again, dragging her bare foot in the sand below. "She's not...reading," she said, her voice barely above a whisper.

Vivien blinked, trying to process this. "At all?"

Crista shook her head. "The speech pathologist in our school district thinks she has dyslexia, but we haven't taken her to a doctor or anything. Mama refuses to believe it, Anthony thinks he can drill it out of her with hours of forced reading, and her teacher thinks she should repeat second grade and...and..."

"And what do *you* think?" Vivien asked.

Crista closed her eyes. "I was going to hold her back until...until...this morning."

"This— What happened this morning?"

"Believe it or not, a conversation with Tessa."

Vivien sucked in a soft breath. "Oh, yeah. She often jokes about her dyslexia."

"Except it's not funny."

"But she's okay."

Crista nodded, glancing over her shoulder at the house behind them.

"She's actually more than okay," she said. "She's the first person who was ever real about it, and the first time I've had hope."

Vivien's heart clenched. "That's awesome. I'm glad you talked to her, Cris."

"She offered to help Nolie," Crista said. "Which is pretty darn classy, considering the things I said last night."

Vivien felt a spark of pride for Tessa's handling of the situation, which made no sense, but it was real. She'd grown incredibly fond of Tessa this past month and realized how much they'd pigeon-holed the woman as flighty, fun-loving, and too pretty for her own good.

"She has a good heart," Vivien said, and meant it. "And I bet she could help Nolie a lot."

Crista bit her lip, again, clearly conflicted. "I know. But..." She made a face. "Talk about consorting with the enemy."

"She's *not* an enemy," Vivien insisted. "She's a kind and spunky and wonderful person who has become a dear friend, and she's a fantastic mentor to Lacey. Even if it's true about Artie, there's no good reason to take it out on Tessa. Oh, I know what Maggie told you, and I know your loyalty lies with her, but...think of what this could do for Nolie."

Crista's shoulders slumped. "I am. I have been. It's all I can think about." She reached for her phone, tapping the screen. "I was reading this article that says a child with dyslexia can benefit the most from learning from adults who also have it and have conquered it. They understand the different way the brain processes words. Anthony and I certainly don't. We don't know how to help."

"But Tessa does," Vivien said gently.

Crista looked at her, her internal struggle written all over her face. Finally, she nodded, though reluctantly. "If Mama ever found out..."

"Does she have to?"

"Well..." Crista groaned. "I cannot lie to that woman."

"She's gone, Cris. She's in the Netherlands, then France, and won't be back until...when?"

"May third at 9:30, which is thirty-three days. And a half. Not that I'm counting."

Vivien laughed at that.

"Viv, do you think I could..." She groaned. "Lie to Maggie? Is it possible?"

"Maybe you wouldn't have to, or at least only by omission. Nolie's your daughter, Crista. Her well-being trumps everything. And, honestly, you can do anything you want, assuming Anthony agrees."

"He might," she said. "And if he does, then I could take Nolie out of school for the rest of the year while Maggie's away. Should I? No, no. It's crazy. What if the truth comes out?"

Vivien dropped her head back, eyes closed. "Are we really that scared of our mother at this age? Why?"

"Because she's the only parent we have," Crista said.

"And I don't know about you, but I'm not willing to lose another one."

"I get that," Vivien said. "I'll cover for you, Cris. If this is going to help Nolie? I will lie to her if I have to. I'd do anything for that little girl, and you know it."

Crista's face folded and tears sprang to her eyes. "Oh, Viv. That's so sweet."

"I love her." She put her hand on Crista's cheek. "And I love you. I promise, if you two stay, we will not let you be the odd man out. I promise this will be different than those summers."

She blinked and a tear fell. "I don't know what's wrong with me," she said on a trapped sob. "I cry all the time lately."

"Because you're under enormous stress," Vivien said. "This is the perfect solution. You get a break, Nolie gets a new kind of teacher, and we get to make up for all those summers when you didn't have a friend. There are plenty around here."

Crista searched her face, thinking hard, clearly having a mental battle.

"You and Nolie can share that upstairs room," Vivien added, trying to seal the deal. "Will she want to come?"

"Of course. She hates school. The only problem is she'll miss her little dance recital."

"A month at the beach should make it up to her," Vivien said. "I love this idea, Crista!"

"Do you think Tessa is...right for the job?"

Vivien smiled, relief washing over her. "I do. You can't believe how she's connected with Lacey. All she does is tease me about stealing my daughter and taking her for her own, so be careful. She's like the Pied Piper and girls of all ages follow her."

"And you promise that Mama will never find out?"

Vivien made a big X on her chest with her finger. "Promise." Then she leaned over and hugged her sister. "Look, I know it's hard for you to rebel in any way, shape, or form, but you're doing the right thing, I know it."

Crista didn't respond, but her expression softened as they separated.

Vivien squeezed her arm one more time before standing. "Are you leaving soon?" she asked. "Or can you stay for a nice Jonah breakfast? They're crazy good."

She shook her head. "This whole thing has just kind of upset my stomach." She picked up the untouched mug. "Thank you for this, but I don't need anything to make me stressier."

"Dump it. And all your worries. Bring them to this seafoam green Gulf along with Nolie. We could use a kid around here."

Crista smiled. "I'm going to drive home to Atlanta right away and talk to Anthony. Assuming he agrees, and I can get her out of school, we'll be back by the weekend." She pushed up, and took Vivien's hand. "I love you."

They hugged hard and Crista went ahead just as Vivien's phone buzzed with a text from Eli.

"I'll catch up with you, Cris." She tapped the phone and read his message.

Eli Lawson: *Hey, guess who's coming to Destin? No, not Kate, LOL. Peter just called and said the*

Pensacola PD is sending him this way for a few weeks to work on a case. They're putting him up at an Airbnb but we'll probably see a lot of him while he's here. In fact, I'm grabbing a bite with him tonight. You cool if I ask him if he can get access to any files from Dad's old case? Just curious. Okay with you?

Peter McCarthy? Now that was a coincidence. She'd just been mooning over him in her diaries. And, of course, since he was a detective over in Pensacola, he'd be a great person to ask for help.

She texted back a thumbs-up emoji, thinking about the man who'd come for dinner not too long ago. A veteran of the divorce wars, he'd encouraged her to take the high road with Ryan. *Look how well that turned out.*

She couldn't quite muster the weak-in-the-knees sensation she used to feel during those teenage summers, but she was certainly looking forward to spending time with Peter.

As she walked up to the house, she hummed the melody of that old song, "Nothing Compares 2 U."

She never did get to slow dance with him to that song, she remembered with a smile.

Huh. *Never say never, Viv.*

Chapter Five

Eli

"I've never in my life heard anything remotely like that." Kate's voice sounded shaky, and not just because she was coming through the speaker on Eli's truck dashboard.

She'd been shocked by his tale of the events with Crista, which he'd just finished telling her as he drove to pick up some materials for the day's work.

He'd shared the whole story of what had transpired, trying to play down Crista's theatrics. Although as soon as she spoke to Tessa, Kate would know the real truth of what happened.

"Yeah, we were all floored," he said. "It almost makes me want to go back to see Frank and Betty Cavallari and ask if they knew about this."

Kate and Eli had visited the much older couple, who'd been "couple friends" with both sets of parents all those years ago. They'd hoped that those old friends might be able to shed light on what caused the Big Breakup between the Wylies and the Lawsons.

But the encounter had left Kate and Eli more confused. Mrs. Cavallari told Kate that Maggie and Artie had had an affair; Mr. Cavallari told Eli that Jo Ellen and

Roger had been involved. Their eighty-something memories were bad, and the affair possibility felt utterly wrong to all of them.

"Do you think you could talk to Jo Ellen, Kate?" Eli asked. "Maybe get a feel for the possibility of this being true or not?"

"I'd rather not."

"Really? Why not?"

"Why would I? Eli, I can't drag her through even the possibility of something like that. She's so tender."

His eyes shuttered as he considered the best way to answer. Kate's mother was still deeply mourning her husband, who'd died last year. If anyone understood how long that pain lasted, it was Eli. It had taken him years to begin to heal after he lost Melissa.

To make matters harder, Jo Ellen, well into her seventies, had fallen and sprained her ankle, which was why Kate had left so suddenly.

But they *had* to ask her. She was the only person alive who might know what happened—other than Maggie, of course.

"Don't you want to know?" he asked.

"No." She laughed. "Sorry if I sound like a broken record, but I'm being honest. You'd want that, right?"

"Of course," he replied, hating that she'd even asked.

The whole conversation felt stilted and distant and... yeah, distant. Did they have a snowball's chance when they were a thousand miles apart? The weeks together last month had been...perfect. Now? Not so perfect.

He pulled into a gas station but before he lined up

with a pump, he parked his truck so he could concentrate on the conversation.

"Listen, Eli, I feel the pain in your voice and, yeah, this is a terrible turn of events." She sighed into the phone, giving him a visual of the way she must look on the other side of this call.

He could see her dark hair with fringed bangs, her sparkly brown eyes, and that wide smile with a hint of dimples. She'd have her glasses...somewhere between where they belonged on her nose and lost on the closest counter or in her pocket.

His heart tightened with affection.

"But we are talking about ancient history," she added, pulling his thoughts away from her looks and back to this problem.

"Not that ancient," he said.

"Thirty years? And both men in question are gone?" Her voice rose with frustration. "Does it really matter anymore?"

He blinked at the question and stared straight ahead. "Are you serious?" he asked on a rasp. "My dad went to prison, where he died."

"Who's to say he wouldn't have died if he hadn't been in prison?" she countered.

"We'll never know, but he was alone—which he likely wouldn't have been at home—and he had...prison stress."

He heard her take a steadying breath. "He committed serious crimes, Eli. Does it really matter who turned him in? You don't question his guilt, do you?"

An old and familiar disgust wound through him. "No, I never have. He was guilty."

"Well, is it relevant how the authorities learned of his...activities?"

"It's relevant to my family," he said, hearing the coolness in his voice. "And, whoa, it matters to my mother."

"Everything matters to Maggie."

He winced, not sure he liked that sentiment, even if he might agree with it.

"I'm sorry," she added quickly, as though she realized that was hurtful. "I know what your father did is a source of true pain for you, Eli. But you need to spread a little of that forgiveness you believe in so much."

Oh. Was there anything a Christian hated more than being reminded that they weren't acting like, well, a Christian?

"I can forgive him—Artie, that is," he said. "I don't like that he felt compelled to ruin my father's life, but—"

"Eli! We don't know any of the details or if this is even true."

"Which is why I want you to ask Jo Ellen, but I understand she's not feeling well."

"She's a wreck," she said. "Is it possible she's getting worse in her grief and not better?" Her voice sounded pained, enough that he put everything out of his head but the need to help her.

"It can," he said, sadly speaking with authority on the subject. "Like a rebound thing."

He closed his eyes and tried to think back to the darkest days of his life.

Not when his father died in prison—though that time was wretched, too—but fifteen years ago when two police officers and an HR representative from the TV station where Melissa worked walked into his office. They came to deliver the news that the station's private plane had gone down and there were no survivors, but to this day, he couldn't recall one word of that conversation.

"I guess grief is not linear," Kate said, sounding very much like the scientist she was.

"No, so...be good to Jo Ellen," he said. "Don't ask her anything that's going to upset her."

"Thanks for understanding, Eli."

"Sure, sure. I just...really worry about all that Crista said. Maggie literally doesn't want us talking to anyone named Wylie..."

Kate gave a wry snort. "Good thing you're fifty-three and a grown man who doesn't have to do what his mother says."

"No, I don't," he countered. "But I love her like you love your mother. She also lost a husband, albeit thirty years ago, and I respect her."

"Enough to...give this up?" she asked on a whisper.

He swallowed. "Of course not."

They were both quiet for a beat, then she sighed. "I have a meeting with the lab staff," she said. "Can we talk tonight?"

"Of course. Have you thought any more about coming down this summer with your kids?" he asked.

"I don't know. Will Maggie allow it?" There was enough tease in her voice to make him laugh.

"Ouch."

"I'm kidding, Eli," she said, sounding a little sorry she'd even made the joke. "We are thinking about it—the kids are chomping at the bit for a Florida vacation."

"Then we'll have to figure out how to make that happen," he said. "Because nothing—and no one—will stop me from seeing you again, Lady Katie."

She gave a gentle laugh, warm enough to erase some of the distance he felt. "I have to run. Talk soon!"

"Bye."

He dropped his head back as the call disconnected. Nothing and no one would stop his feelings for her, that was true. But he sure wasn't looking forward to the fight.

He had a month to figure it out. As always, no matter what challenge he faced, he knew where his help came from. Opening his eyes, he looked up at the blue sky through the windshield.

"You brought Jonah back to me," he whispered to the God he firmly believed heard every word. "Can you work on my mother now?"

He didn't hear any audible response, but, like always, he trusted that his prayer would be answered.

THE BEACHFRONT RESTAURANT known as Pompano Joe's was never quiet, but Eli had been able to snag an outdoor table, so the only noise was from the surf not the crowd. With the setting sun turning the entire beach a thousand shades of orange, he and Peter enjoyed a relaxing dinner of fried seafood and a couple of beers.

Years always faded away when he was with the man he'd known since elementary school. Peter had a rough childhood—his parents divorced, his dad was a gutter drunk, and his mother was never around—but he and Eli had become fast friends playing sixth-grade basketball together.

The older Peter got, the more time he wanted to spend at the Lawsons', so it seemed like a no-brainer to bring him to Destin for seven consecutive summers, straight through to their senior year of college.

They'd been through a lot together, and loved reminiscing, especially here. Peter had his own divorce story, but the tall, sandy-haired man had coped beautifully.

He'd raised two sons and worked tirelessly to bring down the baddies, his law enforcement job being a great source of pride. He'd parlayed his greatest character traits —a keen eye for observation and being a truly kind person—into a fascinating career as a police detective.

After they'd spent most of the meal catching up and laughing about old times, Eli asked about the missing persons case that brought Peter's investigative skills to Destin.

"There's no evidence of foul play," Peter said after he explained that a Pensacola resident had gone missing during a weekend trip to Destin. "The dude could have gone off to Mexico with his mistress. But every lead over there was a dead end, so they sent me here to see if I can retrace the guy's last days before disappearing."

"They're sure he was here?" Eli asked.

"His car was found abandoned near Henderson," he said, referring to the local state park beach. "While I'm here, I'll be combing security footage and getting Ring camera output, interviewing locals near his rental, the bars and restaurant owners, the usual."

"Sounds interesting," Eli said.

Peter grinned. "Mostly I'll be coming to the Summer House to hang out with the Lawsons and the Wylies."

"One Wylie," he said.

Peter gave him a knowing look. "You miss Kate, don't you?"

"Understatement, my friend."

Giving in to a slow smile, Peter lifted his bottle of Heineken. "And here I always thought it was Tessa who had you wrapped around her little finger."

"It was, when I was a moron, er, kid," he joked. "Kate's just...right for me, Pete. She's solid, smart, a really good woman. She makes me laugh and think. I didn't get enough time with her, though. And now she's a thousand miles away, and there's a new complication."

He lifted his brows. "What's that? Anything I can help with?"

"As a matter of fact...you might."

"Hit me."

Eli leaned in, pushing away his nearly finished plate, and gave a very scaled-down report of what Crista had said. He didn't need to get into the family emotion, especially with a man as pragmatic as Peter.

But his friend instantly knew what was needed.

"You want me to find out who turned him in," Peter guessed.

"I certainly don't want to ask you to do anything outside the bounds of law enforcement rules. But...are those files available?"

He huffed a slow breath, closing his eyes to instantly communicate the complications.

"Yes and no and maybe," he said. "First of all, it depends on if the case was investigated at the state or fed level. Knowing what I do about your dad's crimes, I think that jurisdiction started with Atlanta PD, then maybe GBI moved in. Do you know?"

Eli shrugged. "I was twenty-two, mad as hell, embarrassed, and wishing I could climb in a hole where my dad was concerned. Honestly, I did my level best to know nothing except the verdict the day it came in."

"I get that," Peter said. "Looking into the origin of the investigation might be easy, especially if the original tip is in case notes or detective logs. Those leads usually come from the victims—and I presume Artie wasn't one of those—or a colleague acting as a whistleblower. I know a few guys in Atlanta PD who could find out how the case got rolling. If so, I'll get you the information."

"Thanks, man."

"Don't thank me yet," he added. "If that doesn't work, court records and transcripts are public information. Did Artie testify against him?"

"Believe it or not, I don't know," Eli admitted. "I was away at school during the trial and my mother kept everything under a dome of silence. Sorry."

He smiled. "Ah, Maggie. Hey, I remember those were tough days and you've always hated the subject of Roger's crimes. Don't apologize." He took a sip of beer, thinking. "Fulton County DA or the Georgia Attorney General could have information, but...hard to get."

"Like I said, I don't want you to color outside the lines, Pete. If it's easy to find out, great."

"I'll poke around," he said, then narrowed his eyes. "If you really want to know." At Eli's questioning look, he added, "It isn't going to help things with Kate if it's true. Not if Maggie has her way."

"I know." He leaned back, the weight of that still heavy. "I trust a higher power."

"Higher than Maggie?" he cracked. "I didn't know there was one."

Eli chuckled, and finished his beer.

"Now can *I* ask a favor?" Peter put his hand over the check.

"Pay for dinner? No way," Eli said. "I got this."

"Pensacola PD's got this," he said, snagging the check. "And that's not my favor."

"What is it? Name it and claim it, my friend."

"Careful now, big brother."

Eli angled his head, not sure he got that.

"I'd like permission to ask your beautiful sister, Vivien, on a date or six while I'm here." He gave a sly, even shy, smile. "Since you and I are taking the chances we didn't have the insight to take back in the nineties."

"The girls were young in the nineties," he said. "Plus, I'd have killed you if you had put a hand on Viv."

He laughed, then his smile faded. "Would you now?"

"Maybe. But you're the one who's carrying concealed right now. Am I right?"

"Damn right," Peter said on a laugh, snapping the bill away as Eli tried again to grab it. "So let me pay or I'll shoot you."

"Thank you." Eli surrendered with a grateful smile. "Vivien's not a kid, but she's not fully healed. Her divorce isn't even final, so…"

"So go slow and easy." Peter nodded. "Heard, brother. How did it go when she went back and saw her ex a few weeks ago? I advised her to remember that a divorce can last longer than a marriage."

"Not great," Eli said. "Ryan Knight's a jerk, but I'm glad she took your advice because she knows beyond a shadow of a doubt that the marriage is over. As it should be."

"So…I can, uh, help her heal?"

Eli shot him a look. "You can treat my sister like the precious gem she is."

"That's the only way, my friend. You have my word."

After Peter signed the bill, they walked out toward the parking lot, shook hands, and agreed to talk very soon.

Something told Eli that the truth he was after would be hard to find, but if anyone could help him, it was Peter.

And if anyone could help Vivien…it might also be Peter.

Chapter Six

Crista

As she turned onto Old Bluff Road, Crista's whole body grew tight at the sight of her brick Colonial tucked into the Atlanta suburbs. She'd been tense to the point of nauseous since she'd left Destin almost six hours ago, worried about how her husband would respond to this truly crazy idea.

He might not want Crista and Nolie to leave during this rare month with Maggie out of the house. He might not want her to be taught "tricks" by a stranger, especially one Crista had just told him was her—and her mother's—sworn enemy. He might just fight her on it because... lately? They fought a *lot*.

Or maybe she was tense because this orderly, safe, gorgeous sanctuary had changed in the last few years, and her little family seemed to be stretched and ready to snap.

Nolie waded through every day like a tiny soul about to drown in scrambled letters and constant frustration. Even at seven, she sensed something was very wrong in her world, and it didn't help that Anthony and Maggie disagreed openly on the subject, putting Crista in the middle.

Nolie might have dyslexia, but she was a very smart and observant little girl. She knew a war raged around her—because of her. But it wasn't Nolie's fault.

Crista couldn't ignore the impact of Maggie on this house—and on her husband.

For months, Anthony had not been the wonderful man she'd met in the office cafeteria when she worked in an ad agency and he was a software engineer for a company on the fifth floor.

Crista had waited until her early thirties to "settle down" because she had been determined to find a man she knew could be her best friend and lifelong partner. She wanted perfection in her marriage—as in every aspect of her well-ordered life—and she was certain she'd found it in Anthony John Merritt.

An engineer who was definitely not a nerd, he'd swept her off her feet the minute they'd met. Their connection was instant and palpable, a source of joy and happiness that she hadn't even known she was missing in life. But the joy seemed to be evaporating as the years went by, a slow leak that started around the time her mother moved in with them.

Anthony and Maggie had always liked each other— but living together was a whole different ballgame. He enjoyed—and was frequently amused by—Crista's need to have everything "just so," but Maggie's controlling personality was next level.

Maggie had come to stay after her hip replacement surgery a little over three years ago, since they had a comfortable guest suite on the first floor. Nolie had been not quite four and Crista had been turning down free-lance copywriting jobs that would have helped with the steep mortgage on their home.

Maggie brought the ideal solution—she could enter-tain Nolie while Crista worked a few hours, and she insisted on paying rent.

The arrangement made so much sense and had worked out beautifully—at first. It was wonderful to have her mother around, but the longer she lived here, the more the house became...Maggie's. The garden, the deck, the décor, even mealtimes and the menu—all dictated by the strongest personality in the building.

She had an opinion on everything—how much TV they watched, when Nolie played, who they entertained, what they did on weekends, where they went out to dinner.

About a year ago, Anthony got a massive promotion that became a ready excuse to leave early and come home late. Their date nights fizzled, their love life flattened, and their marriage hit a stagnant stage that terrified Crista.

All the while, Nolie went to battle with the books, and Maggie...observed, opined, and ordered all things be done her way.

On a sigh, Crista pulled into her pristine garage. Like everything in her home, the space was so clean you could eat off the gleaming speckled epoxy floor. The tidy stor-age, orderly shelves, and neat lawn equipment was what the advertising industry called the "visual backstory"—

someone who had their life together kept a garage like this.

And like most ads, it was wildly deceptive.

Taking a deep breath, she grabbed her purse and overnight bag and walked toward the kitchen entrance, praying there wouldn't be that trouble she hated on the other side.

She opened the door quietly, hoping it didn't make Aunt Pittypat bark for ten minutes and demand a treat.

"Daddy, I can't! I'm tired." Nolie's whine echoed from the kitchen.

Oh, there was the trouble.

"Honey, focus on the word. Put that pencil down and focus."

"I like to draw pictures. That's a pretty flower."

"Can you spell flower? Can you read it?"

Crista shuttered her eyes and swallowed her dread. "Hello?" she called.

"Mommy's home!" Nolie's voice rang out in joy at the same time Aunt Pittypat barked noisily, the two of them racing through the kitchen and into the mudroom. "Mommy! I missed you!"

"I missed you, too, Nolie-bird!" She dropped the overnight bag to reach for her little girl, scooping her up and burying her face in the locks of dark hair for a great big inhale of love.

She adored this child, her love rocking her from head to toe. Nolie leaned back, her expressive brown eyes—so like Crista's—wide and...watery.

"Have you been crying?" Crista asked, slowly

lowering her slender frame to the floor, aware of the little Yorkie zipping around the floor in excitement.

Her lower lip quivered. "Just...trying...you know... Daddy wants me to..."

"Read," Crista whispered, taking Nolie's hand. "I know."

Anthony came around the mudroom entrance, his footsteps preceding the sight of his six-foot frame in the doorway.

"There you are." He gave a smile, swiping his hand over his close-cropped chestnut hair with a sigh of pure relief. "Yeah. We missed you, Mommy."

Her heart hitched as it always did when he playfully used the term—anytime she saw him, really. She loved him deeply, which was why the distance between them hurt so much.

"Tell Daddy I don't have to read anymore, Mommy." Nolie tugged at her hand. "Tell him, please. I don't want to work today."

Poor kid, she thought, stroking Nolie's silky hair. She shouldn't have to worry about "work" at seven.

"Five-minute break," Anthony said. "Let's get Mommy settled and we'll just finish that last chapter. It's a good story, right, Nolie?"

She rolled her eyes. "I don't know what it's about, Daddy. I don't care."

"It's about a butterfly and a frog." The frustration was clear in his voice, and in the shadows around his eyes. "And you have to read at least one more chapter."

She looked up at Crista with a plea all over her little face, eyes filling again.

"It hurts to read, Mommy," she said on a whisper. "I want to play. I want to dress-up the new Barbie that Grandma Maggie gave me for babysitting Aunt Pittypat."

Anthony grunted. "Barbie dolls aren't going to get you into third grade, kiddo."

She squeezed Crista's hand. "Please, Mommy. Please."

Her heart slipped as she realized she hadn't been home five full minutes, and they'd already approached the crux of their biggest battle—to go to third grade or repeat second.

She wished Nolie didn't know the issue was even on the table—so much pressure for a child—but Anthony had insisted she understand how serious the situation really was.

As if that would make her dyslexia disappear.

"Take a break, honey," Crista said, but looked hard at Anthony. "We need to talk anyway."

"Okay, but tomorrow she has dance after school, and she has got to finish this book."

"We'll read it together tonight before bed," Crista promised Nolie, whose face lit up. She knew "read it together" meant...well, Crista would read it and Nolie would snuggle happily.

Was that so bad?

"Let's go, Pittypat!" Nolie shot toward the door and, for a minute, Crista thought Anthony would block her way. Then he stepped aside and let girl and dog disappear.

"She's got to learn, Cris," he said softly.

"I'm not even in the door yet," she said, hanging her handbag on a hook. "And I have to talk to you."

"Yeah, yeah. Sorry." He backed away to let her through and she slowed her step, looking up at him with an ache in her heart.

Was he really not going to hug and kiss her hello? She couldn't remember the last real kiss they'd shared—well, yes. A rare date night well over a month ago.

Maybe she shouldn't leave. Maybe their marriage would fail because of the effort to be sure Nolie didn't.

He gave an uncertain smile, reaching to give her a perfunctory hug and a light kiss on the forehead.

"We really did miss you," he added.

Did he? Sadly, she didn't know.

"I wasn't gone that long, but, whoa, a lot happened."

"Come on." He gestured her into the kitchen, which was immaculate—a fact she appreciated—and she walked to the cozy corner banquette. The table was covered with a few books, one opened to a page with a bright pink butterfly and so few words, she knew it was meant for a younger child.

"Something to drink?" Anthony asked as he opened the fridge and grabbed a Pellegrino.

"I'll take a bottle of water. Thanks."

She slid onto a cushioned seat, glancing out at the deck, bathed in spring sunshine. The rolling hills beyond were bright green and a few new roses were in bloom in Mama's garden.

"I promised her I'd deadhead them for her," Anthony said, following her gaze. "I don't want Maggie to come back and find unloved rose bushes."

"That's good," she said, taking the water bottle.

He probably didn't want her to come back at all, Crista thought, but Anthony was too nice to say it out loud. They both were—but that didn't mean they weren't thinking it.

"How was the house?" he asked. "I hope they dumped the ridiculous idea of not selling it."

She let out a sigh, not wanting to even think about yet another subject where they didn't see eye to eye. He'd flipped out at the idea of not selling the Destin house.

He'd called the house "the one great thing Maggie ever did for us" and had already created a spreadsheet for how they'd save and invest the windfall.

"No decisions have been made," she finally said. "But the house is spectacular. And it would be an amazing place to take Nolie."

This week, as a matter of fact, but she took a long sip of water before dropping that bomb.

"So, how did they take the news that your father's so-called best friend was the rat who turned him in?" he asked.

She made a face, almost sorry she'd shared that with Anthony when she'd come back from taking Maggie to the airport. Especially now that she was going to actually lean on Tessa Wylie for help.

But she'd been frantic to share the news, and she needed him to understand why she had to deliver it in person, so he'd have to work from home while she went to Destin.

"First of all, I'm not sure I'd call Artie Wylie his *best* friend, but whatever."

He shrugged, gulping some Coke. "Did they agree not to see the daughters? I mean, that was Maggie's edict, right?"

"Actually...one of the daughters was there. Tessa was staying at the house."

His eyes widened. "Seriously? The thick plottens," he joked. "I mean, she is at the top of Maggie's 'names not to mention in my presence' list."

"Yeah. I was shocked to see her," she admitted. "Kind of lost it, to be honest."

His smiled as if he knew quite well what "kind of lost it" meant for Crista.

"You have every right to be upset," he said. "And if Maggie ever found out she'd been there—"

"She has dyslexia."

He stared at her, lowering the bottle, glancing at the open children's book. "I know, Crista. That's why I'm sitting here reading instead of working."

"No, I mean Tessa Wylie has dyslexia."

He leaned back. "Huh. Really. Did you know that when you were kids? Was she...different?"

She shot him a look, hating how they all thought dyslexia was some horrible disease. Maggie refused to say the word, as though that would make it go away. Anthony was obsessed with how it could ruin a person's life. And Crista fretted over what it meant for her daughter's future.

Based on Tessa, they were all wrong.

"She's perfectly normal, and was when we were young. And she came right out and told me it's 'not a death sentence.' I'd appreciate you remembering that."

"I know, I know. But it can make life difficult. Starting with being older than all your peers in school, which I don't want for Nolie." He leaned forward, intensity in his light brown eyes. "When they hold a kid back a few years? That's hard, Crista. And for Nolie? Well, she's already the tallest girl in the dance class and stands out. Imagine in school if she's—"

She held out her hand and cut him off.

"Tessa's managed just fine," she said, not wanting to get into an argument about Nolie's perfectly normal height. "She's an event planner and starting her own business, with Lacey, if you can believe that."

"Lacey isn't working for Ryan?"

"She quit and went down to Destin," she told him. "Jonah's there, too."

"Jonah?" He looked stunned. "Geez, is anyone *not* there?"

"Me. And Nolie."

His brow furrowed, not understanding what she meant.

"Anthony, Tessa might be able to help." She leaned closer and lowered her voice to make her point. "She knows...tricks. She knows how to function in the world with dyslexia and told me over and over it's not so bad. She offered to help Nolie." She swallowed and searched his face. "She might be the answer we need right now."

He stared at her. "An event planner? So not a teacher or tutor with an advanced degree in childhood learning?"

"No, but she's got real-life experience," she said. "Honestly, I was hesitant, too. I don't even like the woman—and I hate her father, who passed away last year."

His brows knit together as he processed all this information with his sharp engineer's brain. But it was his heart that put the real worry in his eyes—a father's heart.

"I don't know, Cris."

"What else can we do? Nolie hates the special classes, and she really hates"—she flicked her hand at the books—"this. So what if it's an unorthodox approach? It's a solution that fell into our lap and Maggie is gone, so I could take her down now. We have to do something or they're going to make her take that test, and then they are going to hold her back!"

It felt like her exclamation echoed in the quiet kitchen, bouncing off the walls like she wanted to, letting the out-of-whack emotions take over.

"I'm not opposed to unorthodox—if it works. And..." He inched closer, narrowing his eyes. "You must be truly desperate if you'll lie to your mother. That's a first."

She fluttered the pages of the frog and butterfly book.

"I'm desperate enough to trust this woman who I'm not even supposed to talk to. Desperate enough to leave you right now, during this rare time when we are finally alone and...Maggie-less."

"I was looking forward to it," he admitted quietly. "But Nolie is more important than anything." He drummed his fingers on the table, systematically going through the pros and cons. "What about school?" he asked.

"Well, I think I could talk to her teacher and explain we're putting her in...a special program in Destin."

"Tessa Teaches."

She huffed a laugh. "Something like that. I mean, she's in second grade, not high school. I can have her back the beginning of May—and I will. Then we can..." She swallowed.

"Face Maggie?" he guessed.

"Take that test."

His eyes closed on a grunt. They both hated that the school wanted to test Nolie to see if she could move up to the next grade level. They didn't do that for very many kids, only those with learning disabilities and stubborn parents. If she failed, she could not move up—the decision was taken out of their hands.

"But if Tessa teaches her some techniques and skills and shortcuts for reading and seeing letters differently?" Crista shrugged. "Maybe she'd pass the test."

He considered that, turning to look out the window as he thought. "I can't leave work for that long," he said. "We have a new product rollout in two weeks."

"I know, but I'll take her. Maybe you can come down for a little bit after the rollout."

He sighed. "I guess it wouldn't hurt us to, um...have a chance to breathe."

The words cracked her heart, and she pressed on his hand. "You don't think that might make things worse?"

He looked at her for a long time, not bothering to argue that things were bad right now. The chasm between them grew bigger every day. A month away might break them completely...or bring them closer when she got back.

"I think this is the right thing to do," he said.

"So do I."

"And you swear you are capable of lying to your mother?" He lifted his brows. "Because when she's not happy, no one's happy."

"I'm not lying," Crista said. "I'm just not telling. And neither are you."

"But Nolie will. She tells Maggie everything."

Crista grimaced. "Oh, I hadn't thought of that. I certainly don't want her to lie, but..."

"Look, if Tessa can really help her, then Maggie will be okay with it. I mean, the sun rises and sets on that kid in Maggie's eyes. She'll be fine."

Crista wasn't so sure of that, but she just felt like this was the right thing to do. Maggie's ire was...a future problem.

"I think we can cross the Maggie bridge when we get to it," she said.

"Agreed." He smiled. "I'm on board if you are, Cris."

She closed her eyes, shocked at how relieved she was. "I'll go tell Nolie. I want to go to her school, and then take her to dance and tell Miss Penny she's going to miss the recital. We can leave in a day or two."

"Whoa." He held up both hands. "That's going to be a problem."

"No, I'll talk to Miss Penny—"

"What about Miss Penny?" Nolie stood in the kitchen, a Barbie in one hand and Aunt Pittypat— wearing a pink doll's dress—in the other arm.

Crista and Anthony shared a look and he gave a silent nod, as if to take the lead.

"Honey, I have very exciting news."

"What?" Her face lit up as she came closer. "I don't have to read?"

"We're going on a trip, just you and me," Crista said. "To the beach in Florida! To a great big, beautiful beach house. Your cousin Lacey will be there and Aunt Vivien and Uncle Eli."

"Really? Can I swim in the ocean?"

"It's the Gulf, but yes, of course. And we're going to stay for a month!"

Her little jaw dropped, but then her eyes grew wide. "I'll miss my recital."

"Oh, honey, I promise you'll have such a great time at the beach, and this is the only time we can go, so..."

"Can I bring the costume dress?" She got on her tiptoes as if she might break into a pirouette right then and there.

"Hundred percent," Crista assured her.

She nodded slowly as if her little mind was clicking

through all possible caveats to this new plan. "And what about Aunt Pittypat?"

Oh. The dog! She turned to Anthony, realizing they'd forgotten that six-pound detail.

"I can't take her to the office," Anthony said, then winked at Nolie. "Especially dressed like that."

Nolie giggled, and snuggled her closer. "Can we bring her, Mommy?"

Holy cow, Crista was pushing her luck with Eli and Vivien. But the dog was so small, and her problems were big. "Absolutely."

"Did you hear, Pitty?" Nolie pressed her face into Aunt Pittypat's snout, spinning with joy. "We're going to the beach!"

Anthony surprised her by putting an arm around Crista's shoulders and pulling her closer. "That's the happiest I've seen her in ages," he murmured.

She agreed, looking up at him, still regretting that they'd miss being together during the weeks without Maggie. "Please come."

"I'll work on it," he assured her, leaning in to give her a real kiss this time, light and on the lips.

The first kiss in a long time, and it gave her hope.

Chapter Seven

Tessa

Tessa navigated the traffic with ease as she and Lacey drove toward Miramar Beach, the midday sun glittering off the Gulf in flashes between the palm trees. The sky was a brilliant blue, the kind of perfect Florida day that made everything feel possible—even building a successful business from the ground up.

Which, as of yesterday, when she'd scheduled this first meeting with yet another potential client, seemed exceedingly possible.

For most of the twenty-minute drive from Destin, Tessa briefed Lacey on the owner of a new bridal salon who'd contacted Tessa Wylie Events to organize a grand opening event.

As they reached the area known locally as "Grand Boulevard," where the salon was located, Tessa had no doubt this client had cash. The upscale shopping and dining area was packed with pedestrians and tourists wandering past cafes, expensive boutiques, and the landmark theater that dominated the center of town.

"This looks like a fun place," Lacey said, looking

around. "Too bad I don't have a cute boyfriend to bring me on a dinner date here."

"Why don't you have a cute boyfriend?" Tessa asked. "I mean back in Atlanta?"

She shrugged. "I've had a few here and there, nothing I wanted to last forever. Why don't you? I know, I know—no man measured up to your dad. Maybe you could let go and fall in love sometime?"

Tessa gave a soft hoot. "You know what I love about you, Lacey? Besides everything? You just ask questions and don't tiptoe over topics."

"Why tiptoe?" she asked. "You're beautiful, funny, smart, and should also have a great guy in your life."

"I'm almost fifty—the great ones are few and far between. You, however, have no such excuse."

"Well, I have a boss who works me day and night," she joked.

"Touché. Oh, here's the parking lot." They still had a few minutes before the meeting, so they decided to take the longer route and check out the local color on their way to the salon.

"Since I have your permission to ask blunt questions," Lacey said as they walked on the wide cobblestone sidewalk, "how are you feeling about Crista coming back today? And staying?"

Tessa exhaled. "Fine, I guess."

Lacey gave her a side-eye. "I ask the blunt questions, I expect honest answers."

Tessa laughed. "Okay, okay. On one hand, I'm kind of psyched to help her daughter. I relate to what that kid is going through. If I can make things easier for her, then that's cool, I think."

"There's a 'but' buried in there."

"Big one." She grinned but felt it fade fast. "Crista thinks my dad was some kind of backstabbing monster, which I refuse to believe. Eli told me she thinks my father turned Roger in to the police. Honestly, I have a hard time believing he'd do that to a friend. He was ethical, yes, but he was also a person who would turn his life upside down to help a friend. Or"—she smiled—"his daughter."

"I get that," Lacey said. "And you need to remember that Crista is harmless. Lots of bark, not too much bite. But my grandmother?" She lifted both hands and backed up a step like she'd hit a forcefield. "Plenty of bite. I mean, I've never really gotten on her bad side and she's famously softer on her grandkids than her kids. Still, whoa, that woman has opinions and likes things done her way or the highway."

Tessa looked skyward, having a few memories of *that* Maggie.

"I can't imagine how she and my chill mother became such tight sorority sisters," she muttered. "And as far as I can tell, Crista is Maggie's lapdog, right? Does exactly what she wants?"

"Well, she's bringing Nolie to get your help, so..." Lacey lifted a shoulder. "She can break a Maggie rule if something is important to her."

"Points for rebellion," Tessa said. "Always warms my heart."

They turned the corner to another street, this one full of modern, neutral-toned buildings, shops on the bottom, offices and maybe some high-end apartments on top. The sidewalk was lined with regal palm trees tucked into sharply manicured beds.

"I think we're here," Lacey said, glancing at her phone.

They slowed their step as they reached a corner storefront with large windows that showcased elegant bridal gowns on glossy mannequins. An understated gold sign read *Lumière* next to the large glass door.

"Lumière," Lacey said. "French for light, I think."

"French for money," Tessa muttered, then winked. "*Ooh là là.*"

"Should we knock or call her?"

"She said she'd leave the door open and..." Tessa pulled the oversized handle. "She did."

They stepped inside, the soft chime of a bell announcing their arrival. The boutique smelled like roses and Chanel No. 5, with a hushed atmosphere and a soft cream-on-cream palette with pops of pale pink.

Crystal chandeliers cast a warm glow over displays of delicate lace, shimmering beaded bodices, and flowing silk skirts. A raised platform with three oversized mirrors stood at the center of the space, framed by blush-toned curtains.

A woman emerged from the back room, a yellow sundress floating down to her ankles, her hair falling like a black veil over her shoulders. She glided toward them, exuding grace and warmth.

"Tessa?" She extended her hand. "I'm Akari Tanaka. Welcome to Lumière."

Shaking her smooth hand, Tessa smiled. "Hello, Akari. What a beautiful name."

"Thank you. It's Japanese for light, and I'm named after my grandmother."

"And Lumière is French for the same thing," Lacey exclaimed. "How cool."

Akari turned and smiled. "Exactly!"

"This is my assistant, Lacey Knight," Tessa said, making the introduction official. "We're both delighted to meet you."

"Thank you so much for coming at such short notice," Akari said. "Please have a seat. Can I get you water or anything to drink?"

"No, thank you." Tessa looked around as they settled into sofas facing each other. "Maybe a tour of this gorgeous place."

"It is stunning," Lacey agreed as she pulled out her tablet, ready to take notes, while Tessa leaned in. "I don't think I've ever been to a bridal salon as elegant as this."

Akari beamed. "Thank you so much. It's my dream after working in other salons for way too many years. I am connected with private dress designers and carrying one-of-a-kind collections. And I'm so excited to be opening. A little nervous, but excited."

"Nothing to worry about," Tessa assured her. "Weddings are a huge business down here. I've done them for years as the event coordinator for the Ritz-Carlton, and I can imagine you'll have no problem attracting the most discerning brides."

"That's what I'm hoping. If they know about it." Akari exhaled. "That's my biggest concern—getting the word out. The launch is so important to get the ball rolling."

Tessa nodded. "That's where we come in. Tell us your vision for the event."

She made a face, wrinkling her delicate nose. "Well, I don't want a party here, since I'd actually prefer not to have food or drink near the dresses, so that's the complication. I want to show off the dresses, set up private appointments, but keep the masses out of this place."

"Of course," Tessa said, looking around and knowing it wouldn't be the right venue at all for a large party.

"But I do want an event with style and drama and fun."

Tessa grinned. "You are speaking my language, Akari. And, I'm sure, exactly what your brides want when they plan their big day."

"I want them to feel the whole wedding just by looking at the dresses, but that's a tall order."

As they talked, Lacey's fingers flew across the keyboard of her tablet. "A first impression is everything," she said. "And it makes sense that you want the brides to associate Lumière with a great event—like their wedding will be."

Akari's eyes lit up. "Yes and yes. But...how?"

Tessa smiled as ideas started ticking in her head. "We can definitely come up with something spectacular to launch the new salon. Do you have any thoughts on a venue if it isn't here? When you close your eyes and imagine walking in, what does it look like?"

"Available in less than a month," she cracked. "I really want to hold this event no later than the end of April, preferably on a Saturday."

Tessa glanced at her phone and touched the calendar. "That will take some fancy magic. But let us worry about that. What would be the perfect atmosphere?"

Akari looked away, narrowing her eyes as she considered the question. "Bright. Sunny. Warm. Very Florida. It doesn't have to be super bougie, but upscale is important. A place that might be a venue for a wedding, if something like that is possible."

In a few weeks? But Tessa didn't want to throw cold water on anything yet. "What do you want guests to come away knowing about Lumière?" she asked.

"Oh, great question. I want to showcase everything—not just the wedding gowns, although they are the bread and butter of this business. But Lumière is more than a wedding dress shop. In the back, there's a separate store for bridesmaid dresses, mother-of-the-bride attire, flower girl dresses, and my secret weapon? Tuxedos and men's formal suits. We're a one-stop shop, and I want to showcase that."

"Beautiful," Lacey said, madly taking notes. "That gives us a lot to work with."

Akari leaned forward. "Do you have any initial ideas?"

Tessa hesitated. She did have a few ideas—a faux

wedding, a champagne brunch, a bridal beauty bar, maybe a big giveaway. But this one would take some thought and a more professional presentation.

"I'd like to tour the entire salon, solidify budget parameters, and take a few days to brainstorm. Then we'll come back to you with an idea that will knock your...veil off."

Akari laughed. "I love that. Let's look around, show you some of our collections, and let your ideas marinate. But be warned—my budget is tight. Probably not what you're used to, so you'll have to get creative."

"I love a challenge," Tessa replied without a moment's hesitation.

The tour and ensuing discussion took almost an hour, but it was spent inspiring Tessa to think big and out of the box.

By the time they said goodbye and set up their next meeting to present their plans, Tessa was humming with excitement.

"So, any ideas?" Lacey asked as they walked down the street back to the parking lot.

"A million of them, but we'll have to do some research and digging. It isn't going to be easy to find the right venue for an event that soon. You?"

Lacey shook her head. "No, but that store made me want to get married."

Tessa laughed and put her arm around the younger woman. "We should work on that, too, faux daughter. Let's find you a husband."

Lacey laughed. "One big idea at a time there, faux momma."

The words squeezed her heart and gave Tessa a bittersweet jolt. "I don't know how I ever thought I could do this business alone, Lacey," she said, giving her a light hug. "You're awesome."

"Aww. You know I'm in heaven and it isn't just the job." Lacey slowed her step and looked hard at Tessa. "I love your style and spunk. I really do."

The compliment warmed her for so many reasons. She clicked with this girl, and she trusted her. And trust didn't always come easy to Tessa.

TESSA PULLED INTO THE DRIVEWAY, easing the car to a stop as she caught sight of an unfamiliar SUV parked near the garage. Her fingers tightened on the steering wheel as she shifted into Park, exhaling slowly through her nose.

"She's *back*," Tessa sang, throwing a look at Lacey. "With offspring."

Lacey smiled as she unlatched her seatbelt. "Nolie's a doll," she said. "A little shy until you get her going, then she never shuts up. Very smart and sweet. Much sweeter than—"

"Her mother?" Tessa joked.

"I was going to say her namesake—Maggie and Nolie both share the real name of Magnolia."

"Huh. Not sure I knew that." Tessa sighed, leaning back against the headrest for a beat before reaching for the door handle. "I'm actually looking forward to seeing if I can help the kid. I only meet adults with dyslexia, but someone who's just figuring out the wobbly life? We might connect."

"I know you will," Lacey said, reaching over the console. "You better, because I don't want to have to talk you into not leaving again. You can't be punished for something your father did."

She shuttered her eyes. "Whatever he did, he had a reason. We may never know it, but I have faith that he didn't act on impulse or intend to hurt anyone."

Lacey nodded a few times. "I believe that, too, and even though I'm a Lawson, I'm on your side."

"Thanks, sweetie, but let's hope there are no 'sides' to be on."

Lacey shrugged, twisting to grab her purse from the backseat. "It all happened long before me," she said. "I never knew my grandfather. I only know that Eli hates him, Maggie worships him, and my mom feels like she was cheated out of having a father."

"Why does Eli hate him?" Tessa asked. "I didn't think that man was capable of hate."

"True," Lacey conceded. "Especially Uncle Eli, who is a man of faith, even if he's quiet about it. Let's just say the fact that his father went to prison for criminal behavior makes him uncomfortable."

"I know that." Tessa gazed at the SUV, the weight of the encounter a few nights ago pressing on her chest.

The things Crista had said weren't small. Her accusations had cut deep.

Even though Crista had walked that back a bit during their early-morning coffee chat, the tension between them remained a wound barely scabbed over.

Lacey pressed her arm. "She can flare fast, but she's always sorry."

"She didn't exactly apologize the next morning," Tessa said, pushing the car door open. "But she tried to be civil. I will, too."

Inside the house, the cool air washed over them as they walked through the open foyer and into the main living area.

Vivien looked up from where she stood near the kitchen island, her face lighting up in a welcoming smile. "Hey, you two! How'd the meeting go?"

Eli was seated at the counter, nursing what looked like an iced tea, and in the dining area, Crista stood near the table, watching over a little girl who was fully engrossed in a coloring book.

Tessa felt an unexpected pang in her chest as she took in the small, dark-haired child, her tiny fingers gripping a purple crayon as she worked furiously. There was a quiet intensity to her. And for the first time, Tessa saw Crista not as a storm of emotions but as a mother, standing protectively near her daughter.

Crista glanced up, her expression unreadable. "Lacey. Tessa."

Nolie looked up, her whole face bright. "Spacey!" She ran to Lacey, who held her arms out, obviously used to the nickname that Jonah had apparently hung on her.

They were all the Lawson cousins, Tessa remembered. Jonah, who wasn't here at the moment, Lacey, Nolie, and the great and awesome Meredith, who she'd yet to meet.

Lacey crouched down and got face to face with Nolie. "So, skipping school for a beach vacay, huh, kiddo?"

"Yes! With Aunt Pittypat!"

"There's another aunt?" Tessa asked, making them all laugh.

"Four-legged, furry, and about the size of a rat," Eli explained.

"A very cute rat," Nolie said, gazing up at Tessa. "She's out on the deck, sleeping. Are you afraid of dogs?"

"Not rat-sized ones named Aunt Pittypat. Are you afraid of strangers?"

"Not pretty ones like you."

"Oh!" Tessa threw her head back and laughed as the others reacted. "You've got my vote for Princess of the Year. I'm Tessa. You must be...let me guess. Named after a flower? Magnolia?"

A slow smile pulled, revealing one missing front tooth with the glint in the gum of one ready to make an appearance. Her eyes were chocolate brown with hair a few shades darker, a little clone of her mother. She stood about four feet, couldn't weigh fifty pounds soaking wet, and still had some baby softness around a sweet, sweet face.

Yeah. She'd love this kid whether she wanted to or not.

"I'm named after my grandmother," Nolie told her.

"What do you know—so am I," she said, aware of Crista's sharp eyes watching the interaction. "She was Theresa Katherine, and my sister and I got her names." She glanced at the child's work. "Whatchya coloring, Nolie?" "Flowers," she said softly. "Messy flowers."

Her heart folded in pity. "There is no such thing as a messy flower," she proclaimed. "Especially from someone named after them. Can I see?"

Nolie glanced at Crista, who gave an imperceptible nod of approval for this stranger, then walked to the table and Tessa followed. She scanned the surface of the dining table that normally functioned as her desk, taking in the scattered crayons, a few torn-out coloring book pages.

There was an open notebook with some scribbles and a lone yellow pencil that had been chewed on at the end. Oh, heavens, she knew that pencil. Could taste the eraser in her mouth to this day.

"You ever get hand cramps when you write?"

"Yes." Nolie nodded hesitantly as she slipped into a chair.

"Same, sister." Tessa leaned over and looked at the letters. Yep, she knew those, too. "Used to happen all the time when I was a kid. And my letters always went a little wiggle-woggly, no matter how hard I tried."

Curiosity and interest flickered in her dark eyes, but she didn't say anything.

"It made school a pain in the butt," Tessa added.

"My grandma says ladies don't say butt," she said, straight-faced. "We say bottom."

"Whoops." Tessa chuckled, as did the others, who all sort of quietly watched the exchange, making her feel very much like the whole Lawson clan was testing her.

Well, she didn't care if she passed their test, but Dad was surely watching. He'd want to see if she'd learned more than how to read and write at that table when she was this girl's age.

"Can I write and color with you?" Tessa asked, sliding into the chair next to Nolie.

The little girl looked surprised and glanced around. She was obviously smart enough to know that some strange adult swooping in and coloring with a kid was not standard operating procedure.

"Sure," Nolie finally said. "But my letters aren't very good."

Tessa grabbed the chewed-up pencil and turned over one of Nolie's coloring pages to the blank side.

"Okay, let's try something fun. Want to know a fun way to make sure your letters don't go ziggy and zaggy?"

Nolie smiled at the words. "That's what they do."

"Did you ever go bowling?" Tessa asked, getting another look at the unexpected question.

"I went to a bowling birthday party for my friend Adeline."

"Perfect. I bet they put those awesome guardrails up so you didn't get gutter balls."

She nodded. "Jason Figsworth got a strike."

"Well, since he's stuck with that name, he deserved it."

Nolie giggled.

"All right, Figsworth," she joked. "What you need for wobbly letters is the same thing you need for a wobbly bowling ball. Guard rails."

Invested, Nolie leaned in and watched Tessa's pen.

"I still do this when I have to write something important," Tessa said, making her dots just the very way Artie had taught her. "Let's spell out something. Give me a word."

"Figsworth," she said with another chuckle.

Tessa smiled, already liking her sense of humor. "Start with an F. Make one, two, three, four, five dots."

"Then you follow them?" Nolie asked, instantly getting it.

Tessa tapped her nose with the pencil. "Ding-ding-ding. We have a smarty-pants in the building." She flipped the pencil and offered it to Nolie. "Now you do it for me."

As she guided Nolie through a simple trick—using dots to create a letter guideline—the little girl relaxed, the tension in her fingers easing.

From a few feet away, Crista watched quietly, her expression unreadable, but certainly not hostile.

Eli's phone rang and he walked back to his office, so Lacey and Vivien came over to sit at the table with them, which Tessa appreciated so it was less like a show.

"You wouldn't believe this bridal salon we went to

today," Lacey said to Vivien. "And we had a great meeting."

As Lacey told them the highlights of meeting with Akari Tanaka at Lumière, Tessa quietly showed Nolie the dot system for writing her name.

Eventually, Crista sat, too, listening to Lacey tell them all about the grand opening they had to plan, but keeping one sharp eye on her daughter.

"So what are you going to do for this event?" Vivien asked.

"That's the million-dollar question," Tessa admitted. "Well, probably not a million, since she already warned us about the budget. We'll do something that makes a splash. And it has to be on April twenty-sixth."

"That's the day of my recital," Nolie chimed in. "But I'm not going. I'll be here."

"Oh. Are you sad?" Tessa asked.

"I brought my dress," she said. "It's pink. We are doing *Dance of the Flowers* from *The Nutcracker*. But my teacher made it *Dance of the Flower Girls*. And we were all going to wear flower girl dresses!"

Tessa gasped, an idea sparking like a flame in her brain.

"*Dance of the Flower Girls?*" she repeated slowly, as if testing the words out loud.

Nolie nodded enthusiastically. "We all carry flowers and come down an aisle like we're at a wedding, but we twirl." She hopped up from her chair and turned in a little circle, her arms delicately lifted like a ballerina. "Like this."

Tessa's eyes widened as a vision clicked into place.

A fashion show. A dancing, moving, twirling fashion show made up completely of the wedding party, flower girls, and, of course, brides.

Tessa's pulse quickened as the idea took shape. "You..." She pointed playfully at Nolie with the chewed-up pencil. "Are a genius!"

Her eyes flashed. "I am?"

"Yes!" Tessa turned toward Lacey, grabbing her arm. "Let's hold a live, elegant fashion show, wedding themed, of course, and the runway is the aisle. And they can dance, just like Figsworth the Flower Girl!"

Nolie buckled with a guffaw that brightened her whole face. But Lacey didn't laugh. She caught the spark instantly.

"Perfect! A wedding-inspired fashion event. Show-casing every piece in Akari's collection—brides, brides-maids, men in tuxedos and..." She turned to Nolie. "Flower girls."

Nolie's eyes flashed as she looked up at Tessa. "Really? Can I be one of them?"

"Can you... Are you *kidding*? You're the star!" She impulsively hugged the child, who squeezed right back. Over her narrow shoulder, she caught Crista's gaze, warm and relieved and hopeful.

She closed her eyes and held the hug, seeing only her dear departed father, who was not a traitor. Somehow, she'd get Crista to believe that, and maybe this child was the answer.

June 12, 1990

Okay, diary, let's just start by saying that tonight was the most horrible night of my entire life. (And that's saying something because Crista is my little sister, and her whole existence is spent annoying me.)

I am writing this under the covers, with my flashlight, because if Kate or Tessa wakes up and see me, they'll demand to know what I'm writing, and I cannot handle the questions right now.

We all got to go to a beach bonfire tonight. Not a boring parent bonfire either—like an actual teenager bonfire. There were probably 30 kids there, maybe more. Mostly older, but teenagers.

Someone had a big boombox playing Poison (the band not the dangerous stuff). A bunch of older girls were dancing in the sand, and the guys stood around trying to look cool.

We weren't even supposed to go at first. It was technically Eli and Peter's thing, but Tessa somehow managed to convince them to let us tag along. Of course, because Tessa can get Eli to do whatever she wants. It's like a superpower. The parents were okay with it because the boys promised to look after us.

Anyway, once we got there, I was happy to

be included. I mean, I was standing around with high schoolers. But then, things took a major turn, and not a good one. Not even close.

I saw Eli and Peter standing off to the side, talking, heads together like they were plotting a bank robbery or something. Obviously, I had to listen. Of course, neither one noticed me so I could hear them talking...about a girl.

Not just any girl. A perfect girl. Her name was Bethany or Brittany or something equally unfairly cool (not named after some movie star from a hundred years ago like moi). And according to Eli and Peter, she was the hottest girl at the bonfire. (Peter's exact words!)

I looked over, and of course, there she was— sitting on the sand, flipping her incredible blond hair and laughing like the entire universe revolved around her. She had on a jean miniskirt and a cropped tank top that was, okay, slightly cooler than my I ♥ New Kids on the Block tee and cutoff shorts.

And Eli and Peter? They were obsessed.

They started plotting how to talk to her, and their ideas just got dumber and dumber.

Okay, she was gorgeous. And cool. She probably had two or three boyfriends back home, while I couldn't even get one boy to look at me— except when Peter ruffled my hair and called me "kiddo" like I was his annoying little cousin. Ugh!

I stared at her and thought...what would it feel like to have boys scheme about how to talk to you? Not one...but two!?

I'll never know.

I tried really hard not to care—I mean, I'm 13 and have a secret crush on a 16-year-old. I'm not technically jealous, but...then Peter ran a hand through his hair and said, "Okay, I'll just go over and talk to her. I'll act natural."

Then he talked to her for like an hour. Eli had to finally drag him away and all they did in the car on the way home was talk about Bethany/Brittany the boy magnet.

I don't think I'm ever going to be the kind of girl that makes boys trip over themselves just to talk to me. I'm never going to have two guys scheme about how to win my attention. I'm just Vivien, the little sister tagalong. I might as well be Crista, at least in Peter's eyes.

But I have Kate and Tessa—Tessa pronounced them "idiots"—and we did have fun singing with the boombox.

U Can't Touch This!

If all they do is talk about her tomorrow, I'll just throw myself into the Gulf. And then Peter will magically realize I exist! And save my life! And perform...that medical kissing thing. Or not.

Going to sleep now.

P.S. If anyone finds this diary when I'm

dead, please burn it immediately. I cannot have anyone knowing I wrote this.

V.

Chapter Eight
Vivien

The call from Fiona Buckman the next morning had taken Vivien completely by surprise. But after a moment on the phone, she remembered the woman she'd been introduced to at a dinner party a week earlier.

Fiona wanted to see and interview her—today. Vivien jumped on the opportunity.

As she left for the meeting, Vivien hoped she had the same luck and energy launching her business as Tessa seemed to have with hers. Other than staging the Summer House, which was why Vivien had come here in the first place, she still had no other accounts for her design and décor venture.

But Fiona not only had a historic house to "redo"—whatever that meant—she ran a property management business that could unlock oodles of work for Vivien. The local Airbnbs were in constant need of a refresh or remodeling, so a client like that could be an amazing launching pad for Vivien Lawson Designs.

As she arrived at the address in the upscale golf-course neighborhood of Indian Bayou, it was instantly clear that Fiona's house was not exactly *historic,* as the woman had said. Pulling into the long driveway and eyeing the corner lot that featured a large Victorian-style house, Vivien would call that a bit of an exaggeration.

Of course, she was the daughter of an architect and Roger Lawson would have dubbed this two-story 1980s build a "McVic"—a faux Victorian. And it wouldn't have been a compliment.

Yes, it had the grand wraparound porch lined with gingerbread trim and wrought-iron railings curling like black lace against the deep green clapboard. The perfunctory towering bay windows gleamed beneath a steeply pitched roof with filigree and fantasy all around.

But it was dated, fake, and screaming for a renovation.

Fiona had said that she'd recently bought the house from the original owner, who'd done nothing to it for decades, and she wanted a complete remodel of the inside.

So today, Vivien's job was to impress the potential client and secure the assignment, or at least leave the door open to writing up a proposal. They'd only talked briefly at the party, but Vivien remembered the sixty-ish widow, and thought her to be no-nonsense and tough.

Which could translate into inflexible and nasty, but hey. After a lifetime under Maggie Lawson? Vivien certainly could handle a woman who knew what she wanted.

Grabbing her laptop bag, Vivien stepped out of her car and glanced down to smooth the outfit that had been heavily vetted by Lacey.

Deciding that Fiona would likely be a style snob, she'd gone with a pale blue silk shell and the pride and joy of her closet—off-white Belgian flax linen trousers that she never wore for fear rain would destroy their luster. She added her beautiful open-toed Steve Madden patent leather slides with a stacked heel for the finishing touch.

Fortunately, it was a cloudless day bathed in Destin sunshine, so she carried her light tweed blue and cream jacket—a Chanel knock-off, but still exquisite. Stepping onto the walkway, she squared her shoulders, adjusted the jacket and laptop, and slid her best bag into place.

Good morning, Ms. Buckman, she practiced in her head. *I'm delighted to—*

What was that noise? She turned left and right, aware of a high-pitched whine, then a clunk, and—

"Oh, my God!" she shrieked as what felt like fifteen nozzles from the sprinkler system rose up and burst to life, gushing water all over her. "*What is happening?*"

She looked from side to side, seeing nothing but shoulder-high streams of water pouring over everything—including her silk and linen.

"Whoa, whoa, whoa!" A man's voice broke through the noise of the sprinklers.

She turned, holding up her hands in a failed attempt to shield herself. She flew off the walkway and leaped toward the grass, which looked bone dry.

But it wasn't, and the slides did indeed *slide*, taking her right down to the ground with a thud that sent her laptop and handbag sailing.

"Hang on!" a man she still couldn't see called. "I got this!"

As fast as it started, the water stopped. A second later, a man dressed in a filthy T-shirt and baggy shorts came darting out of side bushes, rushing toward her.

"You okay?"

She looked up at him, speechless and soaked.

"Oh, man, I'm really sorry. I'm trying to fix the sprinkler system, and you just showed up at the very wrong moment. I didn't see you." He crouched down on one knee, a ballcap and sunglasses hiding his face and whiskers that hadn't seen a razor in a few days showing a mix of gray and black. "Are you hurt?"

She managed a breath and looked down at the soaked pants—with a grass stain!— and the not-really-Chanel jacket strewn on the ground next to one of her shoes.

He followed her gaze and picked up the shoe, holding it out to her on one knee like he was Prince Charming. She could have hit him with it.

"This yours?" he asked.

She snorted at the abject stupidity of the question. "Yes."

"I'm really sorry." He held out his other hand, rising to offer her assistance. "Coast was clear before I went into the bushes to turn on the valve."

She took his hand, which was strong but not callused like she'd expect of the landscaper or whatever he was. She let him guide her to her feet and as she rose, she looked down at her outfit, soaked and destroyed.

Letting out a whimper, she brushed her trousers and tried not to say a very dark word.

"Here." He offered the shoe again, putting it on the ground so she could step in. Then he turned one way, then the other, muttering something as he went for her laptop case.

"I hope this is okay."

After getting it, he grabbed her bag, stuffing God only knew what back into the open top, snagged a pen that must have fallen from the laptop bag, and brought it all to her.

The whole time she stood in shock, the damp clothes cold despite the sun, her hair dripping in her face, and she didn't even want to think about her mascara.

"I'm sorry...ma'am." His voice was deep and rich with regret. "I wasn't sure which way was on with this system. I'm really..." He gave a soft laugh. "Not exactly a sprinkler repair man."

No kidding.

"It's..." She wanted to say "all right" but really? It wasn't. She was wrecked. "I'm, um, supposed to meet..." She angled her head toward the house. "Ms. Buckman."

He cringed as if the very idea pained him. "You want me to cover for you?"

"While I change in my car?" she quipped, taking her belongings and wiping some dirt from the jacket. "It's fine. I'll just step into the bathroom and towel off."

"There's a powder room off the entry." At her surprised look, he added, "I tried to fix some wonky plumbing when she moved in."

"Thanks for the warning," she said dryly. "I'll avoid the faucet."

He chuckled. "Look at that—pretty *and* she has a sense of humor. Don't see that a lot, you know?"

Did he say...pretty? Was this handyman flirting after he'd drenched her? She felt a smile pull despite the fact that she kind of wanted to kill him. Except, yeah, he had a handsome face under the whiskers and shades.

"Thank you..."

"I'm Danny," he said. "Danny Sullivan and I'm—"

The front door flew open, revealing Fiona Buckman standing in the doorway, her smooth white hair contrasted against a black sweater making a daunting impression.

"What is going on?" she demanded.

"Ruh-roh," he muttered under his breath. "Ding-dong, the witch is not dead."

Vivien half-gasped, half-snorted, stunned by his insolence. She hoped Fiona hadn't heard and didn't lump Vivien with this half-baked handyman from hell.

Swiping back some wet hair, she lifted her chin and smiled as if nothing in the world was wrong.

"Little run-in with the sprinkler system," she said, feigning brightness.

"Oh, it works, Danny?"

"We're getting there." He stepped back and touched the brim of his hat in a gesture that was somehow both mocking and chivalrous. "I'll wait until you're inside."

"Come on, come on." Fiona waved her closer. "I'll

give you a towel. You can't possibly ruin the floors because they're all coming out anyway."

With one more glance at—what was his name? Danny the Walking Disaster?—she headed up to the porch.

Inside, Fiona ushered her straight into the powder room. "Honestly, that man's going to be the death of me," she murmured. "There's a towel in there. You'll be fine."

In a room with a black pedestal sink and *ghastly* velvet flocked wallpaper, Vivien tried not to look too hard at herself in the ornate mirror. After an attempt to dry, she donned the jacket, which was damp, but not see-through like her wet silk top.

As ready as she could be, Vivien stepped into the center hall, a two-story affair at the bottom of a massive staircase, just as Fiona joined her.

For the first time, she got a good look around, taking in the dark floors that she certainly wouldn't replace, but might have stripped and re-stained. A heavy brass chandelier that looked like it had been installed when the house was built forty years ago hung from the ceiling, barely casting enough light to make up for heavy gold drapes that covered arched windows in the formal living room.

Yes, it was wretchedly dated. But there was so much potential here—the kind of high-quality woodwork that could be refinished, the detailed moldings that could be modernized without losing their charm.

"Your home is beautiful," Vivien said sincerely,

pausing to admire the dark wood trim up the sides of the stairs as Fiona gestured her toward the back.

"It will be, but now? I can't bear to look around. But getting into Indian Bayou was all that mattered to me. Location is everything, you know, and this one is top notch."

Vivien followed her into a formal dining room, where a massive rosewood dining table dominated the space.

"I bought it furnished," she said, sounding apologetic as she touched the table. "I haven't had a chance to get rid of this."

"I'm not sure I would," Vivien said. "It's an antique and probably the site of many family dinners. We could refinish it and let it star again."

She grunted. "It's firewood to me, but maybe we'll donate it. Sit down."

Vivien almost bristled at the order, and Fiona glanced at her. "You can't ruin the brocade even if you're wet," she said, misinterpreting her reaction. "The chairs are going, too. Everything is."

"Well, that's why I'm here," she said. "We can modernize this home, but maintain the illusion of history and what I'm sure is an amazing legacy."

"Legacy?" Fiona scoffed as she sat at the head of the table. "I have no idea what the *legacy* of this house is, and I don't care. I know what it's going to look like, and I need you to make that happen."

Okay. Some clients had a distinct vision, but they were usually open to some input. Otherwise, Vivien was a hired gun with no creative input. But this was a test, and a lot of other business was on the line, so she just nodded.

"So, I've created a few different vision boards," Vivien began, reaching for her laptop and praying that only the case was wet. "Think of them as idea hubs that create an overall aesthetic. I'd like to know what colors, textures, and styles you respond to, first, then I'll—"

"Oh, no, that won't be necessary," Fiona interrupted, pulling an iPad from a bag on the floor. "I already know exactly what I respond to. I know how the house will look when I'm finished."

Vivien lifted a brow. "Terrific. Tell me—"

"I want everything gone, totally stripped down to the bones, or at least the drywall. All the ghastly wood torn out, all the curves and gaudiness gone. I want sleek, modern, contemporary, organic." She tapped the iPad's screen and handed it to Vivien. "I have a vision board of my own, actually."

Vivien blinked, a little taken aback but quickly recovering. "Oh, well, great! I want you to love the house, so whatever look you're going for, I'll make it happen."

But as she scrolled through Fiona's Pinterest board, Vivien's enthusiasm for the job took a nosedive.

Every image was stark and colorless—white walls, black accents, and cold, sleek lines. It was modern, yes, but also sterile. Appropriate for an ultra-contemporary California hillside home, but an upscale golf community in Destin in a structure that had nooks, crannies, and atmosphere galore?

There was no warmth, no personality, no nod to the

character of the house itself. Vivien couldn't help but think it resembled a high-end hospital rather than a home.

"Okay, so you're definitely wanting a very modern look."

"Yes, I just said that," Fiona replied, her tone clipped. "I would love it if you'd do those concrete floors that are all the rage, too."

Concrete floors in Florida? Vivien had to swallow her whimper of sadness.

"All right. Just from looking around, your house has such beautiful detailing. I think you could find a way to get the clean, contemporary vibe you want but preserve the—"

"Preserve nothing," Fiona said, cutting her off. "I want it all gone. See these white walls?" She gestured toward an inspiration photo. "That's what I want. Clean and spotless, nothing elaborate, fussy, or embellished. Am I clear?"

Crystal.

Vivien glanced toward the kitchen, which she could see from her seat. It did need an update, but there was so much richness and charm in the cabinetry.

"What do you think about refinishing the cabinets to a much lighter, organic wood, adding black finishings and white countertops? It could still be very contemporary but—"

"Are you not hearing me?" Fiona snapped, her voice sharp. "No wood. None. I want it all gone and replaced with sleek, white, clean lines. I like those shiny white European cabinets with no handles. Are you familiar with them?"

In this house? It was so wrong she wanted to cry.

Instead, Vivien bit the inside of her cheek, a flashback to Maggie in her head. She didn't usually—maybe ever—work with clients like this. But...she'd been raised by one.

"Okay," she said evenly. "I can do modern and sleek, definitely. But, respectfully, Fiona, you hired me to design the redecoration of your home, and I really think you could consider some—"

"I hired you because I don't want to do it myself," Fiona said, standing abruptly. "I know the look I want, and this is it." She tapped the iPad again. "So, please, make it happen. I have a business I have to run now that my husband has died. As you may recall, I manage dozens of properties in Destin and all around the Panhandle and 30-A. Those properties always need refreshes, remodels, and redesigns. Do my house right, and you'll go at the top of the list for recommended designers for the owners. Do it wrong and you won't work in Destin again. Do you understand?"

She most certainly did.

Vivien stood as well, forcing a smile. "If you could just email me the link to your inspiration board, I'll get started on finding materials and furnishings right away."

Fiona nodded curtly. "Good." She walked Vivien to the door and offered a brisk goodbye before disappearing back inside.

Standing on the porch, Vivien took a deep breath, letting the warm air steady her nerves. She turned to look at the house again, her designer's eye picking out the details she'd love to keep and others she'd like to change. Yes, it was faux Victorian, but she could work with that and bring out the home's essence. That would be fun.

This would be...work. But it was a stepping stone to more work.

And speaking of stones...she glanced left and right, noticing the sprinklers were running, but were now aimed at the grass and shrubs. Danny was nowhere to be seen, thank goodness, so she walked gingerly to her Highlander and climbed in, turned on the engine, and made a safe getaway.

Just as she turned the corner, she glanced at the side of the house and saw him. He stood halfway up a ladder reaching into a gutter, shirtless now—he'd probably gotten himself soaked. As she slowed at the stop sign, she squinted at him, grudgingly acknowledging that he had a nice physique.

Actually, really nice.

She slid her window down to get a better look just as he turned and stared right at her. Before she could turn and pretend not to be gawking at the man, he tipped his ballcap and grinned.

Blood warmed her face as she breathed out a sigh and turned to face the street.

Great. With luck, she'd never see that hapless handyman again.

A CAR she didn't recognize was parked in the driveway at the Summer House when she returned, making Vivien wish she could slip in unnoticed, rush upstairs, and get these ruined clothes off as soon as possible.

But as she opened the front door and heard male laughter and voices, she knew that wasn't going to be possible.

"Hey, there she is." Eli stepped into the entryway and instantly drew back. "Oof. What happened to you?"

"A wayward sprinkler," she muttered. "Do you mind if I..." She pointed in the general direction of the stairs. "Could you, uh, distract our company?"

"It's Peter, he's not company."

Peter? Oh, she didn't want to see him like—

"There you are, Viv." He came around the corner, looking tall and strong and way more together than she felt. His gaze dropped over her. "Is it raining somewhere?"

"Just over me," she said, fluttering the now destroyed Belgian linen trousers.

Eli pulled out his phone and looked at the screen. "Jonah needs me up in the apartment. Catch you out there, Pete."

He breezed by her, going right out the door she'd just come in, leaving her standing bedraggled in front of the man she once prayed would be her first kiss. She could still see some of the reason why—the dreamy dark eyes and easy smile—but he was an older, wiser, confident detective now, and attractive in a very different way.

He hadn't been her first kiss, but not for lack of writing in her diaries about it.

"I understand you're going to be working in the area," she said. "Missing persons case?"

He nodded. "Routine stuff, but the department rented me a townhouse right off 98, so I'll probably make a pest of myself here."

She laughed. "Just like old times. Can you stay for lunch?"

"I just had mine," he said. "I really just wanted to swing by and see...you."

Her? Then she remembered their last conversation. "To apologize for sending me up the high road, where I crashed?"

He gave a sad smile. "Yeah, Eli told me it didn't go so great with your ex. I still think you did the right thing."

"I did," she said. "Now I know there's a good a reason I'm getting a divorce."

"Exactly. No doubts or second-guessing."

"Yep. I do appreciate your advice, and I hope that Ryan and I can somehow remain civil, if not friends. As you said, divorce lasts a long time." She added a smile. "In fact, I'll be signing those papers in a matter of days."

"Then my timing is perfect," he said. "Maybe a little early, but that's how I roll."

"A little early..." She frowned, not following.

He angled his head as if he couldn't believe she didn't

know. "Too soon to have dinner, Viv? I'd like to go out with you."

He...*what?*

"I didn't want to ask via text—I'm way too old school for that. And I wanted to see your face, and going by that surprised look, Eli didn't warn you I'd be asking."

She felt her face warm with an unexpected blush for the second time in a few minutes.

"No, I...no. He didn't warn me about anything," she said on a laugh. "So...really? A date?"

He smiled. "Just a nice dinner to catch up without the entire Lawson crew breathing down our necks."

"Peter, I..." She was weirdly breathless, certain her hair was falling in still-damp clumps and her mascara might have left raccoon eyes. But he looked like he didn't care about any of that. "Yes, of course. I'd love that."

The look on his face made the whole awkward moment utterly worthwhile.

"I'll call you," he said, taking a step forward. "Eli gave me your number."

"You two are scheming like teenagers, aren't you?" she asked on a chuckle.

"Some things never change, Viv." He stepped closer and for a second she though he was going to lower his face and drop a kiss. But he just tugged one of her wet strands. "Good look for you, Viv. You look pretty," he said softly.

And with that, he stepped out the door, leaving her breathless and shocked and weirdly excited.

The handyman had called her pretty, too. She

couldn't remember the last time she felt pretty—let alone had not one but *two* men tell her she was in the same day.

"Huh." She looked down at her grass-stained, misshapen, ruined Belgian linen pants, smoothing the water bumps left behind. "Who knew these would be my lucky pants?"

Chapter Nine

Eli

After Peter left, Eli went back to work with Jonah, where they were underway on the unfinished apartment. Wiping sweat from his forehead, he surveyed their progress on the skeletal framework of the space. Two-by-fours framed the walls, the rough subfloor creaked underfoot, and open windows let in the warm Florida breeze.

When finished, this addition to the house would consist of two bedrooms, a living area with a small kitchenette, and a large full bath. When he'd drawn out the specs, he knew it was a brilliant use of the are above the three-car garage. It had rental income potential or could add wonderfully livable space and privacy—a working office, a mother-in-law's suite—for whoever bought the house.

If they sold it.

He felt his heart tighten on the subject again. Part of the appeal of keeping this beach house, at least when Vivien approached him with the idea, was that he could open it up to the Wylies as frequent—regular?—guests. A place where he and Kate could meet often and nurture their budding romance.

But if Maggie's beef with the other family was that deep and painful...could they do that? Worse, could he pursue the kind of relationship he wanted with Kate?

Jonah looked up from the bright pink fiberglass insulation he was measuring for the day's work. "Heavy sigh there, dude. Is there a problem with that electric schematic?"

Eli inched back from the box on the wall. "If there was, I'd have to call the electrician who installed it, since I'm not licensed for that. But it's good. I'm just... thinking."

Jonah's gaze stayed direct, his hazel eyes narrowing as he regarded Eli. "You've been weird today."

Eli gave a snort. "You'll have to define weird."

"Not as happy as usual," Jonah replied without missing a beat.

He missed Kate, that was why, but he wasn't sure how to—or if he should—explain that to his son.

Instead, he picked up a Yeti of cold water, taking a drink as he collected his thoughts. "Hey, nothing can bring me down if you're around."

"No pressure or anything," Jonah cracked.

"I don't mean to put pressure on you," he said quickly. "I know I did a lot of that in the past and it cost me."

Jonah shrugged. "I was a pain in the butt who didn't want to be an architect." He grinned, looking like that seven-year-old kid Eli remembered more than the thirty-year-old man he was. "Now I'm the pain in the butt who wants to be a chef."

"Speaking of, any word from the Culinary Arts program?" Since he'd learned about it and applied, Jonah's whole mood had lifted. He'd been in regular contact with Carly, his girlfriend in California whose pregnancy was the impetus to his decision to pursue a career as a chef.

"I'm supposed to find out if I made the first cut today. We'll see if I..." He finished lining up a strip of insulation and held up the measuring tape, snapping it noisily. "...measure up."

"Oh, please. You will."

"Thanks to that letter of recommendation from Kate," Jonah said, then he looked up at Eli—and kept staring.

"What?" Eli said when it became uncomfortable.

"Nothing. It's just...your expression changes when her name gets mentioned. I like to watch for it."

Eli gave him a vile look and cursed his lousy poker face. "Keep measuring and cutting, if you don't mind. Otherwise, we'll never get the insulation in."

"Yeah, yeah. I hate this part, anyway," Jonah said. "When I worked those summers for Uncle Ryan, I did more drywall than anything. I can't wait to get to that. Is he still officially my uncle, by the way? Or do I just call him...Ryan?"

"I don't know," Eli said. "Just Ryan. I think Vivien and Ryan's divorce papers are being signed this week or next, so that's good."

"Good?" He lifted his brows. "Is a divorce ever good?"

"Well, I think Aunt Vivien will be much better off," he said. "And"—he gave a sly smile—"not alone for long."

"What does that mean?"

"Peter was just here and if all went according to plan...he made a date with her."

"Oooh," Jonah dragged out his reaction. "Romance in Destin. Didn't see that twist coming."

Eli smiled. "She always liked him but was a little too young those summers we were here."

"Huh." Jonah rolled the cutter over the insulation with a deft touch.

"Nice work on that, Jonah."

"Thanks." He lifted the perfectly shaped insulation. "Let's get this bad boy in place."

They worked in comfortable silence for a while, the rhythmic sounds of construction filling the space, but Eli could feel something unspoken lingering between them. Finally, Jonah broke the quiet.

"Hey, Dad, can I ask you something?"

Eli looked up, sensing the shift in tone. "Of course. Anything."

Jonah hesitated, his gaze flickering toward the main house. "Do you think it's true what Aunt Crista said? That Kate and Tessa's dad is responsible for your dad dying? Should I call him Grandpa? I never met the guy."

"Just...Roger."

"Okay then, Roger. I mean, I don't feel like it's any of my business, but it's, uh, awkward. And now she's back and no one is mentioning it, so...what do you think?"

Eli ran a hand through his hair, feeling the weight of

the question. "I don't know. And I don't—" He was about to say "care" but that wasn't true. He cared a lot. "It's hard to imagine, but is it fair that the sins of the past should affect the people of today?"

Jonah lifted his eyebrows. "Is that from the Bible?"

"Honestly, I don't think so." He frowned. "Maybe. Look at me. I'm so busy, I can't remember scripture."

Busy obsessing over Kate, he thought, but didn't add that. He merely made a mental note to stick his nose back in the Word of God, where he got his best life advice.

Jonah tucked some insulation in the kitchen wall. "Whatever happened, it must've been pretty bad for the hatred to still run this deep."

"I guess," Eli said, turning to the next pile of insulation.

"So how does this whole old feud affect things with Kate?" Jonah asked.

The question made Eli pause and wonder if this wasn't where Jonah had been headed all along.

"Things with...there are no 'things' with Kate. We're friends and..." His voice faded in the face of Jonah's look.

"I wasn't born yesterday," Jonah muttered.

"I know when you were born," he said. "I was in the room."

"Then be real with me. You and Kate have something good, huh? It's more than just a friendship and after-dinner walks?"

It had started with friendship and after-dinner walks, Eli mused. But the chemistry, attraction, and bond had formed fast and furiously. He could still remember their one and only kiss.

Eli felt a soft smile tugging at the corner of his lips. "Yeah. It really is good. It's amazing, actually."

Jonah's expression shifted ever so slightly. Eli caught it—a flicker of emotion, a moment of hesitation. "That's... that's great, Dad. I'm happy for you."

Eli's heart cracked at Jonah's tone, like there was something more behind his words.

"Well, don't celebrate yet. We live thousands of miles apart, and my mother would..." He tapped the electrical box on the wall next to him. "Blow a fuse and burn the place down—literally, I'm afraid—if she found out I'm in love with—"

He caught himself, but it was too late. Jonah's whole face froze in shock. "Wait... *what?*"

Eli held up a hand. "Hey, it's early days and it's just an expression and I don't even know..." Lying was not in his nature and God hated it. He sighed. "Yeah. I might have fallen in love with her. Or I'm on my way. And she doesn't know that yet, but she will."

Jonah stared at him, then turned away, his jaw tight as he suddenly gave all his concentration to the utility knife he had stabbed into the pink fluff.

Eli stepped closer, sensing his son retreating inward. "You okay?"

Jonah swallowed hard, toying with the knife, visibly fighting an emotion Eli hadn't seen from him in years.

"Yeah, man, yeah, of course. It's just that...it seems

sudden. I mean, she was here for, what, three weeks? Four?"

"I've known Kate for thirty years."

"Long before Mom," he murmured.

Oh, boy. That's where this was going. "Not too long. We said our last goodbyes to the Wylies in 1995, I started my last year at Georgia, and met Mom pretty early that fall."

Eli closed his eyes for a second, remembering the first time he'd seen Melissa DuBois walking across Tate Plaza. He was broken those months—his father under investigation and being charged with crimes Eli didn't understand, his heart still bruised from Tessa's thoughtless rejection of his love.

Melissa—Missy, as she was called by her friends—was the brightest thing he'd seen for months, and he just wanted to bask in her glow.

"Hey, it's cool, Dad," Jonah said. "I don't expect you to be alone forever. It's just..."

"I'm not alone," he said simply. "I have two great children, awesome sisters, and a mostly great mother."

"And memories of Mom," he said, his voice thick.

"Plus the certainty that I'll see your mother again," Eli added.

Jonah's head whipped up as his tool came to a halt. "You can't be sure of that."

"I am," Eli said.

"She didn't...she wasn't..." He shook his head. "I don't believe in religion anyway, and neither did she."

Jonah didn't know that Melissa had started to open

her heart to the Lord. She just hadn't gone public, and she wasn't one hundred percent sure, but she had been reading the Bible the night before she died.

Surely, when that Cessna was spiraling toward Earth, she'd accepted Jesus in her heart. *Surely.*

But now was not the time to debate that. Not when Jonah had that look in his eyes, that grieving, aching hole in his soul that had not been evident—at least not frequently—since he'd arrived here.

Jonah carried his grief like an old, tattered jacket—worn, familiar, something he couldn't bring himself to let go of.

His heart clenching, Eli reached out, resting a firm hand on his son's shoulder. "Jonah, no one could ever replace your mother. She was the most incredible woman. She gave me you and your sister. And she will always be my soul mate."

Jonah nodded, but his eyes were damp. "I know. I don't mean to be childish about this. You deserve to be happy, and like I said, Kate is awesome. She was a natural at the mothering thing. I mean, I'm not sure I'd have stayed here, and I'd have never had the nerve to apply to culinary school if not for her. It's just..."

Eli exhaled, knowing exactly what his son felt. Even after nearly fifteen years, Jonah carried it with him every day. "I know, Jonah. I miss her, too. Every single day. That will never go away."

"Yeah." Jonah's jaw clenched, his hands tightening into fists. "I guess it's just hitting me hard with the anniversary coming up."

Ah, yes, the pain of April. Melissa had died on April twenty-fifth, fifteen years ago.

He hated the day, loathed the anniversary and the memories and the reliving of the loss. He *still* couldn't stand to see azaleas in bloom, bursting in springtime wonder all over the south.

The last time they'd kissed it was in front of a massive pink azalea in their front yard which seemed to explode overnight.

They'd been so delighted with how it looked, and as they held each other on the front walk, his last words were telling her to be careful on that flight today. As if she could control...whatever had gone wrong.

Yes, he despised the day when it rolled around, and it was just a few weeks away.

"I know it's hard this time of year," Eli said, his voice steady. "It's hard for me, too. But hey, we have each other now. That's more than we've had in a long time."

"Yeah, and that's on me, man. I was the one who stayed away." Jonah swiped some of his near-shoulder-length hair back. "I always go back to Atlanta on that day, just so you know."

"You do?" Years had gone by without seeing Jonah. And he'd been there? In Atlanta?

"I go to her grave. First I make sure no one's around, which is why you never saw me. But I go every year and talk to her."

Eli let out a soft groan, not even knowing what to do with that information. Jonah had been in Atlanta, at Melissa's gravesite, and Eli hadn't known it? Her death had gutted all of them, no doubt about it, but, somehow, it hit Jonah harder than everyone else.

He lifted his arm, wanting to hug his son.

"Hey, no mush on the worksite," Jonah joked, backing away. "I need to put my hours in here to pay back your generous loan. You strong enough to bring that drywall up from the garage, old man, or do I have to do it for you?"

Eli knew a solid change of subject and a well-placed joke to derail the conversation when he heard one.

He huffed. "Please. I can carry two sheets at once."

"Then time's awastin', Mr. Lawson. I'll finish the insulation."

But Eli couldn't walk away from this moment that easily. Instead, he reached over and gave Jonah's shoulder another squeeze.

"I'm proud of you, son," he said gruffly. "Taking Carly's pregnancy and her ultimatum so seriously, coming here, finding this new passion for cooking, working for it. Doing what you have to do to be ready to be a father. Your mother would be proud of you. And so am I."

Jonah took a slow breath. "Thanks, Dad." His phone buzzed and he looked relieved as he pulled it out of his pocket. Relief gave way to a huge smile and a soft hoot.

"Well, look at that, will ya? Northwest Florida State College. Make my dreams come true, please." He grinned at Eli and tapped the phone, walking into the other side of the apartment. But without wall insulation, Eli could hear every word on this end.

"Yes, ma'am, this is Jonah Lawson speaking."

Eli looked skyward. "Father, he needs this. Please. Put him in the program where he belongs, where he will flourish, where he might find—"

"An interview? Of course, I can definitely do that. I'm pretty open so..."

Yes! An interview! He'll crush an interview!

After a long silence, he heard Jonah exhale sharply. "Uh, yes... yes, sure. I can do that. I'll see you then."

But he didn't turn around or throw his fist in the air or do a dance on the sub floor. He just stood there with his back to Eli, then slid the phone into his jeans pocket.

"Did I hear you say...interview?" Eli asked.

Very slowly, Jonah turned, shocking Eli with tears in his eyes and no color in his face.

"Yeah, I got an interview. Actually, several of them." Jonah's voice was hollow.

"Son, that's ama—"

"On April twenty-fifth."

Eli's stomach sank. "Well, you know you'll have some serious power in heaven helping make sure you—"

Jonah swallowed hard. "I should have said no. I don't know why I didn't say no."

"Jonah! You can't say no."

"I told you, I always go to Mom's grave that day. I talk to her. I...bring food." He shook his head and swore under his breath. "I can't let her down. She expects me."

And he didn't believe in the afterlife?

Keeping that to himself, Eli took a step closer. "Mom would understand, Jonah. It's unfortunate timing, but we can find other ways to honor her. She would want you to do this interview. She's cheering for you."

Jonah was quiet, then nodded. "Yeah. I know. I'll do it."

Eli placed a firm hand on his son's back. "I'm here for you. I'm with you. If you want, we can go up the day before or the day after."

Jonah's eyes just shuttered. "Whatever. Let's get this insulation done. I'm sick of breathing it." He wiped his eyes as if that's what caused the dampness, and Eli let it go, totally understanding the pain.

Chapter Ten

Crista

Crista hung way too many grocery bags on her arms, weighed down by a trip to Publix. It seemed like the perfect errand to get her out of the house while Tessa "set up shop," as she called it, and invited Nolie to the table for a morning of learning.

She went through the open garage door, the sounds of Eli and Jonah's conversation floating down as they worked on the apartment above. As she climbed the few stairs to the kitchen door, she was already imagining the scene she'd walk into.

Tessa sitting at the dining table, Nolie at her side, deep in concentration as she carefully sounded out words. They'd be bathed in sunlight, the doors open to let that healthy salt air into the room. It would be a quiet, happy moment with none of the stress Nolie experienced when Anthony taught her.

But as she managed to open the kitchen door, she heard a squeal, clapping, and laughter.

Okay, that was—

She froze at the sight of Nolie whirling through the living and dining rooms, both arms extended. Lacey stood next to a whiteboard leaning on the back of one of the barstools, like a homemade presentation board.

Tessa sat at the dining room table, but she was draped over her chair, with a mess of papers, ribbons, pens, and who knew what strewn about.

Aunt Pittypat ran in Nolie's wake, barking wildly, her little tail tick-tocking happily.

A morning of learning? If she'd walked into a preschool, maybe.

"I think the bride should fly in!" Nolie yelled. "With wings!"

"Wings?" Tessa and Lacey squealed.

"Yes!" Nolie exclaimed, flapping her arms. "Wings!"

Tessa pointed to the whiteboard. "Then put it on your list, Flying Figsworth!"

Crista's stomach tightened. This wasn't what she'd expected.

She set one grocery bag down on the kitchen island, clearing her throat, which wasn't enough to get their attention.

"Hello?" she tried, making a quick mental note not to lose it...yet.

Didn't Tessa realize they only had a few weeks? They weren't teaching Nolie how to fly, for heaven's sake!

Tessa, utterly unfazed, looked up from her laptop with a bright smile. "Hey, it's almost like having Kate here again. She's addicted to Publix. Please tell me you got my Essenza."

"If it was on the list, I got it," she said absently,

unwinding her arms from the other bags. "What's going on here?"

"We're storming our brains!" Nolie announced, prancing over. "It's like a big party where all you do is have ideas, Mommy! The first rule? There's no bad idea!"

"And trust me, she's tried," Tessa said, tempering that with a droll smile at Nolie.

Crista took the hug Nolie effortlessly offered, pressing a kiss to her daughter's head.

She was warm, like she'd been playing outside, her hair wild, her face flushed.

She stroked Nolie's damp cheek, tucking a strand behind her ear. "Have you been, um, reading anything?"

"Not a word!" she exclaimed, rolling her eyes dramatically. "This is just for ideas and Tessa says the best ideas come from moving around. So we're dancing!"

She added a giggle and a quick spin—done with more enthusiasm than Crista could remember seeing in a long time.

"Now I have to storm with my brain!" She zipped around the island, joining Tessa and Lacey, who seemed to be much more focused on a project than on Nolie.

Had Tessa forgotten she'd promised to work with the child? Had she just figured she'd tell Nolie to play by herself and call it "brainstorming"?

Crista swallowed, consciously forcing herself not to channel her inner Maggie and insist things be done a certain way. As much as she wanted to blow in here and make demands, she knew she must be patient.

Instead, she turned her attention to methodically

unpacking groceries, her ears trained on the conversation in the living room.

She knew her own tendencies. She knew she could be dramatic, emotional, reactive. She had spent years trying to curb that, especially lately when it seemed like anything could set her off.

But she also knew she had to play this smart. She was here for Nolie, and she needed Tessa's help. Starting yet another war with her wasn't going to accomplish anything.

Still, the irritation simmered beneath her skin as she pulled milk from the bag and slid it into the fridge.

In the living room, the discussion continued.

"Okay, so what if we do a spotlight moment for the flower girl dresses?" Lacey suggested, gesturing to the board.

"Dress," Tessa said. "I'd like to keep it to one—and we know who that is."

"Me!" Nolie shouted. "Oh, oh! I have an idea, Miss Tessa!" She waved her hand like the show off in the front row of a classroom.

"Hit me with it, Figgy."

"What if I have a wand?" Nolie bounced on her toes, waving an imaginary wand. "With ribbons!"

Tessa snapped her fingers. "Nolie, that's brilliant. I love it. Please add it to the list! You know how."

Crista stiffened, leaning to peer over the kitchen island. Nolie grabbed the whiteboard marker, her face alight with excitement.

But as she turned to write, her hand faltered. She got

the first two letters down, "R...I...," but then she stopped. Bs were always tough for her, and "ribbons" had two of them. Nolie's brow furrowed. The marker hovered over the board, her small fingers tightening around it.

What about the dots she'd done yesterday? Crista bit her lip to keep from interfering, but didn't Tessa see the struggle?

Nolie sighed, deflated, and set the marker down. "I can't do it."

Crista's heart squeezed painfully in her chest.

"That's okay," Tessa said, casually and without even looking up. "We can try again on your next big idea."

Was she even *teaching* her?

Nolie's shoulders hunched, and her face fell, and Crista felt it right down to her own toes.

She couldn't stay quiet any longer. "Nolie, sweetie, why don't you go play in our room for a bit? Set up your Barbies? We brought the Dreamhouse."

"We're storming our brains, Mommy!"

Tessa looked up, a question in her eyes that mirrored the sound of Nolie's complaint.

"And you can finish soon, but I need to talk to...the ladies."

With a sigh, she headed upstairs, Aunt Pittypat hot on her heels.

Crista turned and zeroed in on Tessa. "Can I talk to you for a minute?"

Tessa arched an eyebrow. "Sure. What's up?"

"I'm going to make a quick call," Lacey said, disappearing with her phone toward the back of the house, obviously reading the room.

Crista hesitated for a second, then walked to the table.

"I thought you were serious about helping my daughter. I moved heaven and earth to get her out of school and dance, left my husband during our only time without a permanent houseguest, and handed her over to you… hoping for the best. I thought you'd take tutoring her seriously."

Tessa blinked, clearly taken aback. "And what makes you think I'm not?"

Crista swallowed and gestured toward the mess and the white board. "She can't read at grade level, and she needs structure. She needs practice, repetition, study materials—"

"And how has all of that *structure* been working for her so far?" Tessa interrupted, her voice level but firm.

Crista's mouth snapped shut.

She hated it—hated that Tessa was right. The strict tutoring sessions, the rigid study plans—they hadn't been helping. If anything, they'd made Nolie more resistant, more frustrated. But that didn't mean that playtime was the answer.

"Look," Tessa said, leaning forward. "I understand Nolie. I *was* Nolie. If anything, I had an even harder time. But you know what finally worked for me? It wasn't drill sessions or workbooks. It was finding ways to learn *without* realizing I was learning. I figured out how to read and write because I wanted to do more of the things I loved—not because I wanted to be good at school."

Crista nodded slowly, getting that.

"And, you know, I do take this little favor I'm doing very seriously. For one thing, I've been through it and my...my teacher was brilliant. He knew that I did better when I didn't focus, so he let the learning happen organically."

"But she—"

"And since it's been a few years," she continued, "I did some research. Every expert—and by every expert, yes, I mean Dr. Internet—says that movement, multi-sensory activity, and hands-on learning is far better than trying to beat it into her."

"I've heard that, too, but there's no movement when she takes the test to determine if she can go to third grade or not."

"Crista, listen. She's going to learn best when the pressure is off. When it's fun. When it's woven into her everyday life. If we force it, she's just going to shut down. I honestly know that from experience. And that kid?" Tessa laughed. "Little Figsworth is a breath of fresh air I didn't know I needed to inhale. What an awesome daughter you have."

Crista drew back, totally not expecting the compliment or the genuine warmth it shot through her.

"Oh," she said on a whisper. "Yes, thank you. She's... special."

"Smart as a whip, too, which isn't unusual for our kind." Tessa winked. "It's easy to write off a dyslexic person as slow, but we're not. Although it's fun to disarm people who don't give us enough credit."

She was absolutely right. Nolie was bright, and she did learn better without pressure, and nothing had worked, really. And hadn't Crista come here to try something different?

She let out a slow breath. "Okay. Fine. Do it your way. But please—*please*—help her."

Tessa smiled. "Relax, Mom. We got this." With that, she put two fingers in her mouth and let out a shrill whistle that would make a football coach proud. "Lacey! Nolie! Ladies of Tessa Wylie Events! Let's go, we've got a bridal salon to launch!"

The girls came bounding back, and Crista watched as Tessa seamlessly guided the conversation back to their event. But this time, Crista saw something different. She saw how Tessa treated Nolie—not as a struggling kid, but as someone with real ideas, valuable thoughts.

Someone to be taken seriously.

"So about the ribbon wands," Tessa said, circling back. "You think we should have different colors or try and match the dress?"

Nolie lit up just being asked her opinion. "Match the dress for sure! I hope it's pink."

"Me too," Tessa said, pointing to the board. "Write down 'ribbons that match pink dress' so we don't forget."

Nolie grabbed the marker, while Crista felt her whole body tense.

With what appeared to be a whole new confidence,

she marched to the whiteboard and finished the word "ribbons."

Written not quite flawlessly, but the Bs faced the right direction.

She wrote all of it, every word, exactly as Tessa said and her P in pink was perfect. Crista's breath caught. Her eyes burned. *Okay. Maybe it's working.*

Before she could process it fully, her phone buzzed in her pocket. She pulled it out, praying it was Anthony and she could tell him. But her screen lit up with one word, four letters, and...horror.

Mama

"I better take this," she murmured, throwing a look at Lacey. "It's Maggie."

Her niece winced, then mouthed, "Good luck."

As Crista climbed the stairs, she kept her gaze on the scene below—Nolie writing and Tessa watching her carefully.

She knew, in that moment, that nothing—*not even her mother*—was going to get in the way of this.

CRISTA STEPPED INTO THE BEDROOM, shutting the door quietly behind her. She let out a slow breath, pressing her back against the door before glancing at the screen of her phone. The picture of her mother, taken on her seventy-fifth birthday, stared at her from the tiny circle, a smile on her face...but it didn't reach her eyes.

Why was she calling from the Netherlands?

Crista had no idea, but she thanked the good Lord that Maggie hadn't quite figured out how to work Face-Time without help.

She pushed off the door, steeling herself, and finally pressed the button.

"Mama, hi! I'm so glad you got a chance to call. How's your trip?"

"Lovely, Crista. Just beyond my wildest dreams." Her cool, barely-there Georgia accent should have filled Crista with warmth and love. Instead, she felt nothing but dread.

"Tell me about it," she said, hoping her brightness didn't sound fake.

"Oh, the very first day, we went to the oldest botanical gardens in the world in Amsterdam. I loved it, but of course, Martha complained about walking so much. I don't know why she'd take a tour and not walk."

"But it's pretty there?"

"Gorgeous. We did a canal tour the second night and then we spent a whole day at the Keukenhof—castle, gardens, the whole thing."

"Oh, that's nice," Crista said vaguely, perching on the end of the bed, aware of her heart rate kicking up with every passing second.

How could she tell her mother where she was? And why? And—

"I always knew it would be glorious to see the floral blooms in Europe in the spring, but it's outdoing even my expectations. Which were high."

Crista smiled tightly, plucking at a thread on the

comforter. "Aren't they always?" she teased lightly, hoping to keep the conversation easy.

"Yes, well, despite the fact that my phone is mostly useless unless I'm connected to the hotel's Wi-Fi, and even that is spotty, I'm having the most wonderful time," Maggie continued. "You would die if you saw the tulips in Keukenhof. The colors! The sheer expanse of it all! I swear I could spend weeks wandering these gardens and still not see every last bloom."

"I'm so glad to hear that, Mama. I knew it would be a beautiful trip," Crista said, gripping the phone just a little tighter. If she could just keep her mother talking about the trip, maybe they wouldn't have to talk about—

"But I had to call and follow up on our upsetting conversation on the way to the airport," Maggie interjected, her voice shifting slightly. "Did you talk to Eli and Vivien? Do they still want to keep the house that would have you all secure for your futures? And, good heavens, did they have any more contact with...*them*?"

Well...one of *them* was downstairs this very minute teaching Nolie how to read and write. And brainstorm.

Crista tensed, fisting the comforter, her palms damp. How could she tell her?

"Uh, yeah, well... I did talk to them," she said carefully. "In person, actually."

"You went down? Like I suggested?"

That was a suggestion? Please. Maggie Lawson didn't know the meaning of the word *suggestion*.

"Mm-hmm, yes," Crista said.

"And told them to stay away from the Wylies, I

hope," her mother said, her voice sharp enough to slice glass.

Crista swallowed, her pulse hammering. From downstairs, she could still hear the faint sounds of Nolie's laughter—the light, free, musical bubble that she hadn't heard in weeks.

"Yes, that's...what I told them," she said, forcing the words out. "I told them you said that." Not a lie. Not even a tiny white lie.

Maggie exhaled approvingly. "Good. And I do hope they have the financial common sense to recognize that house was meant to be sold, not turned into some ridiculous shrine to a childhood that ended decades ago."

Crista stayed silent, practically chewing a hole on the inside of her cheek, silent for three, four, five rapid heartbeats and a few loud barks from a very worked up Yorkie.

"Crista? Are you okay?" Maggie's voice softened, but it wasn't concern—Crista knew that tone. It was suspicion.

"Yes, I'm fine, just in the middle of it with...Nolie. Trying a new tutor." That was the truth. Sort of.

"Oh, please, all that tutoring," Maggie scoffed. "There is nothing wrong with that child that a little Grandma time won't fix. Is that Pittypat I hear? How's my baby?"

"She's fine. She's...walking a lot." Again, not a lie. Except she was walking on sand, not sidewalk.

"I knew Nolie would take care of her," Maggie said. "She's bright as can be."

"That's exactly what her new tutor just said. Said

she's a...breath of fresh air." She closed her eyes and remembered Tessa's expression when she talked about Nolie.

"I'm telling you she doesn't need a special tutor," her mother said.

Crista pressed her fingers against her temple, silent. There was no point arguing with her mother.

Maggie let out a long sigh, as if she were the one who was exhausted from the conversation. "So, you just stayed the one night in Destin, I presume? Are Vivien and Eli back in Atlanta now, too?"

Crista froze, her heart stuttering in her chest. She knew this moment was coming, knew she'd have to lie. If she told her mother she was here, she'd want to know why she took Nolie out of school and for how long.

It was better she didn't know. Or only found out after Nolie passed the test—and she wouldn't have to tell her who the new tutor was.

If she knew it was Tessa Wylie, she would lose her mind. It would be a betrayal too deep for Maggie to forgive.

Crista took a breath. "Yep, I'm back in Atlanta. I haven't seen Vivien and Eli." At least not since that morning...on the deck of the Summer House.

The lie felt thick on her tongue, but she pushed the words out, forcing a small, tight smile even though no one could see her. "Anyway, I've got to run, Mama. You should rest up before your next big outing."

"Okay, then, goodbye, sweetheart. Kiss Nolie for me. And Pittypat."

"I will. Bye!"

Crista ended the call, dropping her cell phone onto the bed beside her. She stared at the ceiling, her heart thumping from the raw, unfettered *guilt*. But as much as it twisted in her gut, making her literally feel sick to her stomach, she knew one thing with certainty.

Maggie could not mess this up. Not if it was going to change everything for Nolie.

She took a deep breath, rubbing her hands over her face before sitting up. Downstairs, she could hear the muffled sounds of laughter, of conversation.

She pictured Nolie's precious face, the way her smile lit up the room and her eyes sparked with pure, unfiltered bliss. It had been so long since she'd seen that kind of joy on her baby's face.

If the cost of that joy was Maggie's approval? She might have to pay that bill.

Chapter Eleven
Tessa

Tessa stepped into Lumière for the second time that week, inhaling the soft scent of roses and French perfume that filled the boutique. Next to her, she saw Lacey take a deep breath, too, squaring her shoulders as though going into battle.

For some reason, the determination and effort this young woman put into their venture touched Tessa.

With a smile, she put a hand on Lacey's shoulder and added some loving pressure to not merely communicate her confidence in the younger woman, but her trust, too.

"We got this, kiddo."

Before Lacey could answer, another young woman came out and greeted them, introducing herself as Akari's assistant. She offered refreshments and took them to a small but tastefully appointed conference room.

She left them alone, sitting across from each other at a table for six.

"I guess this room is for private planning with brides," Lacey said.

"Or a place for the girl to have an emotional breakdown."

Lacey laughed. "Weddings do bring out the worst in

some women, don't they? I guess it's all the stress of demanding perfection."

Akari swooped into the room, a vision in deep purple today with her long black hair pulled back into a loose bun.

"Who demands perfection?" she asked, catching the end of the conversation.

"I do," Tessa assured her as they both stood to greet their potential client. "And we brought it today."

Akari laughed as they shook hands and exchanged small talk, then she took the seat at the head of the table, with Lacey chatting a little more than usual from nervous excitement.

"I'm so thrilled to see what you've come up with," Akari said.

"We think you're going to love it," Tessa said, while Lacey took out her tablet and set it up where they could all see it. "It's something that will truly capture the essence of Lumière and the joy of a wedding celebration."

Akari clasped her hands together. "Tell me everything!"

Lacey tapped the screen, as they'd practiced, and pulled up the sketches and mood boards they had created.

"What we want our guests to know," Tessa started, "is that Lumière isn't just a store. It's an experience. Everything about it radiates beauty, elegance, and celebration. And what better way to showcase that than a fashion show that replicates a wedding?"

"I like it." Akari leaned in with curiosity.

"We want to create a wedding-inspired runway show, set outdoors in the most picturesque location possible. The runway will be a long, elegant boardwalk from a gorgeous beach house, over the dunes of Destin, right to the sands as white as a wedding dress!"

"Oh!" Akari gasped. "A beach event! I'm intrigued. I do so many weddings on the beach, and it truly captures the spirit of this area."

Buoyed with confidence, Tessa continued. "Think golden-hour light, soft sea breezes, and a stunning backdrop of the Gulf. Guests can mingle on the dune-side seating or watch from the deck of a beachfront mansion that will give them a place to socialize and gather before and after the fashion show."

Lacey tapped on her tablet, ready to show Akari their mock-up of the venue and event.

"And it won't just be the wedding gowns," Tessa assured Akari. "The runway will feature models in your choice of collections, but it will unfold like an actual walk down the aisle, with bridesmaids, groomsmen, key attendants, parents, and, of course, flower girls. Each collection will be showcased, ending with the multiple brides in an array of stunning dresses. Afterwards, we'll have music, dancing, cake, and opportunities for you to meet one on one with guests and arrange private showings at Lumière."

Akari pressed a hand to her chest. "I absolutely love it. Not only can we showcase the clothes, but wedding themes, colors, décor." Then her smile faded. "But, oh, models and a venue—a wedding, if you will—will cost a fortune."

"Not necessarily," Tessa said. "Instead of paid models, who are quite pricey, we suggest you use real people. You may have some customers willing to model, but we also have friends of both sexes and a wide age range who'll do it for free."

"Music to my ears," she said. "And...the venue? Rentals are insane this time of year, even if you could find an empty beach house."

"We have the house—brand new, massive, on the water, and it has a forty-foot boardwalk that was finished last month. If you want, we can identify some rental companies, florists, and food vendors for light snacks, cake, and décor who are willing to work for cost to showcase their wedding offerings, too."

"Brilliant!" Akari cooed.

"It will be a very reasonable budget, but feel highend, elegant, and festive," Tessa said.

"And we have pictures of the Summer House that will be our venue," Lacey added, clicking to one. "We used AI to show you what the seating and décor could look like. We have multiple 'wedding themes' for you to consider."

Akari leaned in and gazed at the screen, pressing her hands together happily as Lacey switched through various options.

The three women spent the next hour going over details—logistics, music, floral arrangements, and seating, and, of course, budget—until Akari finally let out a satis-fied sigh. "Well, in case it isn't obvious, you have the job."

Lacey and Tessa smiled at each other and thanked her for the vote of confidence.

"I'd love if you both promise to be a bride—I'd love to see you two beauties in one of my gowns."

"Oh..." Lacey gave a laugh. "That would be fun."

"But impossible," Tessa said quickly. "I'm going to be fifty this year—not bride material—and we'll be quietly and furiously working the event."

"I understand, but I have a glorious line just for older brides—a little less youthful and more forgiving, not that you need either one. I would very much like to see someone in your age range."

"Whatever you like, Akari," she said, knowing they'd figure something out. "You're the boss."

"Good. That's settled. Let's make this wedding fashion show happen!"

When the meeting was over, Tessa and Lacey practically floated out to Grand Boulevard and back to the parking lot.

"You were awesome in there," Tessa said when they got into the car. "I feel like a proud Mama bear."

"You ran the show and were amazing."

"Please," Tessa scoffed. "I could never have worked that tablet with such ease. Thank you for being such a great member of my team. You made us look totally together."

"Thank you," Lacey said, turning to look at Tessa. "Most people don't share credit the way you do, Tessa. It's so nice to work for someone who isn't all 'me, me, me' about things. And I say that fully acknowledging that my last boss was my very own father, who loved nothing more than stealing credit."

"He even credited another designer with your mother's work," Tessa noted. "But thank you for saying that. I think it's more fun to spread the cheer than try to keep it all for myself. And speaking of credit—I am so glad she agreed to just one flower girl, aren't you?"

"Yes!" Lacey gave a fist bump. "Figsworth will love that. Genius of you to persuade Akari that kids stole the show and were a handful to manage."

"Both of those things are true, but I really wanted to honor the one who came up with the whole idea."

"You're doing such great work on my little cousin," Lacey said. "I thought all you were going to do was help her read and pass a test to get into third grade."

"True, but part of that is building self-assurance. I know firsthand that when you have a learning disability, the first thing to go is confidence. You want to turn shy, even if you're not."

"She's not naturally shy," Lacey told her. "When Nolie was three, she was a bundle of energy and personality, the center of all the family attention at every gathering. Even until she was five or so. But when she got into school and couldn't keep up with the others, she very slowly started to change. Not get withdrawn, exactly, but not as...bold. Unless you're alone with her. Then she comes out of her shell."

"Huh." Tessa considered that interesting piece of insight. "Did anything else change then?"

"Well, three years ago, when Nolie was four, Maggie moved in with Crista and Anthony."

"Why did she do that?" Tessa asked. "Does she have health problems and need help?"

"She had a hip replacement—pretty standard. She decided to stay at Crista's in the downstairs guest suite for her recovery and I guess they all liked her being there enough for her to give up her own home and move in permanently."

"Are you sure they liked it?" Tessa asked, lifting a dubious brow. "Crista's terrified of the woman. Maybe Nolie is, too."

"Everyone's a little afraid of my grandmother," Lacey acknowledged. "But she dotes on Nolie—on all of us grandchildren, to be fair. I think Nolie's shyness is from the struggle in school, and that's also caused tension in the family."

Tessa nodded. "I'm sure it has. Poor kid. Dyslexia is kind of swept under the rug, but it messes with you when you feel like you aren't as smart as everyone else. It chips away at everything—your personality, your self-worth, the way you see the world. That's why I want to help Nolie. Because if she believes in herself, it will make learning easier."

Lacey was quiet for a beat. "It sure would have been

understandable if you had told my Aunt Crista to take a hike. She was really rough on you when she first got here."

Tessa shrugged. "I know, but..."

"But underneath that gorgeous exterior is a heart made of putty and mush," Lacey teased, jabbing her arm playfully.

"Tell anyone and you're dead." Tessa winked at her.

"You're paying it forward," Lacey mused. "Your dad helped you, and now you're helping her."

Tessa tapped her fingers against the steering wheel, thinking. "And we've all shoved the accusations about my dad under the rug, which worries me a little."

"I know," Lacey agreed. "And things under rugs have a way of tripping you up eventually."

Tessa threw her a smile. "Pretty wise for twenty-four, Lace."

She laughed and they talked more about the event, staying on that topic until they pulled into the driveway of the Summer House. Before they could even get out of the car, the front door burst open and Nolie came running out, her hair flying as she threw her arms in the air. "You're back!"

Tessa grinned, scooping the little girl up as she barreled into her. "We are! And guess what? You, my dear Figsworth, are going to be the star of the show."

Nolie's eyes went huge. "I am?"

Tessa nodded. "The grand opening fashion wedding show extravaganza. You're the featured flower girl. Because it was *your* idea."

Nolie squealed, kicking her feet in excitement. "Can we storm our brains some more? I'm so ready!"

Tessa set her down and took her hand. "Absolutely. We need our best team on this. Which means..." She glanced at Lacey. "I think Tessa Wylie Events just gained a third employee."

Nolie gasped. "Me?"

Tessa laughed. "You, kiddo."

Hand-in-hand, they walked inside, where the dining room table was already scattered with notes and sketches.

"I thought we were going to bake cookies, Nolie," Crista said from where she stood in the kitchen with her hands in a mixing bowl.

"You bake, Mommy. We have work to do! Can I write the lists, Tessa?"

"Why don't you read Lacey's notes to me?" she replied, coming around the table and sharing a long look with Crista.

Neither of them spoke, but they didn't have to. They locked gazes, and in that weird space of two seconds... connected.

"Thank you," Crista mouthed.

Tessa smiled and pointed at the mixing bowl. "I like chocolate chip. None of that oatmeal stuff."

"Done and done," Crista said, looking down and fighting a smile.

July 10, 1990

I. Am. Dead. Not literally, of course, but I might as well be because Peter McCarthy just ruined my life in the best possible way.

Okay, let me back up.

It was supposed to be just a normal, completely uneventful afternoon. Kate, Tessa, and I were heading down to the beach, just goofing off like always, and we saw Eli and Peter near the boardwalk, messing around with a volleyball.

Then Tessa—being Tessa—yelled something to Eli about how he wished he had her serve, and Eli—being Eli—immediately challenged us to a match.

That's when everything started unraveling.

Because, you know me. I am not athletic. I am especially not coordinated when Peter McCarthy is ten feet away. But did I say no to playing? No. Of course not. Because I am a fool.

So there we were, an actual game forming, with teams being picked and stakes being raised (nothing serious, just pride and bragging rights). And somehow—I don't know how—I ended up on Peter's team.

I nearly died on the spot when he asked me to play on his side of the sand court.

The first serve came straight toward me, and instead of bumping it like a normal person, I spun my arm like a broken windmill and completely missed. The ball plopped in the sand. And I wanted the ocean to swallow me whole.

Eli thought it was HILARIOUS. Tessa laughed, too. Kate tried to say something encouraging but I was too embarrassed to hear.

And then Peter—PETER—stepped next to me, put a hand on my shoulder (!!!!!), and said, "Hey, no big deal. We've got this."

And just like that, I could breathe again.

But then it got worse. I was determined to not make a fool of myself for the rest of the game, but no such luck. When the next ball came my way, I ran for it—way too fast and not exactly like a gazelle—and completely tripped over my own feet. And wiped out. Face-first into the sand. I didn't even try to get up right away because, honestly, what was the point? My soul had already left my body.

Eli was dying. Kate and Tessa were not helping.

And then Peter McCarthy dropped to his knees next to me—not laughing, not teasing—actually concerned.

"Viv?" His voice was so gentle. "Are you okay?"

I could not respond. I could not basically breathe.

Then, before I could regain consciousness, he

—he brushed sand off my cheek.

Let me repeat that for the people in the back.

PETER MCCARTHY BRUSHED SAND OFF MY FACE.

With his actual hand. His literal fingers. Not in some casual, careless way. But in a slow, sweet, totally unnecessary way.

When I finally managed to move, I sat up too fast and headbutted him.

That's when he laughed.

Not at me—with me (I hope). And then, because he must have sensed that my body was seconds away from dissolving into the sea, he stood up and offered me his hand. Which I took.

Which means I held hands with Peter McCarthy.

Even if it was just for a few seconds, even if it was only so he could pull my pitiful self off the ground, it happened.

I am never washing my hand again. Ever. Because he saw me today. He noticed me. And maybe for one fleeting second, I wasn't just Eli's little sister.

Maybe, in some alternate universe, in some far-off timeline, I could actually be someone that Peter McCarthy likes.

And if that's the case...

Well.

I really need to learn how to play volleyball.

Love,

Vivien

PS: I've officially forgiven him for Bethany/Brittany at the bonfire.

Chapter Twelve
Vivien

As Peter ordered two glasses of pinot grigio, Vivien leaned back and pretended to take in the view from the deck known as a "skybar" in The Edge Seafood Restaurant. Not exactly a high-rise rooftop, but the open-air second-floor dining room was the perfect place for their dinner date.

The golden hues of the setting sun cast a warm glow over everything, and a light breeze carried the scent of salt and citrus. The soft murmur of other diners, the occasional clink of glasses, and the distant hum of motor boats blended into a relaxed ambiance.

A lovely restaurant, yes. But the sights, sounds, and experience Vivien liked the most was sitting across from her.

Peter McCarthy—the object of way too many girlhood fantasies, recipient of more than a few practice pillow kisses, and centerpiece of dozens of diary entries. She'd read one of those entries after getting dressed tonight, recalling the volleyball incident with nothing but affection for the person on that beach who didn't laugh at clumsy Vivien.

And tonight? She was finally on a date with him.

Peter handed the wine menu back to the server, and pinned his dark gaze on her, a brow the same color as his light brown hair flicked with interest.

"Why are you smiling?" he asked.

"I can't smile? I'm out with a great guy in the perfect place, and I'm happy. That's why I'm smiling."

He looked skeptical, leaning in. "That wasn't just an 'I'm having a good time' smile. You were thinking of something that put a...gleam in your eye."

"You're so observant," she said, purposely not sharing her thoughts.

"I'm a detective," he replied, taking his napkin from under the fork and shaking it onto his lap. "I'm observant for a living."

"It's kind of like you can read minds," she murmured.

"If I could, I'd know what put that smile on your face."

"I'll tell you later," she promised. "Now, I just want to bask in the warmth of this sunset over the harbor, and thank you for being so nice and asking me to dinner tonight."

"Nice?" He nodded. "I get that a lot. Not from the bad guys, obviously, but...from the ladies."

"Because you are a considerate, classy, attentive man. That'll earn you a 'nice' from most women." She inched closer. "Which leads me to the obvious question—have there been a lot of ladies since you've been divorced?"

"Not a lot, no. I've had a few...I guess you could call them relationships. But nothing ever really developed. It's fine. I've got a consuming job. Lots of colorful cases."

"Like the one that brought you here? Can you tell me much about it?" she asked, sensing she should take the conversation off the more personal things, at least at the start.

"I can tell you I'm hitting more dead ends than live leads," he said. "This guy just vanished. I'm starting to think he left the country, but we can't find any record of him traveling."

Eli had shared the most basic facts about the case, so Vivien knew a little about what Peter was working on.

"So, he's a Pensacola resident—a salesman, right?" Vivien asked. "And he came here for a long weekend, never went home, and his car was here. That's it? And his family reported him missing?"

"His ex-wife," he said. "But only because he hasn't paid alimony, which could be why he's missing."

"Huh." She winced, thinking of other reasons he might have disappeared. "Could he be...you know?"

"Yeah," he said, understanding the question. "But no body and no sign of foul play and no motive."

"No other family or boss pushing to find him?"

"No one except the ex seems too concerned. Apparently, he's a loner type who likes to travel, but the abandoned car is strange. He's missed a few appointments and his cell phone is off; no record of use for a long time."

"Don't they say the spouse is always under suspicion, or have I watched too many Lifetime movies?"

He smiled. "They're freakishly accurate," he said. "She doesn't really have a motive—their divorce was amicable."

She rolled her eyes. "I believe a wise man once told me there really is no such thing."

"I believe that wise man was me," he acknowledged. "Maybe a tad bitter from all I've seen. But, anyway, we'll figure it out."

They ordered dinners, chatted about the restaurant and how the whole HarborWalk scene hadn't existed when they were kids, sipping their wine.

"So tell me about this client you've reeled in, Vivien," he said. "Pretty impressive to start a business from scratch in a whole new town."

"Well, having Eli and my mother hand me the job to stage the Summer House was a huge boost. Then Tessa coordinated a party and her client's wife introduced me to Fiona, my client."

"Who gave you an outdoor shower as a test of your skills."

She rolled her eyes. "It wasn't her," she said. "It was the incompetent handyman who had no idea where to point a sprinkler system. Why a woman with that much money couldn't hire someone a little more skilled is beyond me."

"Maybe she's difficult to work with and that's all she could get."

Vivien's jaw loosened and she pointed at him playfully. "Right on, Detective McCarthy. She is not an easy client."

"Tell me about her." He seemed genuinely interested, which she appreciated.

"She's a wealthy widow and her husband owned one

of the biggest property management firms in Destin. She's running it now. She bought a big eighties-built faux Victorian in Indian Bayou and wants to do horrible things to it."

He drew back, laughing. "Sounds criminal."

"It is! She wants to take this house—which is admittedly in desperate need of an update and renovation—and turn it into some kind of soulless box of white and gray...nothingness. It won't be easy to design."

"And you have to do exactly what she wants?"

She angled her head. "To a point. Obviously, she holds the checkbook, but I'm hoping to introduce some colors and textures, and possibly put a little life into the place. She wants to strip out some really nice wood accents, too."

Peter studied her, a glimmer of interest and admiration in his dark brown eyes. "I guarantee you'll knock it out of the park."

She felt her cheeks warm slightly at the flattery. "Thank you. It's really a huge opportunity that can lead to more business. That's important because my ex isn't going to send me any clients or projects like he promised."

Peter nodded thoughtfully, both of them quiet while their dinners were served, filling the air with the delicious aroma of grilled seafood.

"So I guess I owe you an apology," he said as they began to eat.

"For what?" She held her fork without taking a bite, unable to imagine what he could apologize for.

"Oh, you know."

She did? Then it dawned on her. "It's fine, Peter."

"No, really, I should have—"

"No." She put her fork down and put a hand over his, resting on the table. "You don't have to apologize for things that happened thirty or thirty-five years ago. I was a dumb kid with a big fat crush and you didn't owe me anything. If anything, I owe you an apology for following you around for all those summers, no doubt making it painfully obvious that you were the number one topic of all my diary entries. I mean, you could barely say a sideways word to me and I was writing, 'Peter McCarthy brushed sand from my face,' in all caps, underlined and heavily hearted. So, no apologies for..."

Her voice faded out as his expression slowly changed from sincere to confused to...seriously amused.

"I was going to apologize for sending you up the high road to make nice with your ex-husband," he said, fighting a chuckle. "But then you gave me what cops call a panic confession."

Very slowly, she lifted her hand as the blood rushed out of her head as she realized...what she'd confessed. "You...didn't know...that?"

He laughed, his broad shoulders shaking. "Not one word."

"Eli...didn't tell you?" she croaked. "Like a bro code thing?"

"He's *your* bro first. Eli is man of honor, and you are his beloved sister. He'd never betray your...what did you call it?" He leaned in, his eyes dancing with mirth. "A *big fat crush?*"

She just stared at him, fighting a smile and a moment of profound embarrassment.

"So I guess my observation skills weren't so great back then," he said. "'Cause, honestly, I had no idea."

She laughed and took a deep drink of wine. "Well, my secret's out now."

"Your diary, huh?"

"I have them all, thanks to Eli," she told him. "He found them before he did demo; they were in an indestructible plastic container with instructions for immediate death to anyone who read them."

He chuckled, searching her face. "What else did you write?"

She let out a sigh, relaxed now, and not feeling judged. "About the time I got a terrible sunburn and you walked a mile to buy me aloe vera."

"I remember that," he said. "We watched *Ferris Bueller's Day Off.*"

"You do remember it!" She gave a little clap. "Yes, we did. And thus began a long crush."

He shook his head, studying her. "I didn't see you as, you know, a girl."

"I know. But you sure saw...Bethany or Brittany...the blonde."

"No recollection," he admitted. "But you were a little more like family than a girl I'd pursue. I'm sorry."

"You do not owe me an apology," she insisted. "You were never anything but kind and, yes, you were more like a brother. Especially in the summers. During the school year, you weren't around much."

"I did sports and…took care of my mom," he said. "My dad wasn't in the picture by the time I was in high school. But in the summers, my mother went up to see my grandmother in New England. I had to choose between a trailer park in New Hampshire or the beach in Destin. Not a tough decision."

She nodded, vaguely aware that he'd had a much tougher upbringing than the Lawson family.

"I'm glad you chose Destin," she said, sensing that it wasn't the right time to dig into his childhood—though she wanted to, and would, eventually.

"And the diaries are here?" he said. "I have to see one."

"Oh, no, you don't. You don't need to see how many different ways a girl can write 'Vivien McCarthy' in pink Flair pen."

He sucked in a breath. "You—"

"I was thirteen. Fourteen. Maybe fifteen, although I haven't gotten that far yet. A kid."

"You were eighteen that last summer," he said. "But I had a lot going on that year. Had to decide if I was going to drop out of school or join the military. It was a complicated time in my life, or I probably would have noticed you." He inched in. "I'm noticing you now. Is that going to make a diary?"

Vivien's breath caught slightly at his words, and she took another sip of wine, looking at him over the rim. "It might. Depends on if you brush sand off my face again."

He reached over the table and grazed her cheek with his knuckle, leveling his gaze at her long enough for her to feel it right down to her toes.

"It's my signature move," he joked with a wink.

"And once again, I swoon."

They both laughed and stayed quiet for a few seconds, enjoying the connection before they continued with the dinner and talked and laughed about a million different memories from the past.

They remembered the time Eli got stung by a jellyfish and Peter announced that the only thing that could save him was to pee on it. And the summer they were stuck inside for three days during a tropical storm, and spent the entire time playing a Monopoly marathon. They remembered meals they'd made, nicknames they'd invented, and a few more girls Eli had obsessed over.

"But no one could hold a candle to Tessa," Peter said. "Especially the last two years. After she turned seventeen, Eli was a goner."

"He was a goner from the day he saw her." She looked skyward. "We all knew it. Even Kate, who felt about him like I did about you."

"Another crush I didn't know about."

"We kept that one very secret because they were sisters and Eli was...oblivious."

He lifted his brows. "Funny thing, though. I sense something real with Kate and Eli now. She's special. Do you think they'll work out?"

Vivien considered the question, narrowing her eyes as she thought. "I think they have a shot, except for the small matter of living a thousand miles apart. And his beliefs are strong. If she's going to be in his life, I'd imagine she'd have to at least give faith a chance."

He nodded. "I've thought of that, although he's low-key about his religion."

They finished eating and lingered over coffee and the conversation until it was well and truly dark. They finally left to walk with the tourists that filled the sprawling shopping and retail center.

As they got downstairs from the second-floor restaurant and stepped outside, Vivien let out a grunt of frustration.

"I left my cardigan on the chair," she said. "I bring one for air-conditioning and always forget it."

"Stay right here," he said. "I'll be back in a second."

She gave him a grateful smile and leaned against the railing, looking out at the lights of the boats all over the harbor.

The strains of music from the restaurant floated down and she took a deep breath, replaying the conversation and feeling...something.

Warmth. Comfort. Security. Peter was a friend, and, yes, in some sense, a brother. She already loved him like that, but could it be more? She didn't know, and considering the fact that her divorce wasn't even final, it really was a moot point.

At the sound of a woman's laugh, she looked up and caught sight of a couple upstairs, something about her pulling Vivien's attention.

Was that Fiona Buckman?

It was! She was too far away to greet, but Vivien leaned back and watched her talking and laughing with a man seated across from her. Well, what do you know? The merry widow was on a date.

Vivien squinted to get a good look at the man in the shadows and soft restaurant light. He had a strong jaw, a handsome face, and the posture of confidence. Wealth, even. Or maybe that was the cut of a shirt that, even from a distance, looked custom made.

Wait a second. Wait *one ever-lovin' second.*

She stood a little straighter, inhaling a sharp breath. Was that the *handyman?* That handsome man who was definitely much younger than—

"Here you go."

"Oh." She turned to see Peter, holding her sheer white sweater. "Thank you. I..."

"Who you stalking?" he asked as he slipped it over her bare shoulders, following her gaze.

"That's Fiona, my client," she said in a whisper, even though the woman couldn't possibly hear her. "And she's out with the hapless handyman! Who has to be ten years younger!"

He looked suitably impressed by the gossip, glancing up again. "Ah, well, that explains why she hires him. He's...handy."

She laughed, taking another look. "I'd have never guessed that. Maybe he moonlights as...an escort?"

He gave that same shrug that said nothing surprised him.

"He is dressed very nicely," she added.

"Maybe he's dipping into her bank account," he speculated. "She wouldn't be the first rich widow to be taken for a ride by a good-looking man."

"He certainly doesn't know his way around a toolbox," she added, concern pressing on her heart. "Do you think he's stealing from her? Or...what's it called when a younger man pursues an older rich woman? Is it a crime?"

"It's called life," he cracked. "But if he exploited or coerced money from her, then we could get him for fraudulent inducement. But the real crime, if it happens, is that she's dumb and, unfortunately, we don't put people in jail for that. Or this place"—he waved toward the crowds—"would be empty."

"So cynical," she teased, giving him a playful elbow nudge.

"Hey, you're the one assuming there's a crime when a man and woman who are"—he peered up again—"maybe ten years apart in age are having dinner together."

"True," she admitted, taking one last look. "But I still think something's up. I'll have to keep an eye on him when I'm over there. What should I look for?"

He considered that as they walked. "Well, first watch for tells, like a new truck or expensive things that a handyman wouldn't own. And see if you can find out if she pays him in cash or—this would be a major red flag— if his handyman's talents extend to helping her with finances."

"Oh, yes, I could see where that would be a problem."

"Also, if he isolates her or she's weirdly defensive

about him. Those could be signs of some kind of manipulation."

She smiled up at him. "Good thoughts, Detective."

"Find out if he has a real job, his own place, or maybe disappears and only shows up when he needs money. Manipulators work in shadows, so shine light on him. If he's a con artist, you'll find out."

"But will Fiona want to know?" she wondered.

"Hey, maybe she's falling for the guy and wants a second chance at life." He leaned into her. "Would that be so bad?"

She laughed as he put an arm around her and guided her through the tourists.

"Keep me posted. I love undercover work, and I'm happy to teach you my powers of observation and deduction..." He gave her shoulders a squeeze. "For a price, of course."

She slowed her step and looked up at him, feeling a smile pull. "A price? And what might that be?"

Was Peter McCarthy finally going to kiss her? Right here in the crowds at HarborWalk? She wasn't sure how she felt about that.

"A small price," he said, turning her toward him and doing the knuckles-on-the-jaw thing again. Whoa, that *was* a power move.

"What is the price?" she whispered, ready to pay it.

"I want to read those diaries."

She threw her head back and laughed. "Not a chance, McCarthy. Not a stinking chance."

Chapter Thirteen

Eli

Eli watched Tessa, Lacey, and Nolie doing... something...on the boardwalk. Prancing and dancing, and so much laughter, he could hear it from his comfortable seat on the deck. Nolie's giggles carried through the air like music to accompany the evening.

He closed his eyes and listened to the sounds, awash with that peace he'd found years ago. The peace that surpassed understanding, the Bible called it.

But he understood *this* peace—there was a glow about the Summer House these days, as warm as the sun that just dipped into the Gulf.

When Crista had shown up and flung accusations, Vivien told him he'd have to build bridges to fix things. Somehow, Tessa had been the architect of this détente, or maybe it was Nolie who got the credit.

No, God got the credit, he thought with a smile. For that and many other miracles happening around him.

For one thing, he'd managed to close some business and design a whole house working remotely from this beachfront haven. Yes, it took the help of his superstar daughter, who managed Acacia Architecture masterfully in his absence.

Meredith fully understood why he was staying down here, and it could be summed up in one word: Jonah. He and his son had connected after years of estrangement and Eli simply didn't want to disappear now. This new bond was another miracle, one that he thanked the Lord for every day.

And that wasn't the only great change on the horizon. Vivien was out this very moment on a date with a fine man. Eli loved the idea of his little sister falling for his best friend, which reminded him of those Hallmark movies Melissa used to watch constantly.

At the memory of his late wife, he sucked in a soft breath, realizing he hadn't thought about her much today.

Not that he obsessed over her—he'd learned years ago to pack up his grief in order to survive and thrive. But that baggage was opened frequently enough, usually upon waking, a few times during his day, and late at night, before bed. When he prayed, he never failed to thank God for having given him Melissa in the first place, and stayed secure in the knowledge and the promise that he would see her again.

But today? The Melissa thoughts had been light. And the Kate thoughts...

He puffed out a breath. The Kate thoughts were darn near constant and made him want yet another miracle.

Jonah came outside, sauntering toward the sitting area with his ubiquitous dish towel over his shoulder, having just cleaned up after a delicious dinner. But his expression was serious as he plopped down in a chair, enough that Eli frowned.

"What's up?" Eli asked.

He sighed. "I really miss Carly."

Eli gave a tight smile, understanding the sentiment. Maybe he needed two miracles from God, one for him and one for his son.

Jonah didn't talk much about the girlfriend he'd left in California. She'd told Jonah she hadn't thought he was mature enough to be a father, and that prompted major changes in the young man. All good changes, but would it be enough for Carly to let him back into her life—and the life of the baby that would be born in a matter of weeks?

"Have you talked to her recently?" he asked.

"I try to contact her every day, but she's not always available. Sometimes she doesn't text back."

Eli hadn't really heard too much about this woman, but nothing he had gleaned from Jonah made him too excited about her. He didn't really know the spirit of her ultimatum—if he passed, would she stay with him? Would she give him access to their child? Would she share the responsibilities?

Eli didn't know any of this, but hoped Jonah did. And no matter what the answers to those questions were, Eli would support his son.

"If you want to keep that woman in your life, show her you care by calling her every single day and sharing your life," Eli said. "Even if she doesn't always call back."

Jonah sighed and nodded. "Yeah, I guess."

"What does she think about the Culinary Arts program?" Eli asked.

"She's kind of like...she'll believe it when she sees it."

"Then she'll believe it very soon. When you get accepted."

Jonah's eyes shuttered and he dropped his head back. "*If* I get accepted."

Just then, Vivien stepped out on the deck, looking fresh from the sea breeze, her expression glowing. Her dark gold hair was tousled and there was a lightness in her step that Eli hadn't seen in a long time.

"Hey, boys. How's life in the Summer House?" She slipped off her sandals and made her way to the sofa, plopping down. "I hear laughter on the beach."

"Where there is Nolie, there is laughter," Jonah joked.

"Where's Pete?" Eli asked. "Everything go okay tonight?"

"He has to do an early call with his investigative team, so he headed back to his place. And, yes, we had a wonderful time." Her cheeks flushed a little as she slid Eli a look. "I can't believe you never told him about the mountain of a crush I had on him. Thank you."

He flicked his hands. "I got your back, little sister. Unless *you* told him."

"He coerced it out of me," she said, propping her feet on the coffee table. "I forgot he's a professional interrogator. Oh, and we may have seen a crime in action. I think my new client, Fiona, might be getting scammed by her unqualified yet handsome handyman. I'm going to keep an eye on him, per Peter's instructions."

"We have an announcement!" Nolie came running up the spiral steps from the first floor, breathless as she rushed across the deck with Pittypat clutched in one arm. "Everybody in the living room!"

Tessa and Lacey followed a moment later.

"Listen to the child, will ya?" Tessa pointed inside. "We have news and need everyone. Where's Crista?"

As they gathered inside, Crista came downstairs in pajamas, her hair damp from a shower, her phone in her hand. "Nolie, I have Daddy on the phone, and he wants to talk to you."

"I can't talk now," she said, her voice high with excitement. "We have an announcement! Sit down, Mommy!"

"I'll put him on FaceTime," Crista said, touching the phone as she joined them and gave everyone a chance to say hi to Anthony.

"Okay, okay." Tessa clapped like a schoolteacher. "Do we have a quorum? All accounted for?"

All but Kate, Eli thought, but he just listened to the buzz of the group as they gathered in the living room.

Tessa turned to Nolie. "Would you like to do the honors, Figgie?"

Nolie gasped, looking between Tessa and Lacey. "Me? Really? I get to say it?"

Crista's eyes softened and she whispered into the phone, "It's a nickname. Tessa calls her Figsworth." She waited a beat. "Yes, like the boy in her class. I honestly don't know. But, please, just watch."

Eli observed the exchange and wondered if Anthony might not fully appreciate what was going on down here. Eli hoped he could see that even Crista's posture was relaxed. He knew that Anthony was opposed to them keeping this house—a subject they'd danced around these past few days. Still, Eli was glad his brother-in-law was a witness to...whatever they were about to witness.

"Go for it, kiddo," Lacey encouraged.

"Daddy's watching, too," Crista told her.

Nolie beamed, standing up and dramatically tossing her hands in the air. "As you know, Tessa and Lacey's party business got a big job."

"Your business, too," Tessa interjected. "You have a title, Figsworth."

She giggled and looked right at the phone. "I'm the Junior Joy Co...co..."

"Coordinator," Tessa supplied gently. "Play your cards right and you'll be the Senior Joy Coordinator."

Nolie tried to be serious, but obviously was having too much fun as they cheered her new title.

She scooped up Pittypat and held her the very same way Eli had seen Maggie hold the dog, and with the same love.

"You're all going to be in a wedding!" she hollered, then twirled in a perfect pirouette. "And so am I!"

The whole group reacted with surprise, gasps, and questions, and poor Nolie lost control of her crowd, spiraling into giggles.

"You tell them, Tessa," she said, smashing her face into Pittypat. "You."

"All right, all right." Tessa slipped into a chair and looked at them. "As you know, we've landed the grand opening event for Lumière, a bridal salon, and we're doing a runway fashion show. It's going to be held here, and that boardwalk will be the runway—and the aisle."

Again, they reacted and Eli raised his brows. "Very cool," he said. "Where will the guests be?"

"We're going to set up tents and chairs on either side of the boardwalk down to the beach," Lacey said. "And people can watch from the deck—assuming that's okay with you guys who own it. Mom, Aunt Crista, Uncle Eli?"

The three of them exchanged a quick look, no one wanting to quash any joy.

"Of course," he said, quickly speaking for all. "We can throw a party here."

"Budget is somewhat tight, of course," Tessa added. "So to save money, we're trying to get some free models." She waited a beat, then grinned. "Including everyone in this room."

Jonah sat up straighter. "Wait—what?"

Eli raised an eyebrow. "And what exactly are Jonah and I supposed to wear in this spectacle? We're not brides."

"You will be grooms or groomsmen," Tessa said. "Jonah will make a handsome young husband-to-be and Eli, Akari really wants to emphasize the 'seasoned' bridal party."

He shot both brows up. "Meaning...old?"

She shrugged. "Apparently lots of people of a *certain*

age are getting married down here in Destin, and she's catering to the market."

Eli exchanged a look with Jonah, who groaned and ran a hand through his hair. "I don't know about this."

"Well, I do," Tessa said cheerfully. "We need good-looking warm bodies, so that means everyone in this room and a few who are not. Is that Crista's husband on the phone? Come on down and watch your daughter be the one and only featured Flower Girl. I'm sure you'd make a very nice groomsman, too."

"Come, Daddy!" Nolie squealed and danced over to the phone.

While they talked and Vivien peppered them with questions, Jonah leaned closer to Eli.

"Kate should be here, Dad," he said under his breath.

"Yeah," he agreed. "It'd be great if she could come. But she's busy with work and her kids."

"Even for a long weekend?" Jonah pressed. "She could bring them down."

"But her mother..."

"If you want to keep that woman in your life, show her you care by calling her every single day and sharing your life." Jonah lifted a brow. "Or so a wise man once told me five minutes ago."

"A very wise man," Eli joked. "Who would probably get turned down if he asked."

"Only one way to find out." Jonah reached for his phone, flipping it playfully in the air. "So sayeth this wise man."

On a sigh, Eli nodded. "I'll call her."

"We'll call her," Jonah said. "'Cause one of us isn't going to take no for an answer. Come on, old—er, I mean, *seasoned* man. To the deck."

As the chatter died down, Eli followed his son back out to the deck, aware of the strange mix of nerves and anticipation that he always felt when he called Kate. But today, they were stronger than usual because he really wanted her to come down for a visit.

Jonah walked to the sitting area, sat down, and placed his feet on the firepit table. Then he gestured for Eli to come closer so they could both talk.

The phone rang a few times before Kate answered.

"Jonah? What's up?"

Jonah grinned. "Surprise, it's your favorite father-son duo. You've got both of us."

Kate laughed, the sound of her voice warm and delighted. "Eli! Hi! What's going on?"

Just hearing her voice made him feel better. "Hey, Kate. How's brutally cold and not very sunny Ithaca?"

She laughed. "We had an unseasonably high warm spell of forty-seven today. Everyone wore shorts. But there's snow on the way later this week. How are things down there? I hear that apartment is coming along."

"We're doing drywall," Jonah said. "Which sounds worse than it is—we've actually been having a lot of fun."

Eli's heart soared just thinking about how this boy who'd been so distant for years could now pronounce drywalling to be fun. Kate deserved so much credit for encouraging him.

"How's life in the lab?" Jonah asked.

Locking his hands behind his head, Eli closed his eyes and listened to her chat about her latest experiment—still working on capacitors and....something else he honestly didn't understand—and the goings-on at Cornell's science departments.

"It's all pretty dull," she added. "Tell me about the house. How's it going with Crista? And Tessa? Is everything okay?"

"Why don't you come and see for yourself?" Eli asked.

"Oh, you know—"

"Hold on there, Lady Katie," he said. "We called with an idea that is completely doable."

She was quiet for a second, then gave a little laugh. "All right, you two, I'm listening."

Jonah took the lead, launching into an explanation of the fashion show—very kindly complimenting Tessa for her adept inclusion of Nolie.

"That's so sweet," Kate said softly. "Who knew she had such a maternal streak?"

"She also has a sadistic streak," Jonah said, "because she wants us in her show. We're being forced against our will to wear tuxedos and parade our fine selves up and down the boardwalk in front of champagne-sipping guests."

She trilled a laugh. "I'd like to see that."

"Exactly," Eli said, leaning forward and giving Jonah a smile. "Why don't you and the kids come and be part of it?"

"Oh, we would but my mother—"

"Bring her," Eli said without giving it too much thought. Too bad if his mother would have a cow. She wasn't here and...neither was Kate. "I'll send you all round-trip tickets for a Thursday to Monday visit to sunshine and...fashion."

"Oh!" He heard the soft intake of her breath, the genuine surprise and gratitude she conveyed with just one syllable. "Eli! That would be..."

"Perfect," he finished for her. "Right?"

"We know you want to support Tessa's new business, so..." Jonah gave a soft laugh. "You really need to say yes."

"Jo Ellen, too?" she asked, sounding uncertain.

"She doesn't hate the Lawsons, right?" Jonah asked. "That weirdness is only on my side of the family. Bring her down."

"Assuming her ankle's doing better," Eli said, knowing the classy thing to do was to also give her a way to say no.

"Her ankle is fine and..." She let out a sigh that he couldn't interpret, but, oh, he could imagine her face. And he ached to see it in person.

"Please, Kate," he said softly. "We all miss you so much down here."

She was quiet for a beat...then two...then Eli braced for her to say no.

"Okay," she said slowly. "We'll make the journey family style." Then she laughed again. "Did you even tell me the date?"

Jonah filled her in on the timing and Eli just listened,

unable to wipe the smile from his face. They talked a little more and he promised to call her tomorrow, although he knew he'd be texting her before bed.

After they said goodbye, the two of them sat in silence for a moment. But Jonah broke it with a sigh as he turned to Eli.

"She could be it, huh?"

"Maybe," Eli said. "It's a long shot, but God specializes in miracles, so..."

Jonah made a face. "Not always. Sometimes He just punishes us."

Of course, Jonah didn't share his faith, and this had to bring up mixed emotions in a boy who still reeled from the loss of his mother.

"God doesn't punish," Eli said quietly. "But he allows us to endure trials and challenges and difficult paths, in the hopes that we'll turn to Him for help."

Jonah stared straight ahead at the black Gulf, now lit only by a three-quarter moon behind a cloud.

"I don't think I could take it if it were anyone else," he finally said. "But Kate? She's so...she's..." He swallowed. "I really like her, and you seem happy."

"A good woman can do that. She can heal you." He inched closer. "Why don't you go call Carly and check on her?"

He sighed again, then stood, swiping his hair back. "Maybe I will," he said. "Maybe I will. Thanks, Dad."

"Thank *you*," Eli countered.

He stayed right where he was when Jonah took his

phone and went inside, the echo of Kate's laugh in his ears. It was the prettiest sound he could imagine, and he couldn't wait to hear it again.

Chapter Fourteen

Crista

"You have got to be kidding me."

Crista grimaced at Anthony's words, spoken into her ear the moment she took him off FaceTime so she could say goodbye.

"Isn't it sweet that—"

"Crista! I didn't send you two down there so she could...*play*! She's missing school, a recital, and all of our lessons because you promised she would come home knowing how to read."

On a sigh, she pressed the phone hard to her ear and rushed upstairs for privacy.

"You don't understand," she said as she slipped into her room and closed the door.

"No, Cris, I don't. What about dancing in a fashion show is going to get her into third grade?"

It was a fair question—one she probably would have asked herself if she'd been watching through the phone and not here for the past week or so.

She tried to gather her thoughts. "It's a process, Anthony."

"We don't have time for a *process*," he shot back. "She needs to read, write, and do math without mixing up her sixes and nines in a few weeks. I'm glad she's having fun and getting to be a fake flower girl or whatever, but it isn't going to get her to pass that test."

"I actually think this is working," she said after a beat. "She's getting confident, and her personality is returning."

"Well, that's great," he said. "But nothing would give her as much confidence as opening a book and reading it."

She closed her eyes and dropped on the bed with a heavy sigh, exhausted by the conversation and the feeling of being torn in two.

"And if she doesn't pass, I have Plan B," Anthony said.

"Oh?" She put the phone down, touching the speaker button so she could get comfortable. "What is it?"

"The Hawthorne Academy."

Crista snorted at the mention of a dream school with the highest acclaim, especially for kids who had trouble in mainstream public schools. "Right. Did you win the lottery?"

"You did," he said softly.

For a second, she frowned, then realized exactly what he meant.

"That house is worth enough, even split three ways, to pay for Hawthorne and still have money left over for college," he said, confirming her suspicions. "Which she'd get into at the right age if she isn't held back."

Crista let out a small grunt. Talk about being torn!

"Are you kidding, Anthony? That would put me smack dab in the middle of...things."

"In the middle of what?" he asked, just enough tenderness in his voice to soften her. "Until Eli and Vivien cooked up this 'keep the house' plan, everyone was very excited about selling it. The whole family was overjoyed that Maggie had secretly held onto this gold-mine that would translate into a cash bonanza for all three Lawson siblings. Just because you're having a nice vacation, are you willing to walk away from that kind of money? Are they?"

She pushed off the bed, needing to walk off the emotion ricocheting through her. She didn't want to get dramatic and theatrical—it wouldn't win this argument.

Centering herself, she walked back to the phone. "Listen, it's hard to put a price on a place like this," she said softly.

"It's not that hard, Cris. Look at Zillow. The price is high, the market is strong, and Nolie is *our only child*. The only thing that matters to you and me is Nolie's future. Am I right?"

He wasn't wrong.

"We'll take vacations down there, I promise," he said, using the logic that always talked her off an emotional ledge, but tonight? She really didn't want to hear it.

"It's not the same."

"We can go to Destin every summer like you did as a kid and stay somewhere else. But you need to break the news to Eli and Vivien that your vote is 'sell' and, Cris, honey, you guys need to come home. I miss you so much and we're just frittering away these great weeks without Maggie."

She flinched at the words, sad that he felt that way about her mother.

"If you leave tomorrow morning, Nolie won't have missed much school, and she can still make the recital. That's the only dancing she needs to do."

"Miss the bridal show event? She'd be brokenhearted!" She squeezed her eyes shut, struggling with the rise of her emotions. "I don't think you realize how happy she is, Anthony. She's blossoming down here."

"I don't doubt that, but she will not be happy when she is the only eight-year-old in second grade. Or, worse, in high school when she's a sixteen-year-old freshman."

"That's not going..." Her words faded out, knowing her arguments wouldn't hold up against his. Nolie did need to stay with her grade level.

She dropped back on the bed, feeling sick and like she couldn't grab hold of all her emotions.

"Mommy?" The door opened a crack and instantly Crista shot up and tapped the speaker button on her phone. She didn't want Anthony to break this news to her. Crista had to do that, but not tonight. Not when she was this happy.

"Hey, I gotta run," she said to Anthony. "I'll call you tomorrow."

"Tell Nolie I love her," he said. "And, Cris, I love you, too. Don't forget that."

She let out a sigh. "I won't. Bye." As she disconnected the call, Nolie came in.

"It's just me," she said with a giggle in her voice. "Figsworth."

Crista laughed and reached for her, giving her way too tight a squeeze. "Figsworth needs to get her PJs on, brush her teeth, and get some sleep."

"I will, Mommy. Can we read tonight?"

She drew back, not expecting that. "You want me to read?"

Nolie smiled up at her. "Let me try it tonight, okay?"

Her heart rolled around. "Of course. I can't wait." She bent over and kissed her daughter's silky dark hair, fluttering a few locks in her fingers. "I love you so much, Nolie-bird."

So much that Crista would once again be the odd man out in Destin.

CRISTA WOKE at almost one in the morning, with Nolie next to her, her quiet breaths the only sound she could hear. The weight on her chest increased with every second she got closer to tomorrow when she had to face the task of breaking her daughter's heart.

Back to Atlanta? Miss the fashion show? Leave the beach?

Nolie would wail.

No, no. She'd cry quietly—Crista was the wailer in the family. Nolie would just let the tears roll down her cheeks with shuddering sighs and...silence.

She flipped back the comforter and climbed out of

bed, unnaturally hot and heavy with discomfort. Her chest burned like she'd had one too many bites of Jonah's salsa.

Walking to the window, she peered out to the long view of the dunes and a slice of the beach, drawn to the moonlight and the sand.

Turning, she checked Nolie, who wouldn't wake until six in the morning, when she would burst to life and rush downstairs, ready to be...Figsworth, the Junior Joy Coordinator.

Quieting a whimper that rose in her stinging chest, Crista walked silently to the door and slipped out, not really sure where she was going. She paused at the door to Eli's bedroom and looked down the hall to the primary suite, where Vivien and Lacey were sound asleep.

Tessa slept on the main floor in the guest suite and Jonah was down on the first floor.

No one was awake to help her, and she didn't have the heart to knock on one of these closed doors and have a breakdown. Or ask for a Tums.

She walked down the steps to the lower level, lit only by a single soft light in the kitchen. But the moon was out and even though it was barely three-quarters, it lit the boardwalk, the dunes, and the beach beyond.

They didn't use the alarm system, so she unlocked and slid the heavy glass door that led to the deck and, in a moment, she was downstairs and walking barefoot over the boardwalk.

The boardwalk where Nolie would dance, dropping

rose petals and joy, her eyes on fire with her mission, her brain focused on something that certainly wasn't...words.

Was Anthony right?

As she reached the end of the boardwalk, she stepped down and let the soft sand sift between her toes. Soothed by the feeling, she looked side to side, not surprised that this beach—as close to "private" as it could get—was utterly deserted.

The tide was high, though, and close, rolling in with the gentle and steady rhythm that Crista always thought of as beach music.

Listening to it, she gazed out and then squinted as something caught her eye in the water. A flicker. A shimmer.

Was that her imagination or some kind of light? Curious, she walked toward the surf and suddenly—there it was again. A glow, a brief pulse of blue light swirled beneath the surface.

Her breath catching, she crouched down, her heart rate rising as she reached out to the water. Dragging her fingers through the wet sand at the edge of the tide, a ripple of glowing blue spread from her fingertips, dancing like liquid stars.

Was that...magic?

"Are you okay?"

She gasped and spun around, seeing the shadow of a figure on the boardwalk. The moonlight caught the light of Tessa's hair, clipped up on her head.

"Yes." Crista stood. "What are you doing down here?"

"Checking on you," she said. "I could see you from my deck." She gestured behind her and Crista's gaze moved to the house, seeing a light on the far right where Tessa's room was. "I couldn't sleep, and I saw you. I wanted to be sure you're all right."

She huffed out a breath, fighting the urge to dump it all on this woman's shoulders. Instead, she turned to the water.

"Did you see that?"

"The blue light?" Tessa stepped off the boardwalk onto the sand, walking closer. "It's bioluminescence."

"Oh, I've heard of that," Crista said, looking at the water, a little sad it wasn't magic. "I don't know if I've ever seen it in person." She knelt down again, moving her hands to send trails of glowing blue through the water.

"You've never seen it here at the beach?" Tessa asked, slowing her step when she reached Crista. "Of course, you'd have to be up in the middle of the night."

"I was too young for that," she said with a wistful smile. "I was always tucked into bed before your big adventures. Though I do remember you all talking about it—and other things that intrigued me."

"Sorry we cut you out, Crista. You were young and we were teenagers."

"I know. But now..." She looked out at the water, catching the blue sparkle here and there. "Sometimes I feel like I missed out on a lot."

Which was yet another reason she wanted to keep this house and let Nolie have those experiences.

"Well, this only happens certain nights when the

water is right. And don't ask me what causes it," Tessa added with a laugh. "That's Kate's department. My sister is the scientist. I just thought it was blue magic."

"I was just thinking that," Crista said, slowly rising. "And, boy, could I use a little."

Tessa looked up and stood, too, brushing her wet fingers on her sleep pants. "Wanna talk about it?"

"More than I want my next breath, but..."

"But it's me, not Vivien or Eli." Tessa gave a playful jab in Crista's arm. "Come on, you can unload. I won't judge."

Crista raised a brow.

"Hey," Tessa said. "What's said in the blue magic stays in the blue magic. We can walk and talk. Hike up those fancy PJs, Cris."

"Well, it does involve you, so..."

"Oh, wait." Tessa held up her hand, stopping as she bent over to roll up her sleep pants. "If this is about my dad, then no, I don't—"

"It's not, no, I promise," Crista said quickly. "It's about...Nolie."

"What about her?" Even in the dim light, she could see true concern in Tessa's topaz-colored eyes, and that touched her.

"You really like her, don't you?"

"Figsworth?" Tessa snorted. "I love that kid."

"You're very good with her," Crista said. "No one's ever been that...easy-breezy, you know. You would have been a good mother."

Tessa's eyes shuttered and she looked away. "Well, I wasn't. What's going on with her?"

"Anthony wants us to come home," she said on a sigh. "Tomorrow."

"What?" She froze mid-step. "You can't leave! Tell him to..." She kicked the sand with her bare foot. "Pound some of that. We got a fashion show to run."

"But that's—"

"And a third-grade test to pass."

Crista looked at her. "Do you think she can?" she asked softly.

"Not today, but soon. I know she can."

"She did read beautifully to me tonight," Crista said. "She fell asleep by page four though—"

"Exhausted from being the Junior Joy Coordinator."

Crista smiled. "Exhausted from having fun and coming out of her shell and not thinking about reading, writing, or math. That's what Anthony can't see, you know."

"Exactly." Tessa pointed to her. "The less she worries about it, the more she learns. I think she can read just about anything that's age and level appropriate. Slowly, yeah. But she can read and comprehend. She can write pretty well, too. I mean, I don't expect essays from a seven-year-old, but the kid does a mean to-do list."

Crista gave a dry laugh. "And really, what else matters to the child of a control freak?"

"You're not a control freak," Tessa said. "You're...a mom. And a darn good one. A little hot-headed, but that makes you passionate."

Crista put a hand on her chest, surprised that the compliment eased her heartburn. "Thank you."

"But about the math..." Tessa said.

"Yeah?"

"We're not quite there," she admitted. "It's funny because math wasn't really my challenge. Lists of numbers, yes—I still get a little queasy at the sight of a spreadsheet, not gonna lie. I just don't know if she can do...I don't know what you call it. Number grouping? Like when you look at a group of things and instinctively know how many there are."

"The teachers call it 'quick-look counting' in school, and, yes, it's a struggle for her," Crista said. "I don't know why but she hasn't quite unlocked that yet. The learning specialist at school called it 'subitizing.'"

"Eesh, there's a word for you."

"Really," Crista agreed. "By third grade, she needs that skill. She needs to look at a circle and know there are seven stars inside it."

Tessa nodded slowly, thinking. "Let me work on that. Unless...you leave in the morning."

Crista closed her eyes at the thought. "Oh, there will be tears."

"Yeah, mine," Tessa said.

Once again, Crista's heart folded that this woman—a virtual stranger who Crista had literally attacked when they'd met—cared so much for Nolie. They were all going to be in tears tomorrow.

"Maybe I can put Anthony off for a day or two. Just while you work on the quick-look counting."

Tessa slowed her step and crossed her arms, studying Crista intently. "What if she passed the third-grade test before you leave?"

"She can't. They don't give it until early May."

"There must be a few online samples and practice tests that we can give her. That was one of my—" Tessa checked herself and continued, "One way I managed to pass was by taking practice tests over and over. My, um, tutor was a teacher, so he knew that if I wasn't too surprised by the types of things I was tested on, even if the content was different, I was relaxed and did better."

Crista eyed her. "This tutor you loved so much—it was Artie, wasn't it?"

She nodded.

For a moment, neither spoke, then Tessa said, "I bet we can find third-grade entrance exams online. Would you look for them?"

"Of course."

"So, if she took one or two or more tests, and passed them all?" Tessa asked. "Would Anthony get off your case and let her stay? And then he could come down for the fashion show and see how happy she is with his own two eyes. Plus, he can see the tests and know you did the right thing."

She made it sound so easy, but maybe that was Tessa's gift. It was probably the very reason she was so good with Nolie. Good heavens, why hadn't this woman had a child?

"What do we have to lose?" Tessa pressed.

"Nothing," Crista agreed. "I'll tell him tomorrow."

"Good. Let's turn around and get some sleep," Tessa said, pivoting in the sand, the move turning the bioluminescence alive under her feet. "Oh, look at that. Blue magic."

Feeling better than she had in hours, Crista laughed softly. "It really is."

"That's magic, too, you know." Tessa pointed to the Summer House, the lone light from her room guiding them closer. "The old cottage and this new mansion. Magic."

And Crista's heart fell again, remembering her other problem. "Don't get attached," she said softly. "I don't think we're going to keep it."

"Seriously?" Tessa glanced at her, a note of real concern in her voice. "I thought...Vivien and Eli..."

"I know. And everyone is kind of dug in, living like it's a family home." Crista shook her head. "But that house is an enormous amount of financial security. Way too much to give up."

"Don't tell me, this is Anthony speaking." Tessa made a face. "I don't think I'm going to like this guy."

"He's a good guy—mostly. We've hit a few rocky patches, especially..." She hesitated, not sure if she should share this with a virtual stranger. But, really, was Tessa a stranger? Not exactly. And it felt so good to get it off her chest. "My mother living with us has...added pressure."

Tessa snorted. "Maggie Lawson? Pressure? I can't imagine."

That made Crista smile. "She does have a way of

making you see people through her lens, which is somewhat unforgiving."

"Like the way you're looking at my father."

Crista didn't answer, feeling more like she was walking a tightrope instead of a sandy beach. And falling off would hurt.

The fact was, her true loyalties were always going to be with her mother. And Anthony, of course.

"Anyway," she said quickly. "Neither Anthony nor my mother can see the need to own this beach house. Anthony understands finance and investments and the profit from the sale of this house could pay for...all kinds of things, including every bit of Nolie's education."

"Ohh." Tessa let out a groan. "I get that, but... summers at the beach are a different kind of education."

Crista knew that, but kept it to herself.

"I think that eventually Eli and Vivien will do the numbers and see how that kind of money could change their lives and secure their futures," she said instead. "Keeping a house we never knew we had is just a silly pipe dream."

Even as she said the words, they felt like the sand under her feet had moved to her mouth. It wasn't a silly pipe dream, but Anthony was right about the money.

"Anyway, thank you, Tessa," she added softly as they brushed off the sand from their feet. "This really helped me."

"Anytime." She smiled, but it seemed tighter than when she'd arrived. "You look for those practice tests and I'll work on the subsi...thing."

"I will warn you," Crista said. "She hates that kind of math. Will do anything to avoid it."

Tessa flicked her hand. "Trust me, darlin'. She won't even know she learned it."

With that, she gave a quick wave and hustled down the boardwalk, leaving Crista alone on the beach, a little surprised she'd left so abruptly.

Crista turned to the water, looking to see the teal and turquoise shimmer again. If Nolie passed that test, she promised herself, Crista would bring her down here in the middle of the night to see this.

Blue magic, indeed.

Chapter Fifteen
Tessa

Tessa hadn't slept well after her conversation with Crista on the beach. Not that the bomb Crista had dropped was a shocker to her—there were days when she found it hard to believe that the Lawson family would really keep this home. They were, in fact, sitting on a goldmine.

If she had to decide between a gorgeous beach house or a couple of million dollars, Tessa had to honestly say she didn't know what she'd do. Money was a necessary evil and the Summer House was a luxury.

Not to mention the fact that Tessa simply couldn't count on living here even if they owned it. It was one thing to spend a summer at Vivien's invitation, but even that would come to an end.

She needed enough time to establish her business and actually earn a steady income before she found something to rent. Could that be done by November, when the Lawsons would make the decision?

Hard to say. She wasn't paying Lacey anything but a small percentage of what they'd make off this event, and yet she was out meeting with florists today.

As she stepped out of her room to get coffee and start

the day, she heard someone in the laundry room... moaning?

"What's going on in there?" she called before she reached the door, biting back a laugh. "'Cause it doesn't sound good."

"It isn't good," Vivien said, sticking her head out and holding something off-white. "I'm thinking I might have to say goodbye to these forever."

"What...oh, these are those pretty pants you... yikes." Tessa took a look at the weird wrinkles and some discoloration on the expensive trousers. "Yeah. Water stains?"

"I looked up Belgian linen and tried to follow the directions to dry them properly, but..." Vivien made a face. "I'm sad because I loved them."

"I can see why." Tessa turned the pant legs one way then the other. "Let me ask Akari, the bridal salon owner. She's an expert with fine fabric. Can I take them to her at my next meeting?"

"Yes! Thank you!" Vivien beamed at her. "You know what you're an expert in, Tessa?"

"I believe you once called me a 'goodtime girl,' Viv. So I'm going to guess I'm an expert in fun."

"You are," Vivien said on a laugh. "Also in problem-solving."

Tessa inched back, not expecting that. "Huh. Thanks."

"I talked to Crista this morning and she's over the moon about your idea to give Nolie a practice test! Look how you've turned that situation around."

"Which situation?" Tessa asked. "How wrong she is about my dad or Nolie's learning challenges?"

"Both."

"So you don't think my dad had anything to do with your father going to prison?" Tessa asked.

Vivien considered that, searching Tessa's face. "I don't know. I don't really want to think about it."

"Well, I get that. But once Maggie's in the picture..."

"She's not going to be in the picture," Vivien said confidently, leaning on the countertop over the washing machine. "For one thing, she's announced that she will never step foot in this place, for reasons none of us know or understand. But when my mother makes a decision, she doesn't change her mind. And for another, I'm hoping we don't sell."

That wasn't quite as strong as "we're not selling" but Tessa clung to the words even though she very much doubted they would come true.

"What?" Vivien asked, narrowing her eyes at Tessa. "What's that look for?"

Tessa let out a sigh. "I think that when push comes to shove, you all might realize the power of that kind of money."

"Power, shmower, Tess," Vivien said lightly. "I love it here. There's a ton of work for me if I can get it, and I would love to live here. And you—"

"Cannot be the world's most fun squatter forever."

Vivien grabbed her shoulders. "You're not squatting."

"I ain't payin' rent, honey."

Vivien flicked her hand. "We'll figure something out.

You've given my daughter—who was lost in her career search—a job she loves. She practically danced out of here this morning to go see the florist, so happy you've trusted her with that meeting."

"I'd trust her with anything," Tessa said, and meant it. "I adore that girl and plan to steal her from you and make her mine."

Vivien smiled at their ongoing joke. "I'm serious, Tess. You've also given Nolie a real chance of getting into third grade and that will change Crista's life."

Tessa managed a shrug.

"And now you're saving my Belgian linen pants!" Vivien exclaimed. "The rent is paid, my friend."

Laughing, she gave Vivien a hug, loving her for the sentiment. It didn't change the fact that Tessa was free-loading. And that was fine for a summer, but beyond that?

"Tessa!" Nolie came blasting through the hall, her dark eyes lit up. "It's Flyer Day!"

"What's that?" Vivien asked, smiling at the child.

"The day we make Flyers, Aunt Vivien," she said with a touch of exasperation. Like, who didn't know what Flyer Day was?

Tessa laughed. "The fashion show is open to the public, though I don't expect a stampede on the beach. Still, we're doing old-school flyers to take to any wedding-related businesses, and the hotels that host bachelorette parties and such. Nolie's helping me make them. And," she added, remembering her promise to Crista, "we're working on an event layout, which will be lots of pictures and numbers."

Nolie gave a shadow of a grimace at the word "numbers" but it was gone in an instant, and so was she.

"I'll be in our office, Tessa!"

"Just need my coffee, Figsworth!" She turned to Vivien. "The office is—"

"The dining room table, I know."

"Yeah, sorry about that."

"Don't be," Vivien said, then leaned in. "We're not showing the place."

Yet, Tessa thought as she shared a smile with Vivien.

"Tessa! I'm ready to work!"

"You better go, boss." Vivien gave her a nudge. "Or your Junior Joy Coordinator will fire you."

Laughing at that, Tessa headed toward the dining room "office" by way of the coffee pot.

They'd likely come to their senses soon, and Tessa... well, she needed a backup plan for life.

"Can we dance the letters, Tessa?" Nolie asked, bouncing lightly on the balls of her feet, watching the screen intently. "You say the letter and I dance it?"

"I know the game," she said, moving the cursor to put the finishing touches on her PicMonkey-created flyer. "Let's do..." She looked up at the top. "Wedding Fashion Show."

"I can, I can!" Nolie let out an excited squeal and jumped into position in the middle of the living room.

Their little game had become a favorite of hers, a way to practice spelling that didn't feel like work. Each letter had a movement—a kick for W, a twirl for E, jazz hands for D, and so on. It was active, engaging, and, most importantly, it worked.

Tessa finished the flyer, while Nolie called out each letter and did her dance, her face alight with joy. As Tessa saved the file, she looked over her laptop at the little girl, Vivien's kind words echoing in her head.

Dad would be so pleased. He'd always played games like this.

"This is *sooo* much fun. I wish we could stay in Destin forever!" Nolie suddenly dropped onto the couch and swung her legs over the armrest. "I never want to go back to stupid school!"

Tessa's fingers hovered over the keyboard. The words hit harder than she expected. She felt exactly like that seven-year-old child. Who—if she couldn't do her quick number groups– would be gone in a day or two.

"All right," she said, standing up. "Get the white board and my notebook, Figsworth. We have a new project."

Nolie perked back up. "Oh, yes! What did you call it? The map?"

"An event map is extremely important, especially when we have to set up groups of chairs." She went to the white board and drew two long parallel lines down the middle. "This is the boardwalk."

"Our runway!"

"Yes," Tessa said on a laugh, marveling at how bright the child was. "And these are where we are going to have to put chairs."

She made six large circles, three on each side. "We should have about forty people in the VIP tents, so we need to mix them into groups. We could divide forty by six."

"I can't do that," Nolie said softly, coming closer.

"No one can, Figsworth! But, we can figure out how many of these..." She drew a figure that looked like a lower-case H. "Pretend this is a chair."

"It's a little H."

"Excellent. For our purposes, it's a chair," she said. "We need to put forty Hs in these six boxes, but we don't want it evenly divided. Some should have five, six, or seven."

Now, if she could get Nolie to help put these chairs in circles, they'd be on their way to learning...what was the word? Subitizing?

She handed the marker to Nolie. "You want to give it a shot?"

Nolie's eyes widened. "Um, can I spell out letters some more?"

"But I need you to do this," Tessa encouraged. "Just take your time."

Nolie studied the board, chewing on her bottom lip. She started pointing to the tables, mumbling numbers under her breath.

"Let's do it this way," Tessa said, picking up another marker. "We could—"

"No, no, no."

"No, you don't want to try?" Tessa guessed, not sure what she meant.

"No, I don't want help," Nolie said, a determined frown furrowing her baby-smooth brow. "I want to do it myself."

Tessa smiled and put a hand on her shoulder, her whole body aching for how easy it was to love this child.

Yes, she thought with a wistful punch of sadness, she would have been a good mother. She might have been—

"Your phone's ringing," Nolie said on a whisper as she stood in front of the board.

"Oh, I didn't even hear it." Tessa turned and picked up the vibrating device, gasping when she saw the name.

Gerald Varick.

Why the heck would her old boss from the Ritz-Carlton call her?

"I better take this call," she said. "Don't get frustrated, okay? If it's too hard, just put them into even groups of seven. We'll knock two out later."

Nolie looked up, a shade of panic in her eyes at the fast math.

"Just relax," Tessa said quickly. "I'll be back in a jiffy."

She didn't want Gerry's call to go to voicemail, so she hustled off with the phone, heading outside to the empty deck.

"Gerry Varick," she said after accepting the call. "This is a surprise."

"Tessa! So good to hear your voice." At the familiar, smooth reply, Tessa lowered herself to the sofa, picturing the thinning hair and pudgy countenance of the Ritz's Regional Director of Conference Services.

She'd reported directly to him the whole time she'd worked there, and they'd had a cordial, if not close, relationship.

It hurt when he'd fired her. He simply didn't believe that she had nothing to do with the very unhappy guest... who happened to be dating the same man Tessa had been seeing. It had been ugly and frustrating, and Gerry's lack of faith in her had hurt.

"Well, it's a surprise to hear your voice," she said, happy she didn't need to sugarcoat the conversation.

"I know, I know," he said. "I'm just glad that whole... business is behind us."

Was it? She bit back the question and waited to find out why he was calling. No doubt he just needed to find a file or locate a client contact.

"Listen, Tessa, it turns out...we—well, I—owe you an apology. We got it wrong."

Tessa blinked. "What?"

"You took the fall for something that someone else did."

She snorted. "I know," she said. "I told you that. Or tried to."

He sighed noisily. "I'm ashamed to say that the

employee responsible for the whole thing was, in fact, Jeanine Margolis."

"The person who got my job," she said dryly. "Shocker, Gerry."

"It was a difficult situation all around."

Difficult for *who?* For the wealthy client she'd briefly dated who'd brought a different woman to his event? Then things at the resort went south for that woman— due to circumstances completely out of Tessa's control.

That client had not only assumed Tessa was to blame, but he'd taken his complaint to an old college buddy, who was in the C-suite of the Ritz's parent company.

Bottom line? Tessa was kicked to the curb and never given a chance to defend herself.

"I think it's fair to say that Jeanine, uh, set you up to take the fall for her mistakes."

Mistakes? Tessa almost snorted. Jeanine sabotaged the poor guest's stay and made it look like Tessa had done the damage.

Damage that had left her essentially homeless and squatting at the unfinished Summer House before she was shamefully discovered by Vivien and Eli.

So, big picture, she was glad it happened. But the "how" still stung.

"So why are you calling, Gerry? I mean, I accept the apology, so—"

"We shouldn't have let you go," Gerald continued. "You were one of our best. No one does a party like Tessa Wylie. And we'd like to fix that."

Tessa's grip on the phone tightened, completely ignoring the attempt at flattery. "Fix it... how?"

"Come back," he said. "Your old position is yours, with full benefits, back pay, a raise, and new staff now that Jeanine is gone. You'd be back coordinating luxury events at all of our East Coast properties, doing what you do best."

Tessa felt like she'd been doused in cold water. Or...a backup plan.

"I—" She shook her head, pressing her fingers to her temple. "Gerry, I don't know what to say."

"Just think about it," he said. "This is where you belong. Our events have prestige and run smoothly because your capable hands were on the project."

Oh, please. Her capable hands were cut off at the knuckles the minute someone in power decided she should take the fall.

"This could offer you a lot of stability," he said. "And you know I'm retiring in two years, so..."

So she could have his job?

She squeezed her eyes shut and when she opened them, she looked right out at the horizon, the snow-white sands, and the jade and turquoise water that shimmered with...magic. Not stability and not a future. Just...magic.

"I'll think about it," she said finally. "I have a lot going on right now."

"Of course. Take your time. Talk soon, Tessa."

"Sure."

She hung up and stared at her phone, then back out to that beautiful vista. It would hurt to give it up.

"Tessa! Look! Look what I did!"

It would hurt to give up Figsworth, too.

On a sigh, she pushed up and walked back into the house, bracing herself. She expected Nolie to have given up, wiped the board clean, and drawn stick flowers—her go-to response when the math got too...mathy.

She stopped dead in her tracks at the neat circles, the tiny Hs representing chairs, and—best of all—the numbers next to each circle—7, 6, 3, 8, 5, 6, and 5.

Which added up to...she had to use a few fingers but, it was indeed *forty*.

"That table is a little crowded," Nolie said, pointing to the eight. "But I thought that's where we'd sit with my mommy and daddy, right up front. And you and Lacey and Uncle Eli and Aunt Vivien, and Jonah. I made a list...here. It's eight, but I'm small. And if that's too many, I'll sit on my daddy's lap when I'm not dancing."

Tessa blinked, everything blurring through tears. "I'd say...you understand the concept."

Nolie smiled. "I just needed to think a little, but I did it."

"You *did* it!" Tessa swooped in and scooped Nolie up, twirling her around while the little girl giggled. "And you nailed it!"

She set her down and looked again at the white board, pride swelling in her chest.

Nolie bounced on her toes. "Can I dance now?"

"Like you're carried by the wind, Figsworth."

Nolie pirouetted away and Tessa stared at the circles, momentarily forgetting about Gerry and his job offer, which, of course, she had to consider. But right now, these circles and numbers and that spinning top of a child were all that mattered.

July 24, 1990

I have got to start standing up for myself.

I say that a lot, don't I? I should make a sign and tape it to my back. You know, the one that doesn't have a spine. But today was yet another example of how I, Vivien Lawson, am a complete and total doormat. Not even a fancy, welcome-to-our-beach-house kind of doormat. Just a plain old brown one that gets stepped on every single day.

Let me explain.

Today was the worst and it's all because I am too nice.

It all started with the boogie board.

Tessa, Kate, and I were at the beach with Eli and Peter, plus some of their summer friends from around here. The waves were perfect—big enough to ride, but not so big that you'd get annihilated and end up with a bathing suit full of sand (been there, NOT FUN). I was beyond excited because I actually had a brand-new boogie board this year, not a hand-me-down from Eli that smelled like old sunscreen and teenage boy. It was mine. A neon pink and green beauty with a rad design that looked like the cover of this Lisa Frank notebook.

So there I was, about to finally get a turn to ride the waves, when HE showed up.

Not Peter. That would've been a different kind of dramatic diary entry. No, it was Dustin Mathers. Otherwise known as Eli's random summer friend who just appears every year and acts like he owns the place. He's fifteen, thinks he's God's gift to the Gulf of Mexico, and worst of all—he never brings his own stuff. Ever. Not a towel, not a frisbee, and certainly not a boogie board.

You see where this is going.

He asked me to borrow my boogie board, grinning his Dustin Mathers grin.

I wanted to say no. I should've said no! But...I didn't want to be the bratty little sister. I didn't want to make a scene.

So what did I do?

I said yes. I handed over my perfect, un-scratched, first-time-ever-mine boogie board to Dustin Mathers.

And what did he do? Did he treat it with respect? Did he use it for a few minutes and then return it as a normal person would?

OF COURSE NOT.

No, he took it out, rode one wave, and I could already tell he was goofing off and acting like a total idiot.

Did I march up to him and take it back? No. Because I am a wimp. Instead, I just stood there, watching helplessly as the stupid boy wiped out repeatedly on my board, dragging it through the sand, kicking it, probably spitting on it, for all I know. And just when I thought it couldn't get any worse?

IT SNAPPED.

My brand-new, beautiful, Lisa-Frank-esque boogie board was now two sad, broken pieces, floating in the shallow waves like a warning to all future people-pleasers.

Eli was mad at the guy, but what good did that do?

Why am I like this?! Did Dustin Mathers buy me a new boogie board? No. He gave a half-hearted apology and went to go play football with his other idiot friends.

And I, Vivien the Spineless, just nodded and told him it was fine.

So here I am, sitting on my bed, boogie board-less and FUMING. I wish I was firm and strong. I want to be one of those super confident girls who just says no when she wants to say no. Like Tessa.

No more letting people walk all over me just to keep the peace. I mean it this time.

Okay, but let's be real. If Peter asked to borrow anything, I would probably hand it over in a heartbeat.

So I guess I still have some work to do.
Love,
Vivien (who really needs a backbone. And a new boogie board.)

Chapter Sixteen
Vivien

The words she'd read in her old diary that morning haunted Vivien the whole time she drove to Fiona Buckman's house.

She'd called herself a doormat way back then? She didn't even remember having those thoughts or feelings as a young girl. As an adult, especially after twenty-five years with Ryan? Yes, she'd frequently used the term and always hated it.

In fact, since leaving her marriage and starting over on her own, she'd vowed mightily not to be walked over, pushed around, or let people use her desire to avoid conflict as a way to manipulate her.

But...as a kid? *Eesh.* Why hadn't she paid attention to that? Why hadn't her mother drummed it out of her?

Because Maggie was the victor in those old conflicts.

These days, she had better sounding boards. When discussing that particular weakness with Lacey or even, at times, with her trusted brother, they both pointed out that Vivien came by her desire to please others naturally —a middle child, daughter of an uber-controlling mother, and a strong incentive to stay out of arguments.

But here she was, facing fifty and the realization that

she'd *always* been that way. Why didn't she have the nerve to tell Dustin Mathers to take a hike and save her brand-new pink and green boogie board?

Well, she did now. Or at least she was aware of the problem and ready to change it for the next half of her life. So today, when Fiona tried to—

The dashboard lit with an incoming call and the name derailed her train of thought, and in a very good way. Speaking of that very young Vivien—wouldn't she be delighted to know that thirty-some years later, she was dating Peter McCarthy?

Okay, *dating* was a stretch. They hadn't been out again since their dinner date, but they texted daily and talked a few times on the phone. This was going...somewhere. She wasn't sure where, but she was ready to enjoy the ride.

"Good morning, Detective," she answered warmly, imagining his sweet eyes, neatly cut hair, and that smile that still made her a teeny-tiny bit weak in the knees. "Catch any baddies today?"

He chuckled. "Not yet, Viv. But it's only eleven. How about you? Beautifying the world one window treatment at a time?"

She laughed, but wrinkled her nose. "Actually, I'm on my way to see a client and I'm already stressed out about it."

"Why?" he asked, sounding genuinely concerned.

She thought about all the reasons why Fiona Buckman's text had her uptight this morning.

At the top of the list was reason number one: she was

more than a little terrified of the woman. And reason number two: Fiona reminded Vivien of Maggie. And that added a shiver of fear at the possibility that her mother could somehow discover that all of her kids—including Crista!—were currently and happily defying her.

But she didn't want to go into all that with Peter.

"Well, her text was brief and...chilly," she told him. "It was a demand that I be there at eleven with no explanation. I'm worried something in the design doesn't work."

"Oh, is this the cougar being scammed by a second-rate handyman?"

She snorted at the description. "Same client, yes. And, sadly, my only one other than the Summer House. But I haven't seen the hapless handyman around her house for a while."

"Have you sniffed around to find out if he's up to no good?"

"Last time I met with her, she was barking orders so fast, I didn't mention anything. And I stopped over late yesterday to see some carpentry work, but she wasn't home. Her housekeeper let me in, and there was no sign of her young paramour—er, associate."

"Well, maybe we're just misunderstanding the whole situation," he said. "Because mistakes do happen. I'm beginning to think this guy I'm looking for was never even in Destin. No one recognizes his picture anywhere, and he left zero tracks. I'm frustrated."

"That's so strange. How does a person just disappear? I'd think there'd be a full manhunt out for him." Vivien checked the clock to make sure she wasn't running late for this appointment, wishing she could just linger and talk to Peter about his case for an hour.

"We've got quite a few law enforcement people looking into it, but without a body, motive, or the media behind it, this could go on for weeks very quietly. I kind of hope it does."

"You do? I'd think you'd want to wrap up the case."

"But not my time in Destin," he said, his voice just a little lower and more intimate. She got the message, and it made her smile.

"You're only an hour or so away in Pensacola," she said.

"Too far for spontaneity, which I happen to like. So how about we have lunch after your meeting?"

"Oh, I love that idea," she said. "I should be done in an hour. Can I meet you somewhere?"

"The Back Porch?"

She gave a soft laugh. "I forgot about that restaurant. It's still there?"

"Bigger and better than when we were kids. It's a Destin landmark. Meet you at twelve-thirty?"

"I'll be there," she promised, turning into the entrance to Indian Bayou.

As she drove to Fiona's house, she tried to imagine why the woman would have sent that icy text ordering her to come over at eleven. It was so...*Maggie.*

Vivien had to cancel an appointment with the owner of a high-end kitchen business, one that could have led to new clients. But she didn't want to disappoint Fiona.

Could she be getting fired? No, no, no.

Maybe Fiona had another job for her at one of her rental properties, she thought optimistically. Or maybe she was just a lousy texter and everything she wrote came across like she was angry.

When she pulled up to the Victorian, Vivien glanced around but saw no sign of Hapless Handy. There was a very sharp BMW sedan parked on the street, though, so maybe one of Fiona's friends was here.

Then why would she demand Vivien come over?

Oh! That was it! New business! Fiona had invited a friend to meet Vivien, go over the work she'd done so far, and look at her portfolio. Perfect!

Lifted by the thought, she parked behind the BMW and grabbed her bag and tablet, glancing at the house and its grand but aging façade. She so badly hoped Fiona could see beyond her obsession with stripping it down to something cold and soulless.

Baby steps, though. The carpenter had finished the new molding around the stairs, removing the gaudy mahogany and replacing it with a warm light oak trim. And Vivien had left all the samples for the kitchen update on the table days ago, so surely by now Fiona had at least picked the new backsplash and pulls.

Smoothing the simple cotton sheath she'd worn, she made her way up the walk toward the front steps, eyeing the improvement in the shrubbery. Maybe Hapless had managed to figure out the irrigation system in between taking Fiona out for dinner and emptying her bank account.

She pushed the thought from her head and braced for the woman who would open the door. Glancing down, she eyed a worn doormat—and took it as a stark reminder of how *not* to behave.

Vivien exhaled sharply, straightening her spine as she knocked on the frightfully showy front door. Please let a replacement be in the budget, she thought, just as the door opened.

Fiona was as impeccably put together as ever, from her sleek white bob to her crisp navy linen dress and sensible pumps. But her pursed lips and miserable scowl spoke volumes and made Vivien's stomach sink.

Instantly, she knew she wasn't here to be introduced to a friend who needed her services.

"Come in, Vivien," Fiona said, stepping aside. "We have a *problem*. Maybe more than one."

Oh, boy. Here we go.

Vivien stepped into the heavily air-conditioned home, immediately regretting the decision not to wear that light sweater she was always leaving behind.

"What's the problem?" she asked as Fiona closed the door behind her.

"You don't listen, that's the problem."

Vivien swallowed and turned to the woman. "What did I not hear?"

"Apparently, everything. Let's start with the staircase molding."

"Is something wrong with it?" Vivien asked, stepping closer to the molding in question.

The oak blended seamlessly with the home's original

craftsmanship and looked, to Vivien, like it had always been there.

"I *despise* this," Fiona announced, waving a hand toward the molding as if it physically pained her to look at it. "Didn't you *hear a word I said?* I don't want wood finishings! I want sleek, clean, *modern.*"

Vivien swallowed her frustration. "Fiona, I did listen to you. You have to have something there."

"I don't agree. Why can't I just have the drywall?"

"Because it will look unfinished," Vivien said. "I chose this wood and style because it complements both modern design and the original character of the house. It keeps things fresh without eliminating charm."

"Charm?" Fiona scoffed. "This isn't a bed-and-breakfast, Vivien. I don't want *charm.* I want *clean.*"

Vivien clenched her jaw. "The house will feel *sterile* if we strip it of all its natural warmth."

Fiona crossed her arms. "No, it will feel *clean.* And that's exactly what I want. This wood nonsense? It needs to go. Maybe *you* need to go."

Vivien inhaled deeply, transported to a bedroom in Atlanta, looking at a bed she thought she'd made perfectly but...Maggie found flaws. Maggie looked disappointed and poor little Vivien wanted to crawl under that bed and cry.

But she wasn't *poor little Vivien,* and this woman wasn't her mother. "I truly believe that once the entire design comes together, you'll see how—"

"Enough." Fiona held up a hand. "I don't need

convincing, Vivien. I hired you to execute *my* vision, not to push *yours*."

Vivien felt the words hit like a slap. She understood, she really did—this was *Fiona's* home, after all. But what Fiona was asking for wasn't just an aesthetic choice. It was a gutting of everything that made this house special.

She thought about every time she had bitten her tongue to keep the peace, every time she had let someone else's voice drown out her own. It was instinctual at this point. But this time? This time, she couldn't do it.

She straightened her spine. "If I'm going to redesign this entire house, I am going to preserve its character. I can make it modern and contemporary, but I don't want it to look like an asylum and neither do you."

Fiona's brows lifted, and for a brief moment, there was silence.

"Well. That's a shame." She rubbed her hands together as if suddenly she was as stressed as Vivien. "I would really prefer if you followed my direction. It would make this much easier. You don't want me to find a different designer, do you?"

Vivien's stomach clenched at the threat, and she remembered there was a fine line between having a backbone and being...out of a job. "I'll do some research and get back to you with new ideas."

Fiona walked past her, heading toward the front door. "Now, the other problem is in the kitchen."

Vivien followed, thinking of the array of selections she'd left for Fiona to consider. "You don't like the countertops, backsplash, paint, or flooring."

"The paint will be white. Pure white, like all the walls. The flooring will be white tile, the quartz is fine, but the backsplash? No blue curves in this kitchen. Is that clear?" Sweeping into the room, she pointed to the tables, the samples obviously untouched. "Because this is... awful."

She made it sound like Vivien had formed the porcelain with her own hands. "Let me guess. White?"

"Carry the quartz up the wall," she said.

Vivien nodded. "I love that idea, but it's very expensive. Would you consider a dark blue cabinet color then? Just to bring some dimension into the room."

Fiona sighed, long enough that Vivien thought she might have made headway. "No," she said. "I'll stick with white."

Of course she would. Vivien wanted to argue, to plead her case, but she knew it wouldn't matter. She was skating on some seriously thin ice, and it was as cold and unforgiving as this woman and her sterile, one-dimensional asylum.

"Now, I don't have any more time," Fiona announced, swooping up her phone from the counter. "I have a video call scheduled. Danny's upstairs, so if you want him to rip out that heinous wood, he can. Well, he can try."

Danny was...upstairs? Like, in her bedroom? That was *his* car in front of the house? Not the wheels of any handyman she knew.

Fiona flipped over the phone and checked the time. "I have two minutes until this call. I'll be in my office, and

I do not want to be disturbed." She waved the phone at the table. "Get these eyesore samples out of here."

Before she could respond, Fiona turned on her heel and walked to the front of the house, closing the door of the first-floor office with a thud.

Vivien huffed out a breath, alone with her "eyesore" samples and a sick, sick feeling.

She had tried to stand up to the woman, but Fiona Buckman was a living, breathing bulldozer and even someone with a spine as strong as that quartz couldn't fight the woman.

Tear out the molding?

She gave a whimper and walked back out to the staircase, glancing at the closed door to the study, hearing Fiona's voice on the other side. Kneeling down, she ran a finger over the wood and wondered if she could just paint it the same color as the wall—that oh-so-vibrant pure white. Then it would just blend—

"That's a ridiculous amount of money."

She froze at the man's voice, glancing up to where she heard it, and heavy footsteps crossing the open hallway.

It was Hapless Handy...talking about money.

"I'm not going to do that to her," Danny said, lowering his voice as if he thought someone—maybe the woman he was currently swindling—might hear him.

Vivien stepped back, out of his line of vision if he came to the top of the stairs.

"Fifty grand and not a penny more," he said. "I know she doesn't pay attention to her cash flow, but we'll get caught short if we go any higher."

Caught...*doing what?* Emptying her account? And did he have a partner in this con?

His voice got louder as he came down the stairs, so now she couldn't move. "I'm at Fiona's, of course. Where else would I be, Harry?"

Harry? Who was—

"Hello, again." He reached the bottom of the stairs, a half-smile pulling at his face as he spotted her on the other side of the railing. "Hey, I gotta run," he said into the phone, tapping the screen without taking his eyes off her.

Was he wondering how much she'd heard?

She straightened and took a good look, searching for clues. But all she saw was a man wearing a dark T-shirt and khaki shorts, a toolbox in one hand and his phone in the other. He was taller than she remembered, and now she could really see his face.

He was about fifty, so not exactly a "much younger lover," although Fiona was at least sixty. He had black hair with threads of silver at the temples, and blue-gray eyes that seemed to spark with humor, as if he *knew* she *knew* and didn't care.

"If she told you I can take off that wood she hates?" He angled his head toward the molding. "The answer is no. I don't have the time or the talent."

"But you do have a toolbox," she said.

He gave a mirthless laugh. "Please. It's a prop. But I'm starting to get the hang of it."

He wasn't even going to *try* and pretend he was a handyman?

"I was thinking we could paint it the same color as the wall," she said.

"Don't look at me," he replied. "Paint is way above my pay grade."

Was he *serious?*

"Look, I'm just here because I love the woman, okay? And you have to in order to work for her...as I think, based on your expression, you figured out."

"You...love her?" She tried, and failed, to keep the disbelief out of her voice.

"Well, I can't say no to her." He looked past her to the office, Fiona's muffled voice coming through the door. "So, call that love if you want."

He smiled and it changed his whole face, taking it from standard handsome features to...yeah, above standard handsome. She pushed the thought away and narrowed her eyes, trying to remember all the things Peter told her to look for—the money flow, expensive things, if he isolated Fiona.

"So, if that's a prop...and painting is out of your league, why are you here?"

He studied her for a moment, looking like he might confide something, but then he shrugged.

"Look, she lost her husband a year ago and made the classic widow's error—she bought a house she doesn't know what to do with, has a business she might not know how to run, and inherited a mountain of money and needs help with it. And I'm not kidding when I say no one will work for her. The list is short. Basically, you and me."

"She needs your help handling a mountain of money?"

He grinned then glanced down at his watch—a *Rolex*.

"Handling money *is* in my pay grade." Then he grunted. "I'm late. See you around, Vivien. Unless she chews you up and spits you out like the last two designers. And the electrician. And the moron who installed the sprinkler system that I have, I'm happy to inform you, finally fixed."

Laughing, he breezed by her and went out the door and, a few seconds later, she heard the purr of that German machine he drove.

Wait...what the heck just happened? Was he conning Fiona? Sleeping with her? A real boyfriend? She'd been widowed for less than a year! And had a *mountain of inheritance?*

And what had he said to "Harry" on the call...she doesn't pay attention to her cash flow? How convenient for him and his Rolex and BMW. The poor woman probably thinks he loves her, too.

Should she tell Fiona, or would that put Vivien right in the crosshairs like...the last two designers?

Dang. She was in a bind, and it didn't look like there was any easy way out.

Chapter Seventeen

Eli

The clang of the weight plates echoed across the gym as Eli pushed up the barbell, arms straining, his breath measured. Peter stood over him, hands poised beneath the bar, ready to catch it if needed.

"C'mon, two more," Peter urged, his voice even, calm.

Eli gritted his teeth and pushed through one more rep before racking the barbell. He exhaled, shaking out his arms, before he sat up and wiped his forehead with his towel.

Peter grinned, offering him a fist bump. "Not bad for an old guy."

"Hey, I held my own," Eli shot back, rolling his shoulders. "Plus, we're not old. We're *seasoned*."

Peter chuckled. "Yeah, yeah, but you know I had you on the squats the other day."

"Debatable," Eli muttered, grabbing his water bottle and taking a sip. "Anyway, you're a cop and have to train for a living. I'm an architect and the only thing that needs to be in shape is my pencil."

"Honestly, you're in great shape, Eli. Not..." He tipped his head to a small group of younger men just finishing up on the Smith machine. "Like those Gen Whatevers."

Eli followed his gaze, checking out the boys who looked like Jonah's peers. "Yeah, not a gray hair in the bunch and so much T, I can smell the stuff."

Peter laughed as the guys came closer to the bench press station. One of them, the bulkiest with a full sleeve tattoo, gave a nod.

"You guys done?" he asked.

"It's all yours," Peter told them, stepping back.

The two of them watched as the guy and his friends proceeded to absolutely destroy their previous numbers. By the time the kid re-racked the weight, Peter let out a low whistle.

"All right, I've officially hit my limit of humiliation for the day," he said.

Eli laughed. "Yeah, let's call it."

They grabbed their towels and water bottles, stopped in the locker room to wash up and get their keys and phones.

A few minutes later, they stepped outside into the warm Florida sun. The air was thick with spring humidity and the scent of freshly cut grass from the park across the street. They plopped down on a bench just outside the gym, taking some time to catch their breath.

"So, speaking of being an architect..." Peter gave him a look. "You letting Meredith run your company now?"

Eli laughed softly. "Basically. I'm doing everything remote these days, with Zoom calls. Truth?"

Peter shot him a look. "Hey, it's me."

Eli took a deep drink of water and looked out toward the sunshine, thinking of the hours he'd been spending with his son finishing the apartment. "I just don't want to leave Jonah while he's waiting to find out if he got into the Culinary Arts program. And, honestly, man, it's been years since we talked this much. The thing that's keeping me here is my son."

"Hey, that's great, Eli."

"It is," he agreed. "He's shared a lot about Carly, who is still keeping him at arm's length while he gets his act together. We've talked about Melissa's death a little, something he's never really been comfortable addressing with me. And we've talked about...life, fatherhood, sports. All the stuff I've missed so much since he's been away and growing up."

"I get that. And it's way more important than work."

"Work's important, too, but between Meredith and setting up a drafting desk in the back office? I'm able to cover all the bases."

"Well done." Peter leaned forward, elbows on his knees. "And if I may ask...how are things with Kate?"

"Oh, yeah, you can ask." Eli stretched out his legs as he considered his response. "Fact is, I miss her more than I thought I would."

"Ah." He gave a smile that made Eli think his friend knew that.

"It's weird, Pete. We haven't known each other as adults for that long, but it feels... right. Like something I don't want to lose."

Peter nodded. "She's coming back soon, right? For a long weekend at the end of the month?"

"Yeah," Eli said, unable to wipe the smile from his face. "She and her kids—and Jo Ellen—are coming for that fashion show Tessa and Lacey are organizing for the bridal shop. It should be a good time."

Peter chuckled. "Yeah, I know all about that. I had lunch with Vivien the other day and somehow, I got roped into being one of the models." He rolled his eyes. "Don't say a word, Lawson."

But Eli was already cracking up. "You? On a runway? This I have to see."

"Hey, I'll have you know I can pull off a tux," Peter shot back.

"I don't doubt it," Eli said, then he eyed his friend. "So...if *I* may ask," he joked, echoing Peter from earlier. "Vivien, huh?"

Peter looked out toward the street, lifting his chin and scratching some beard growth. "Yep. Vivien."

"Don't forget she's still my little sister." He gave him an elbow jab. "Hurt her and someone will die."

Peter laughed. "I'm not going to hurt her," he said. "But there's definitely some chemistry there. I think. I don't know. It's early days. And I know she hasn't even signed divorce papers yet, so I'm keeping it very chill."

Eli nodded as he regarded the other man. There was no one he'd trust more with Vivien, but was she ready for another relationship? Even with a guy as great as Peter? And did Eli have a say in that? Probably not, but he might try anyway.

"So, uh..." He hesitated, then asked, "You thinking it could turn into something serious, Pete?"

"Maybe. I mean, it has potential. But I don't know how long she's staying in Destin, which is over an hour from Pensacola. Not a thousand-mile challenge like you and Kate, but still not easy to build a relationship."

"If it's real and strong and lasting, that's just an obstacle," Eli said. "Plus, I firmly believe God opens doors when He wants you to go through them."

Peter gave the tight smile of a non-believer, but one who fully respected Eli's faith. "I guess Vivien's proximity depends on what happens with the house," he said. "You haven't made a decision whether or not to sell it, have you?"

Eli leaned back against the bench. "Nope. We haven't made a final decision. There are a lot of things to consider—people's lives and jobs, the upkeep on a place like that, and, of course, the cash cow of selling it. But it's only April. We've got time to figure it out. Right now, everything's on the table."

They sat in comfortable silence for a moment, letting the sun warm their tired muscles. Then Peter shifted, his posture changing slightly. He turned toward Eli, his expression more serious.

"Look," Peter said, lowering his voice slightly. "I have some information about your father's files."

Eli sat up straighter. "You do? You holding out on me?"

"I don't mean to be. I'm just not sure if it's going to

answer your questions or give you a whole bunch of new ones."

Eli stared at him, aware of how tight his chest grew. "What is it?"

"Well, I called in a favor and was able to get some old files from the initial investigation."

"That's legal, right?" Eli said. "I don't want you to go one inch outside the law."

"I didn't and I won't, you can be sure of it. The files were heavily redacted, and I wasn't allowed to take any pictures or make copies. I did determine that, yes, there was an informant. He requested—and was granted—anonymity. At least from the filings I read."

"Oh." Eli leaned back against the stone wall with a punch of disappointment. Anonymity was such a non-answer. "Is that SOP in a thirty-year-old case that was long closed?"

"It's not exactly *standard* operating procedure," Peter said. "But it's definitely a decision made at the discretion of that department's chief. It might mean Feds were involved in later stages of the investigation. Those guys lock everything forever and throw away the key."

Eli nodded. "All it tells us is that there was an anonymous source, and for whatever reason, the police honored that request. Is that normal?"

"Oh, yeah. If they think the informant could be in danger or if they want to go back to him and negotiate for more information or even if they're protecting their source from being called in as a witness. Lots of reasons,"

Peter said. "But it doesn't answer the question of whether or not it was Artie."

Eli frowned, processing. "So Maggie might have been wrong."

"Maybe," Peter said carefully. "I mean, it's still possible. But this isn't the smoking gun that proves Artie was the one who turned him in."

"Is that the end of it, then? All you can get your hands on?"

"Not necessarily," he said. "I've got a contact within the Atlanta PD now, and that file gave me some names I could call or places I might look."

"Don't go to any trouble, Pete."

He shot a "get real" look. "You know I want to help you, and it's no trouble. I just don't know if you'll like what I find."

"Well, without finding anything, all we have to go on is Maggie's word and we know what she says."

"Jo Ellen's coming down," Peter reminded him. "Could you talk to her?"

"Maybe. Kate said she hates the subject—thinks it's ancient history that we should forget."

"In other words, you don't want to ruin your weekend by dredging up the past?"

Eli nodded. "But I also do not want to plow into a serious relationship with this potentially hanging over our heads. I mean, the implications are major. Our mothers hate each other—or at least one does. While I happily don't need my mother's approval anymore, I have no interest in breaking up our family, or Maggie's old heart. It's a layer of complication."

"Especially if Artie did turn him in just because he wanted to take the high road or thought it was the ethically correct thing to do," Peter said.

"Exactly. And if it turns out that Artie did maliciously betray my father, regardless of how 'right' he was and how guilty my dad was? Well, can we get past that?"

"Then this is at least a little hopeful," Peter said. "It doesn't confirm that it was Artie. Maybe Maggie's wrong."

Eli exhaled slowly, clinging to that hope. "Maybe this was a misunderstanding, and the families can resolve things. Then...Kate and I might have a real chance."

Peter gave him a small smile. "Wouldn't be the worst outcome."

Eli nodded, determination settling in. "I need to tell Vivien. And Crista. And Tessa. They should know about this."

Peter clapped a hand on Eli's shoulder. "Then go do it. Let's get back here after a day of rest. We need to bulk up for the fashion show."

Eli chuckled, standing up and shaking his head. But as they said goodbye and he walked to his car, he had to say a power prayer that "anonymous" was not Artie Wylie. *Please, God.*

"Anonymous?"

"Redacted?"

"*What?*"

The questions volleyed at Eli by the three women on the deck with him were understandable, despite his best efforts to explain what Peter had told him. It was just enough information to be dangerous, confusing, and frustrating.

Eli had called Vivien on his way back to the Summer House and asked her to gather Crista and Tessa with some privacy, which was probably why Lacey had taken Nolie down to the beach to play. Jonah was up in the apartment finishing the bathroom's tile floor.

That meant Eli was able to be alone with these three—who very much deserved to know what Peter had told him.

He'd tried to call Kate from the car, but she was in a meeting; he'd fill her in later.

For now, he had to navigate the reactions of three very different women with three very different agendas as far as Artie Wylie and Roger Lawson—and their wives—were concerned.

"Well, that's our answer," Tessa said.

"How is *anonymous* an answer?" Crista snapped back, her stress palpable from the minute this conversation started.

"My father wouldn't do anything *anonymously*. He'd call that cheap, cowardly, and shameful. If he reported a criminal act, he'd proudly put his name on the documentation and give all his reasons for turning the bad guy in."

Vivien sighed. "Tess, can you do us a favor and

refrain from calling our father a 'bad guy'? We know what he did."

Her eyes shuttered. "Sorry. I'm just defending my dad. You know I will to the death."

"Well, our father has already met his death," Crista muttered. "And no one's defending him."

For a moment, no one spoke as they let the comment settle over them. The only sound was the rustle of the palm fronds and Nolie's voice from the beach, an ironic contrast to the tension straining across the deck.

"I'm certain that my dad would have signed his name."

"Was the name redacted?" Vivien asked. "Or was the tipster called 'anonymous' through the whole document?"

"You know, I'm not sure, but Peter might know. He wasn't allowed to copy or take pictures of the files."

"Doesn't that seem weird to you?" Vivien asked. "I mean, it's a thirty-year-old closed case and Dad's long gone, so..."

Eli shrugged. "I asked Peter, and he said it's at the chief's discretion. Or that the FBI got involved at some point, because they are very tight with clearances and files no matter how old the case."

Crista folded her arms, her dark brows knit with the strain of the conversation. She rose from her seat and walked to the railing, leaning against it to watch Nolie play, sighing repeatedly as she put her hand on her stomach like she could feel the stress right in her gut.

"Our mother insisted it was Artie," she said suddenly,

turning toward the rest of them. "Why would she make up something like that?"

Vivien's posture was calm but cautious as she leaned forward, her gaze on Crista. "Maybe she believed it to be true. Maybe she needed someone to blame. Maybe Roger told her that to ease his own guilt. There are a lot of reasons, but it doesn't necessarily make it a fact. Anonymous doesn't automatically translate into Artie."

"Thank you!" Tessa exclaimed. "Nothing translates into Artie."

"But he's not exonerated," Crista said.

Eli watched the flicker of anger in Tessa's eyes, the way her lips pressed together before she spoke. "If the source was anonymous, then that means there's no proof it was him. That means my father doesn't have to be the villain in this story."

"You want to believe that," Crista replied. "I get it. But it also doesn't prove it was someone else."

"Remember," Eli said, feeling a fight brewing. "Peter said he has connections and some more trails to follow. We could still learn something more definitive. But with this question—"

Crista let out a sharp breath. "What question? Maggie said Artie turned him in and that was the cause of their big falling out. Why would she lie? Why else would they end a long friendship?"

"Kate and Jo Ellen are coming in a few weeks," he said. "So we can—"

"I can't." Crista threw both hands in the air, one of her common gestures when she was losing the battle with her emotions. "I can't do this. I can't have this conversation or let Artie off the hook for being anonymous. I don't think I can continue to hobnob with...his family."

"Crista!" Vivien launched out of her seat. "Don't do this. We've made so much progress. You and Tessa and—"

"That's a Band-Aid that isn't going to heal the wound," she said, taking a step away. "And the wound is deep. Dad died in prison. Do you think that would have happened if he'd been home? Mom would have called an ambulance at the first pang in his chest and he could very well be alive today. But he was alone, in a cell!"

Tears sprang to her eyes, surprising Eli because she hadn't cried in so many days.

"You can't blame me for your father's death," Tessa ground out.

"I'm not blaming you," Crista insisted. "I just... promised my mother and..." She turned again, swiping at tears she obviously didn't want to shed. "I've lost sight of everything."

Her murmured words were carried on the breeze, but Eli heard them and he and Vivien both went to her.

"Come on, Cris," Eli said. "You know that's not true. Nolie's made progress."

At the mention of Nolie's name, they all looked down at the beach, watching the child dance in the sand while Aunt Pittypat scampered around her. Lacey was clapping and singing a song, the two of them laughing in the sunshine, bathed in what Eli thought of as the enchantment of Destin.

Crista looked at him, something dark flickering in her eyes. Guilt, maybe. A mother's worry and a daughter's doubt. Then her expression hardened and she pushed off the railing, past all of them.

"Anthony's right," she said softly. "She's just playing. Not learning."

Tessa flinched like she'd been struck.

"Are you kidding me?" Her voice wavered, but anger burned behind it. "You promised you'd stay if she passed the third-grade test. We're taking it today. That's why she's down there. We thought she could decompress and—"

Crista shook her head, taking a step back. "I can't do it, Tessa. I just can't. I don't know what's wrong with me, but I've been programmed my whole life to hate a Wylie."

"*Programmed* is right," Tessa said with a bitter laugh. "Do you ever think for yourself, Crista Merritt? Or just follow the orders of your Queen Maggie or your husband?"

Crista stared at her, breathing so hard her nostrils flared. She opened her mouth to say something, then slammed it shut.

"Crista, please—"

She shook off Vivien's attempt to make peace. "I'm packing our things," she ground out. "Nolie and I will be gone this afternoon."

With that, she strode inside, leaving them in silent shock.

Eli exhaled sharply. He wanted to stop her, but knew

she needed to calm down. His eyes met Vivien's, who looked as troubled as he felt.

And Tessa looked gutted. She swallowed hard, then lifted her chin, her breath shaky as she shifted her gaze to the beach and it landed on Nolie.

"I made a promise and a commitment," she said, voice steady but fierce. "And Artie Wylie's daughter doesn't break either one."

With that, she walked off, leaving Eli and Vivien standing in the wreckage of the argument.

Back to square one, Eli thought. Back to broken bridges, and fractured families.

Chapter Eighteen
Crista

Fear? Anger? Temper tantrums and accusations? Humming with emotions that seemed more in control of her than anything else?

Crista Merritt, what is wrong with you?

Even for her, the reaction to the "anonymous informant" news was over the top. Was she afraid of the truth? Worried it would get her in trouble with her mother? Cause a setback for Nolie? Somehow break up her marriage or family or her relationship with Eli or Vivien?

Deeply frustrated and out of sorts, Crista closed the door to her bedroom and dropped on the bed, giving in to a full-body sob that made no sense to her. She'd been doing so well at controlling her emotions until...until that day Mama had told her the truth about Artie turning Dad in to the authorities.

Maybe before that. Maybe when her mother had broken the news that they owned this house. That's about when the "wilder than usual" emotional reactions had started. It was like a switch flipped that day and she'd been hanging by a thread for weeks and weeks now.

She fell back on the bed and stared up at the ceiling,

trying so hard to understand and control this personal rollercoaster. Maybe she needed medication.

No, no. Maybe it was the stress of Nolie possibly having to repeat second grade. Or that feeling that every flaw in her life was magnified by her mother's judgmental eye. Even the distance from Anthony that they'd tried to fix with, what? One date night a while ago.

Who could blame him for being distant? She was *unstable*.

But now this revelation about Dad. She closed her eyes and moaned, the very thought of her father in jail making her feel literally sick. She'd only been a child when he was arrested, and it had scared the daylights out of her. She hadn't understood what was happening and, goodness, her mother certainly hadn't bothered to enlighten her.

Everyone thought Crista was "too young" to know what was going on. The next thing she knew, Mama was crying at the dining room table and told her that Daddy had died in jail from a broken heart.

It didn't take a shrink to know it was that day that Crista Lawson became a stressed-out perfectionist and drama queen. If only she could be "perfect"—her life, her home, her hair, her everything—then maybe she wouldn't lose *both* parents.

Those days, those years, were scary and gloomy and the only thing she could cling to was...Maggie.

And now, years later, she had to wonder—what if Artie Wylie had kept his mouth shut?

Would Dad have been arrested? Could he have

climbed out of the hole of debt and fraud he'd dug himself into without getting caught? Could he have confided in his brilliant wife, who might have thought of a way out? Maybe he could have turned himself in for a lighter sentence and been on probation at home when his heart stopped beating?

Would Crista's whole life have been different?

She felt the sting of tears on her cheeks and tried to push up to get the packing started, knowing she'd painted herself into a corner and Anthony expected her home tomorrow. He'd given her a day's reprieve, but...

Sighing, she closed her eyes, the weight of bone-deep fatigue pressing down on her. She felt that little wave of dizziness that sometimes happened right before she drifted off, and she just didn't have the strength to stand or...move.

All she could do was escape in...sleep.

"Hey. Crista? Are you in there?"

The voice came from way in the distance, soft and familiar.

"Crista?"

She blinked, inhaling a sharp breath, yanked from a deep slumber. How long had she crashed?

Pushing up, she grabbed the phone on the bed next to her, her jaw dropping when she saw the time. An hour and a half!

"Can I come in, please? I have to tell you something."

It was Tessa, she realized, shaking off the fog of an unwelcome afternoon nap. Mustering her energy, she pushed to the floor and walked to the door, opening it slowly, as if she didn't know what would be waiting on the other side.

"I have to show you something."

She stared at the other woman, something shifting in her heart. Tessa had tried with Nolie—her techniques were questionable, but she got an A for effort.

"You have to look at this." Tessa held her iPad out.

Still a little confused, but awake now, she stepped back, silently inviting Tessa into the room. "What is it?"

"Are you okay?" Tessa frowned. "I mean, I know you're upset but you look..."

"I fell asleep," she said. "I just conked out for an hour. No clue why."

"Stress," Tessa said. "But this might help." She held the iPad out again, showing a form that Crista didn't recognize.

"What?" Crista frowned at it, trying to make sense of the words...

Georgia State Department of Education...Elementary School Placement Exam

She instantly recognized the name of the test from research she'd done earlier and shared with Tessa.

For Practice Only ~ Results Not Official

"Oh..." She looked up at Tessa. "She took it?"

"Twice. Both times the same result." She pointed to the form, sliding her finger over the name Magnolia Merritt, the date, and the test type—*Third Grade Readiness Evaluation*.

"Oh, my."

"Keep reading," Tessa said, tapping the screen so it went to the next page.

Overall score: Pass

Pass? Crista closed her eyes, literally swaying.

"You okay?"

"I'm just a little...dizzy."

Tessa giggled. "I know. I was, too. This happened twice, Crista. I have both scores. Look at these numbers!"

"I can't..." She felt woozy again. "I just... Read them to me." She took a few steps back to the bed, so overwhelmed by relief and emotion that she felt her entire body vibrating.

"Reading Comprehension," Tessa said. "Eighty-one-beautiful-percent."

"No!"

"They call that, 'Meets Expectations,'" Tessa said. "I call it a massive victory! And get this! Math was even higher! Every single category, Crista—exceeds, meets, or approaching grade-level expectation. She passed with flying colors!"

Crista put her hand over her mouth, not even able to comprehend all the feelings ricocheting through her body.

"Does Nolie know?" Crista asked.

"I didn't even tell her it was a test," Tessa said. "I told her it was a game. A game she aced! Our girl is *going* to third grade!"

Our girl. Good heavens, this was a dear woman. A good, dear, kind woman who cared about Nolie.

She blinked at Tessa, fighting for calm with a few deep breaths. "I'm...I'm sorry, Tessa."

Inching back, Tessa's smile wavered as she searched Crista's face. "Are you going to whack out on me again for something that happened thirty years ago and I had no control over?"

Tears burned Crista's lids. Shame, regret, and another wave of utter lack of self-control. "No, I'm not. I'm literally apologizing. I'm sorry for...all that."

Tessa's shoulders dropped as she stepped closer. "It's okay."

"No, actually, it's not," Crista said. "I don't know why I acted like that. You didn't deserve it. You deserve my gratitude."

On a long sigh, Tessa dropped onto the bed, placing the iPad between them. "I'm just really proud of Nolie."

"You should be," Crista said. "You've done something in a few weeks that we haven't been able to do the whole school year. Not even close."

"Because I'm dyslexic, too," Tessa said gently. "Remember that, okay? It's like I speak her language and you don't."

"You do speak her language," Crista said. "I've honestly never seen her connect so easily with anyone outside of our family. I should be throwing my arms around you in appreciation and yet..." She put her hand on her stomach, dread making it roll.

Because when her mother found out it was Tessa Wylie who'd helped Nolie get into third grade, there would be hell to pay.

"Crista?" Tessa leaned in. "You okay? You look a little...green around the gills, if you know what I mean."

"I'm fine. It's the emotion. The revelations. The guilt." She closed her eyes and took a deep breath. "I think that's what's really getting to me."

"Let it go," Tessa said. "You have nothing to feel guilty about. First of all, your mother is putting ridiculous parameters around your life. Around all of you. She gives you this house to keep or sell but it comes with a caveat that says, 'Don't breathe the same air as a Wylie'?"

Crista laughed. "That's what Vivien has said from the beginning. Could this be an unconditional gift? Does Maggie Lawson know the meaning of that?" She cringed as she said the words. "Oh, listen to me. I never say anything bad about my mother. I always defend her."

"You're a good daughter, but you have to put *your* daughter first. Her needs, her education, and, well, her tutor, who happens to be a Wylie." Tessa smiled. "Does it matter, if Nolie is thriving?"

Crista searched the beautiful face of the woman sitting next to her. "You were always a little nicer to me than any of the other 'big kids' at the house," she said, as surprised as Tessa was at the unexpected change of subject. But she realized she'd wanted to say it for a while now.

"You might not remember," she continued, "but when I had to be in a sleeping bag on the floor, I almost always woke up in your bed."

"'Cause I was scared I'd walk on you when I sneaked in late from a night swim with some cute boy."

"But you cared," Crista said. "I think I knew that when I handed Nolie to you. You have a caring heart."

Tessa rolled her eyes. "Don't let that get out. It'll ruin my hard-earned reputation as cold-hearted—"

"No." Crista put her hand on Tessa's arm. "You're not cold-hearted. You actually would have made a spectacular mother. Nolie is proof of that."

Tessa's soft expression slowly grew...harder. Cooler. Slightly distant. "Well, I wasn't." She picked up the iPad. "Now, do you want to tell Anth—" She froze. "What's wrong, Crista?"

Crista stood, almost unable to talk as her throat thickened. "I think...I'm going to be sick."

She didn't wait for Tessa to react, but tore into the ensuite and flung the toilet seat up.

"Crista?"

She waved her off and leaned over, getting almost instant relief when her whole lunch came back up.

After a moment, she stood up and turned to the sink, flipping on the water to rinse her mouth. When she looked up into the mirror, she didn't meet her own gaze but Tessa's.

The other woman stood right behind her, quiet, with a very knowing look in her eyes.

"It's like I can't control anything," Crista whispered. "Mood, food, tears..."

"When was your last period?"

Crista froze and blinked. "What?"

"Are you on birth control?"

"No, but I'm forty-three and Nolie took years to conceive and…"

"Exhaustion. Dizzy. Throwing up?" Tessa lifted a brow. "Didn't you mention heartburn the other night? And let's not forget those mood swings."

"No. It's not…" Well, there *was* that date night a month or so ago. It *was* possible.

Tessa raised a questioning brow, silent.

"Please," Crista said, pressing a washcloth to her lips. "Keep this between us. I'll have to…be sure."

"Are you happy about it?" Tessa asked softly.

Crista just looked at her. "I'm…just stunned. It would be…wow. Yeah, impossible but…oh, my goodness." Reeling, she reached out and hugged Tessa, aching to hold someone close at this most confusing, shocking, unbelievable moment.

She squeezed Tessa, who gave her a light hug back, and when they separated, she could have sworn the other woman had tears in her eyes, too.

How sweet she was to care.

"I was so wrong about you, Tessa," Crista admitted gruffly.

Tessa mustered a smile, but it didn't quite reach her eyes. "Your secret's safe with me," she said. "Better call your husband and tell him the big news."

"About Nolie or…" She touched her stomach.

"Both."

No, not both, Crista thought as Tessa gave a wink and a wave and left her alone in the bathroom.

She'd just tell him about Nolie. And the other thing?

She needed to take a test. She still simply couldn't believe it.

"Passed? Like passed for real?" Anthony's voice rose as he asked the question for the fourth time. "And you're sure that it's the same test?"

"Not exactly the same, but conceptually, yes. It was a third grade entrance exam for the state of Georgia and she passed!"

She heard Anthony sigh and then laugh and her whole being suddenly ached for him. This was the longest they'd ever been apart, and she could feel the absence down to her toes.

"I miss you, Anth," she whispered into the phone, the temptation to tell him what just happened so strong. But she had to be sure—this could absolutely be some weird fluke and then he'd be disappointed.

Wouldn't he? Or would this upset him? Another expense, another form of stress...

"Oh, Cris, honey," he said, his voice soft and loving. "There are no words for how I miss you. Both of you. This house is so empty! I even miss that darn dog."

She laughed, feeling lighthearted and lightheaded. "Pittypat's a beach regular now. You wouldn't believe how she wakes up and demands to go down that boardwalk."

"The one where you're having a fashion show?"

She stayed quiet for a beat, letting the question sink

in. "I thought you said Nolie and I had to come home and she'd miss that."

He let out a moan. "A moment of pure selfishness and stupidity. Of course she's staying."

"Oh, Anthony!" She bit her lip and, oh, yeah, here came the tears again. "Please come for the fashion show. Although...I have to warn you, Kate Wylie, her teenage kids, and her mother will be here, too."

"Warn me? I'm not Maggie. I don't have some imaginary issue with these people I've never even met. But will I have to dress up like I'm in a wedding?"

"Probably." She smiled, tamping down the burn in her gut that she had every time she thought about telling Maggie how she and Nolie had spent this month.

"I can be there on Friday afternoon," Anthony said, pulling her back into the conversation. "Would that be okay?"

"Yes! Of course. Nolie's in our room, but we'll get her an air mattress. She'll be over the moon, Anthony. She'll be so happy. I am." She swiped a tear, just accepting that they flowed constantly now. "And we'll keep working with her, of course! Tessa isn't done, I'm sure, there's more to—"

"Crista," he whispered, cutting her off.

"Yes?"

"I love you."

The words squeezed the air out of her lungs. So much that she couldn't even respond.

"I really do, Cris. I've been hard on you and all you've done was care about her. I've been demanding and scared and..." His voice cracked. "I love you so much. You're an amazing mother."

She closed her eyes and held her breath, the only way she could keep from bursting out a way too premature announcement. She wasn't even remotely sure how she felt about the possibility, so there was no way to balance his reaction.

"I love you, too," she managed. "It's been a really stressful time with Nolie and Maggie..."

"Yeah, Maggie. Too bad she's so dead-set against keeping that house. You might be able to talk me into giving up the cash just so she'd have a second place to go. Or we would."

She flinched. "You've had enough, huh?"

"No, no. I love her, and I know you two are close, it's just that sometimes we need a break from having her... witness our life."

He was so right. And if there was a baby? Oh, boy. A mess of stress.

"Well, if we end up keeping this house, it would be a nice place for us to escape as a family," she said. "Nolie loves every grain of sand and every ray of sunshine."

He chuckled. "That kid is too much, isn't she? Passed! Look out, third grade, here she comes!"

His voice rose with joy, and it lifted every cell in her body. Once again, she had to fight the temptation to tell him her news, but she just closed her eyes.

"I can't wait to see you, Anthony."

"Oh, I'll be there. And I'll wear a tux for that thing. I'll do it for Nolie. I'd do anything for that kid. And you."

She squeezed the phone, wishing she could hold him. "I know. You're a wonderful father and husband."

"I'll be better, Cris. I promise."

"And I'll be less emotional," she countered. *Just maybe not for...eight more months.*

But she didn't say a word, just promised that she and Nolie would FaceTime him tonight.

Would she tell him then? No. If she was pregnant, she'd tell him in person when he came down. She wanted to be with him when he found out.

It was only when she hung up that she realized how much she wanted that test to be positive.

Chapter Nineteen
Tessa

For reasons only she knew, Tessa was still reeling after yesterday's...*situation* with Crista. It wasn't that Crista was having some possible pregnancy symptoms, although that did kind of throw Tessa off a bit.

No, it was the fact that yet another person had told her what a great mother she would have been. No one understood why that stung. And she was so tired of carrying her secret around. Maybe she'd tell Kate when she came in next weekend. Maybe she'd tell the whole world. Maybe they'd stop reminding her of a decision she could not undo.

For the past two hours, she'd been able to put the emotions on a backburner while she and Laccy had a long and incredibly productive meeting at Lumière. After it ended, they stepped into the sunshine of Miramar Beach, riding high from how much Akari loved the plans for the fashion show event.

Lacey darn near skipped over the cobblestone sidewalk with untethered joy, as exuberant as Nolie would be.

"We were awesome!" she sang as she clutched the

packet of notes and reference photos Akari had given them, fanning herself dramatically with the stack of papers. "Did you hear how excited she was? I swear, we are *so* good at this."

Tessa chuckled at her, turning the corner to catch the rays of a sun dipping toward the horizon, casting an ethereal glow over the rows of upscale boutiques and cafés.

"Wow, what an evening," she said, taking a deep inhale.

"It's amazing," Lacey agreed. "Let's go celebrate with a glass of wine. Isn't that cute place, Vin'tij, on the next block?"

"It is," Tessa said, trying to decide if she wanted to settle into the bistro and bask in Lacey's happiness. Normally, nothing would have stopped her, but her heart was still unreasonably heavy.

"Come on." Lacey tugged her arm. "One glass of something bubbly to toast our enormous success."

Tessa shook her head. "One client does not an enormous success make, my young protégé."

"We have the Bat Mitzvah next month, and you've had three new business leads," Lacey replied. "Akari said she gave our name to several people looking for wedding planners. You can plan a wedding."

"In my sleep," she said, letting Lacey lead her. "All right, all right. One drink. Let's go."

Vin'tij Wine Boutique & Bistro was a perfect spot—trendy but relaxed, with a cozy, artsy atmosphere. They grabbed a high-top table near the window, each ordering a sparkling rosé. They decided to split a baked focaccia because Tessa never met a triple cream brie she could resist.

The place hummed with soft jazz music, and the pink-hued sunset spilled through the large windows, making the ambiance feel even more charmed.

Tessa sighed as the drinks were served in tall flutes, their deep rose color looking so refreshing.

Lacey raised her glass. "To Tessa Wylie Events—the best company I've ever worked for."

Tessa clinked her glass against Lacey's, laughing. "You're either wildly optimistic or drunk on the smell of the stuff."

"Neither one," Lacey insisted. "I just can't believe how smoothly everything is coming together. Akari was *so* excited about the show."

"We need everyone involved to catch the vision," Tessa said. "I'm not sure Eli and Jonah are *thrilled* about their new careers in male modeling."

"Jonah is still pretending to be annoyed, but I swear I saw him checking his reflection before we left today. *He's* into it. Uncle Eli, though? That's gonna take some convincing."

They laughed about it while the appetizer was served, wafting the aroma of warm brie and caramelized onions between them.

"And we'll need more brides, of course," Tessa added.

"You need to step up, Tess." Lacey pointed at her with a slice of cheese-covered bread. "Why don't you want to wear a wedding dress?"

Tessa groaned, putting her own bread back down on the small plate in front of her. "Oh, Lace, don't start."

"It's just that you're so pretty and you have a great figure. Honestly, for that 'second brides' collection? You're perfect. In every way, you're perfect."

"Kate will do it." She took a bite and tried to enjoy the rich flavor.

"You should, too."

Tessa wanted to roll her eyes, but Lacey studied her so intently, she suddenly felt uncomfortable.

"What?" Tessa asked, touching her lips. "Do I have cheese on my face?"

"I'm just thinking..." Lacey leaned back in her chair, her smile stretching. "Tessa, can I just say that I love this job?"

"Oh, Lacey, that's—"

"No, no, let me get this out. I've had two sips, so it's not the rosé talking. This is the first time I've ever felt like I'm actually *doing* something. Like I wake up and want to work. That's never happened before."

"That's because you've finally found something that excites you," Tessa told her, knowing the feeling all too well. "You're not just punching a clock for a paycheck, especially considering the paltry sum I've paid you. But you're building something."

"All that's true, but it's more than that." Lacey leaned forward, her expression turning more serious. "I never met anyone like you. I just love you, honestly. I believe in you, and I trust you."

Tessa stared at her, the echo of old Gerry's voice and

offer still in her ear, knowing that if she took it, this girl would be hurt.

"Because nothing good ever lasts in my life," Lacey continued. "I can't seem to get traction and I'm going to be twenty-five. Twenty-*five*."

Tessa knew she should laugh and make a joke like, "Oh, to be twenty-five again," but the number hit with a little more impact than it should, making Tessa look down. She'd been twenty-five herself...and that was twenty-five years ago, so...

"I mean, I keep waiting for the other shoe to drop," Lacey plowed on. "I'm a bit of a quitter...or at least I have been when it comes to work. But this? I don't want to quit. I don't want anything to go wrong."

Tessa sighed, a punch of guilt making her want to be honest—she *had* to be honest.

"It might change, Lace," she finally said. "You need to know that."

Lacey froze, her chatter quieting. "What do you mean?"

"I mean..." She huffed out a breath. "I have to be straight with you. The Ritz has offered me my old job back."

"*What?*" Lacey mouthed the word, turning a little pale.

Tessa took a long sip of her drink, delaying the news that would truly affect Lacey. Finally, she exhaled.

"Nothing is definite or decided, but I have agreed to think about it."

"What's to think about?" Lacey shot back. "They

treated you so unfairly! That isn't where you belong! You're here and...we've got a business and...this is so much fun and...." She swallowed. "Please don't leave, Tessa."

The words pressed on her heart. "Lacey, it's a really good job with benefits and I live in luxury for nothing. I wouldn't have to worry about where I'm going to be sleeping in six months."

"You'll be living with us at the Summer House!"

"We can't be sure about that," Tessa said. "Crista hasn't agreed not to sell yet and...you don't know what's going on in her life. She could change her mind and take the cash."

Tessa was already certain that's what Crista would do if she had another baby. They'd sell the Summer House and have a nest egg for two kids.

Lacey shook her head furiously, as if she just didn't want to hear that. "My mom and Uncle Eli will convince her. And even if they don't, we could stay here and build the business. Find a place to live and—"

"Or I could try and get you a job at the Ritz."

She closed her mouth and stared. "I...I...I don't want to work at the Ritz," she admitted softly. "Thank you for that, but I don't love the corporate world. There's something about being in this together, with no boss—well, you, and you're amazing—and the freedom of owning a piece of something built from nothing. It's just so thrilling to me."

"Then you could start your own business," Tessa said.

"Not without you! Tessa! I love you!"

This time she said it loud enough that half the restaurant probably heard, and a few people chuckled at the heartfelt admission.

But not Tessa. She couldn't laugh. She couldn't. The words scraped over the most tender place in Tessa's heart, opening an old wound and making it bleed.

Probably because that wound had resurfaced lately.

"Lacey, please, I—"

"No, no, you have to know this. You can't think about going back to the Ritz. We *need* you here. *I* need you here. Forget friend. Forget aunt. Forget mentor. You're like a second *mother* to me, Tessa. That's how much I love you. And you would have been—"

"Stop!" Tessa rasped the word. "Please don't say that again."

"Oh, my—Tessa! You're crying!" Lacey was up in a flash, rounding the small table, wrapping Tessa in a hug. "I'm so sorry. I didn't mean to say something to upset you. And if you have to take the job—"

"No, it's not the job, Lacey."

"Then what? What did I say?" She frowned, thinking hard. "That we need you? That I love you? That you're like a second...mother?"

"Just...don't say that," Tessa whispered. "It's hard for me to hear."

"Because you've never had a child?" Lacey drew back, nothing but concern in her blue eyes. "That doesn't make you..." She let out a breath. "Or is it..."

Tessa closed her eyes, a tear spilling. Tears she *never* shed except when she thought about…

"Or is it because you *have* had a child?" Lacey finished on the softest breath.

Tessa froze, silent and unable to lift her gaze and meet Lacey's.

All Tessa would have to do was look at Lacey and the secret would be out. It would no longer be something that only Tessa and her father knew. And someone, somewhere, with a twenty-five-year-old adopted son.

The only person on the face of the planet who knew Tessa's truth was gone. The person who'd flown to her side and taken her to the hospital and arranged everything, the whole time keeping her secret—and keeping it until the day he died—was gone.

Oh, Dad. I miss you.

Now she was alone with her old history pressing down on her shoulders like a lead weight, lifted by this sweet girl who wasn't her daughter but might as well be.

After what felt like an eternity, she looked up and stared at Lacey, who had no more questions in her blue eyes. Only love, sympathy, understanding, and…more love.

"Have you…had a child, Tessa?"

Tessa swallowed and surrendered. "How did you know?" she asked on a breaking whisper.

"I don't know. I just…sensed it. You change when someone talks about you being a mother. The light kind of goes out of your eyes and I…honestly, I really don't know. I felt it, though."

"Very intuitive of you," Tessa murmured. "I've never told Kate or my mother. They never guessed."

Lacey snagged her barstool and pulled it so close, their legs were touching when she sat down. "Tell me everything. I will never repeat it to a soul, but you need to share this."

She nodded. She was right. Tessa needed to share this more than anything. And she trusted Lacey, deeply.

"It happened when I was twenty-four," she started, then smiled. "Exactly your age."

"What happened?"

"I was working for Carnival Cruise. Nothing glamorous, believe me. I was a waitress on a ship that sailed out of Port Canaveral, over on the east coast of Florida. I met a guy who was on a party cruise with his buddies, and we hit it off and..." She lifted a shoulder, not proud of her past. "I did some dumb things—chief among them not using protection. A couple months after that, I realized I hadn't gotten my period and..." She made a face.

"Oh, Tess. Did you tell him?"

"Please." She looked toward the ceiling and scoffed. "I didn't actually like him enough to give him my number. How's that for irony? I don't even remember what town he was from. It was essentially a weekend hookup and..." She groaned. "Ah, Lacey, I'm so ashamed."

"Don't be. What did you do?"

She closed her eyes, going back to those terrifying days. She'd had options, but none of them felt right.

"I turned to the only man who understood right from wrong, and who wouldn't judge me."

"Artie Wylie," Lacey guessed.

Tessa nodded. "He was my, you know, go-to parent. Not my mom. But Dad? Yeah. He came down to Florida, and we talked and talked, and he helped me figure out what I wanted to do, and that was to arrange an adoption through a local agency."

Lacey just squeezed her hand, quiet.

"I had a baby boy. And here's the sum total of what I know about him: He was seven pounds and ten ounces, nineteen inches long, and born at seven sixteen PM on February 19, 2000, in Holmes Regional Medical Center in Melbourne, Florida."

"Oh, he just had a birthday two months ago."

Tessa gave a soft laugh. "Yes, and that was the day I got fired from the Ritz. I was driving aimlessly up the coast, crying my fool eyes out like I always do that day, and I saw the sign for Destin and I..."

"Wanted comfort," Lacey finished, rubbing Tessa's hand gently. "Do you know his name?"

"Nope and I don't want to," she said. "I pray he's happy, healthy, and well-loved."

Lacey just let out a long sigh, leaning closer and dropping her head on Tessa's shoulder. "You poor thing, carrying that around all alone."

"It was easier that way. I couldn't tell Jo Ellen or Kate. I didn't want to be a disappointment, but my dad?" She gave a dry laugh. "For some reason, it was impossible for me to disappoint the man. God knows I tried, but his love was unconditional with a capital *un*."

"And the adoption? You never tried to—"

"No. No, no, no. I couldn't insert myself into his life. No, he's better off not knowing me."

"How can you even say something like that?" Lacey asked. "You're the most amazing, beautiful, wonderful person ever."

Tessa laughed. "Oh, keep drinking, Lace. Pretty soon I'll be a saint and not..." Her smile faded. "A dumb blonde disappointment."

"You are so wrong," Lacey said. "You have the absolute most wrong sense of self-worth. I meant it when I said I love you."

"And I must love you right back," Tessa said. "Your mother thinks I'm joking when I say I want you for my daughter...but I think there's truth in all humor."

"Tessa. You've been through so much. So much."

Tessa blinked rapidly, trying to keep the flood of tears at bay. "Just a life, Lace. A complicated life driven by decisions I can't undo."

"Do you wish you'd kept the baby and raised him yourself?" Lacey asked gently.

"I don't like to travel that road not taken," Tessa said. "Regrets are foolish and not fun. I like fun."

Lacey laughed softly, but grew serious. "Is this why you like fun? Because you gave up a baby?"

"Pffft. I like fun because it's fun. But, if I'm being completely honest, I do wish I had a grown son right now. It would be nice. Maybe to be a grandmother someday."

"Hottest one ever."

She pointed playfully at Lacey. "Hey, maybe you, my pretend daughter, will give me one."

"Not soon, but yeah. Someday." She squeezed Tessa's hands again. "You could probably find him, you know. It wouldn't be—"

"No." She narrowed her eyes. "And I don't want anyone to know this, Lacey. Not your mother, not my sister, no one in the world. Can you keep my secret?"

"Yes, I promise not to tell any of them. Are you sure your dad didn't tell your mother?"

"Positive. He could keep a secret like no one's business. And I mean it—Kate would be devastated to find out I went through that and never told her."

"Why didn't you tell her?" Lacey asked. "You two are close."

"Close...*ish*," she replied. "At the time, Kate was in grad school and...we weren't that tight, since I was out to sea so much on that cruise ship. We frequently went long, long times without seeing each other. She never questioned my being out of sight all that time."

Lacey settled back on her seat, picking up her flute. "I won't toast to little seven-pound Holmes."

Tessa laughed. "That was the name of the hospital. I told you, I don't know his name."

"Don't you want to know?" Lacey asked, clearly struggling with that. "I mean, aren't you curious?"

"Sometimes, but I feel like this is better. My dad was very clear that I signed a contract, I gave the baby up for adoption, and that was legal and binding."

"He *was* a law ethics professor," Lacey said.

"He was also my rock," Tessa added, then smiled. "And now you are." She made a face. "No pressure or anything."

"I don't feel any pressure," Lacey assured her. "But..."

"No buts, Lace. I've made my decision, and I will live with it."

"*But...*" she continued. "You cannot take that Ritz-Carlton job or..."

Tessa's eyes widened. "Are you blackmailing me?"

"Never." Lacey laughed. "But don't do it, please. I can't stand to lose you."

Tessa smiled, deeply happy she had this young woman in her life and pretty sure she couldn't stand to lose her, either.

Chapter Twenty
Vivien

Rogue.

Vivien had gone totally rogue with Sherwin-Williams Alabaster when her client had asked for Pure White. Well, she'd asked for "pure white" as a description—Fiona probably didn't know there was also a paint color *called* Pure White. Not that anyone with eyes or a soul would call it a *color*.

Standing in Fiona Buckman's entryway, Vivien leaned back and looked up at the nearly twenty feet of freshly painted wall in the two-story center hall, thrilled with her decision to go a tiny bit rogue. Two shades of warmth, but it made all the difference in the world. The walls hugged a person now, whereas plain white was like a blinding light that screamed *do not enter, do not relax,* and, whatever you do, *do not feel at home.*

This was absolutely the opposite.

Since the interaction over the molding and samples well over a week ago, Vivien felt like she'd found a balance with her strong-willed client. She'd talked about it with Lacey, mulled it over with Tessa, and even shared her feelings with Peter—and they'd all encouraged her to speak her mind since she'd been hired for her expertise.

Vivien had made some compromises, and she'd talked Fiona into a few things, too.

Best of all, Hapless Handy seemed to have disappeared. Maybe they'd...broken up.

Right now, with Fiona gone and just workers here, Vivien could concentrate on the space around her, which was truly getting prettier with every visit.

It was still modern and clean, but not sterile. Fiona didn't want sterile—she only thought she did. What she wanted was fresh and uncluttered, modern but still a bit organic.

Which was exactly what the Alabaster had accomplished.

She heard the hammers and electric saws from the kitchen, happy that the new counters were in—soft white quartz with delicate veining, timeless and elegant.

As she walked through the house, Vivien nodded to herself, checking out each room as she moved, peeking into Fiona's office. That was the room they were scheduled to discuss today, when Fiona returned from a meeting at the beach.

Vivien couldn't wait to rip out the carpet and tackle those hideous window treatments.

"Mrs. Buckman?" A man's voice called from the front door. "I got a mirror delivery!"

Oh, the entryway mirror she'd chosen had arrived! Excited to see it, she rushed back to the front of the house, knowing this was another slightly rogue move.

"Mrs. Buckman's not here, but I'm her designer," she

told the man as he handed her a clipboard to sign. "I can't wait to see this."

Fiona wanted something big, cold, and frameless. Vivien had found something big, warm, and trimmed with a beveled edge that had a vintage-meets-modern vibe she just loved. No wood, no brass, no antique anything, but plenty of impact.

She watched as the men carefully uncrated the very expensive seventy-inch-tall mirror she'd found at a sweet little design studio down on 30A. She watched and directed as they pulled the massive glass free of the packaging and leaned it against the painfully bare wall in the entryway.

"It's perfect!" She pressed her hands together, delighted by how the curved corners fit the space and the angled edges caught the light. It was timeless, but slightly historic, simple but not at all artless.

"This is going to make such a statement," she murmured, stepping closer as the men adjusted it.

"Want us to center it a little more?" one of them asked.

Vivien was about to respond when the front door opened behind her and Fiona came into view through the mirror.

"What on *God's green earth* is that?" Her voice was as sharp as the glass that reflected her.

"Isn't it gorgeous?" Vivien exclaimed, knowing that enthusiasm sometimes softened Fiona's opinions.

But this time, she looked horrified.

"It's...it's...it's not..." She closed her eyes as if she were rooting to the center of the earth for composure. "I hate it." She marched closer to the glass, looking like she intended to smash it into oblivion for seven times seven years of bad luck. "This is not what I wanted. I *loathe* vintage."

Vivien's stomach sank. "But Fiona, it's a statement piece. A frameless mirror would look—"

"I *want* a frameless mirror." Fiona cut her off. "Something modern. Clean. Not this... *thing*."

Vivien exhaled slowly. *Okay, deep breath. You can find a compromise.* "I know you wanted modern, but I promise you this is going to elevate the whole space. It's not gaudy, there's no gold or—"

"Vivien," Fiona interrupted with a pointed glare. "Get rid of it."

Vivien clenched her jaw, swallowing the frustration burning in her throat. "Okay," she forced out. "I'll take care of it."

Fiona turned on her heel, walking into the house. Vivien followed cautiously, already sensing deep in her bones what was about to happen. Going rogue might not have been a good idea.

Fiona froze in the middle of her soaring two stories and stared at the walls.

And then, slowly, she turned back to Vivien, her expression unreadable. "In what universe, Vivien, is this pure white?"

Vivien lifted her chin, preparing for war. "It's Alabaster."

"This is *not* the color I picked."

Vivien's pulse pounded and, once again, she was thrown down a memory hole, staring at her mother, who merely lifted one eyebrow and made her kids cower. But this wasn't Maggie Lawson!

"You hired me for my professional—"

Fiona's sharp inhale cut her off.

"I told you *white*," she snapped, stepping forward. "I told you *exactly* what I wanted, and this is *not* it. Pure, unadulterated, plain white. Why can't you just *listen*?"

Vivien clenched her teeth. "It *is* white. It's just a softer white, Fiona. Pure white would make this house feel—"

"I don't care how it *feels*," Fiona seethed. "I care about what I *asked for*."

Vivien swallowed hard, her hands tightening into fists at her sides. This was it. The moment. The moment where she either stood up for herself or caved like she always did.

She took a breath and straightened her back as if a ramrod held it up.

"If I'm going to design this house, Fiona, I'm going to preserve its character," Vivien said, her voice calm but firm. "I can make it modern. I can make it contemporary. But I will *not* make it soulless."

Fiona's mouth pressed into a thin line. "Then I'll find someone else."

The words sliced through Vivien's chest. For a second, she didn't move. Didn't breathe.

Then Fiona turned to the workers. "Stop everything. Get rid of the mirror. Repaint the walls. And Vivien—"

She turned back, her voice like steel. "You can leave now and please don't come back. We're finished."

Vivien stared at her, then nodded stiffly. "Understood."

She turned on her heel, grabbed her bag on the floor the entryway, and walked out of the house without another word.

Her legs felt like lead as she made her way to her SUV, her chest tight, her hands shaking. She had stood up for herself. She had spoken her mind. And now?

She was fired.

So much for a backbone. At least doormats got a paycheck.

As she reached her car parked on the street, she heard a loud motor and spotted the BMW sports car owned—or at least driven by—good old Hapless.

He parked right behind her Highlander, shut off the engine, and climbed out. He wore a fitted and wildly expensive white linen shirt, the sleeves rolled up to reveal his forearms...and that expensive watch on his wrist.

Definitely not a handyman's wardrobe.

He flashed a smile and took off his sunglasses, as though he needed to get a better look at her.

Vivien rolled her eyes. *Perfect. Just what I need. A run-in with the con artist.*

She opened the driver's door, hoping they could get away with a cursory nod, but he just kept coming, regarding her closely.

"You okay?" he asked, the tone of the question both off-putting and a little...personal.

"I'm fine."

"You sure? Because you look like someone just ran over your puppy."

Vivien exhaled, pressing her fingers to her temple. "Not my puppy, just my job. I'm leaving—for good." She added a tight smile. "She's all yours."

Danny tilted his head, stepping closer. "Oh, man. Did my *delightful* sister fire you?"

Vivien blinked, whipping around so hard she felt hair. "Your...*sister?*"

"Yeah," he said, looking surprised. "You didn't know that?"

"She's...your...*what?*"

He laughed. "Eleven years older, but don't tell her that. Actually, don't tell her anything if you want to live. But I take it you learned that the hard way."

Vivien gaped at him, her brain short-circuiting. *Sister?*

She replayed every assumption she'd made about him and how very, very wrong she'd been.

"Is that why you aren't...such a great handyman?"

He threw his head back with a hearty laugh that came right from his chest—the chest she'd once seen shirtless and had admittedly stared at. The move showed beautiful straight teeth, a strong neck, and...and...

His *sister?*

"I'm the worst handyman in the county, possibly the state," he said. "However, she's been through a dozen of them, several plumbers and electricians, three housekeepers, and two landscapers. I think there's an underground network of service professionals who've blacklisted Fiona. So..." He lifted a shoulder. "I attempt to help but that's not my, uh, thing."

She blew out a breath. "I apologize."

"For what?"

She studied him for a minute, not wanting to tell him what she'd assumed. The absolute worst.

"No!" He leaned forward, a mix of shock and amusement in his eyes as he figured it out. "You thought... How could you?"

"I saw you having dinner, and..."

"You thought I'm some kind of player trying to..." He cracked up. "I'm taking her to dinner right now. I do every week. Still, that's rich. I can't wait to tell her."

"Please don't. She already hates me and every decision I ever made."

His smile faltered. "I'm sorry," he said.

"It's not your fault I didn't listen to her on paint. And the mirror. And...everything."

"I think the house looks great," he said. "I might have you do mine next."

She eyed him, slowly shaking her head. "I don't think so."

"Well, I'm still sorry my sister..." He huffed out a breath. "She has issues."

"You think?"

"And I can tell you this from experience," he added. "She will come crawling back."

Vivien scoffed. "I doubt it."

He gave a knowing smile. "She will, but you, like all

the other professionals she burns through, will say no. Can't say I blame you, but, whoa. Now I have to decorate her house, and it won't be pretty."

She laughed softly, liking him despite how much she didn't want to.

"So, let's keep the lines of communication open, okay?" he asked. "Maybe I can secretly pick your designer's brain, and I'll pay you instead of her."

She just smiled and shook her head, not sure what to make of him. "Whatever."

"Why don't you give me your number?" he said. "Better yet, why don't you let me take you to dinner? It would give me a chance to tell you a little about my sister, who really isn't a wicked witch."

Vivien inched back, her stomach doing a completely unexpected flutter. Was the hapless handyman asking her *on a date* or was he just being nice because she'd gotten fired?

"I'll think about it," she said, purposely vague.

He lifted a shoulder. "I'll take thinking. It's not a no."

"Not a yes, either."

He chuckled. "Good. I like to have a goal. And I'll get your number from my sister, if you don't mind. Right after I tell her how much I love the paint and...the mirror, was it?"

Vivien exhaled another laugh. "Yes, the big one in the hall."

"What didn't she like about it?"

"Everything."

He looked skyward. "Sounds like Fi. We'll be in touch, Vivien."

She nodded and climbed into the driver's seat, watching him head up to the house.

What just happened?

As she drove away, she realized she wasn't thinking about being fired anymore.

She was thinking about *him*.

It was late in the day when Vivien pushed open the front door of the Summer House, stepping inside with a sigh so heavy it could have knocked over one of the perfectly arranged vases on the entryway table.

The cool air-conditioning hit her skin, but it did nothing to ease the heat still clinging to her after the latest disaster at Fiona Buckman's house.

She rounded the corner to the empty living area, letting her bag slide from her shoulder and drop onto the kitchen island with a thud. She leaned forward, gripping the edge of the marble surface, slumping.

It was official. She'd lost her first big client.

She closed her eyes for a moment, trying to shove down the sting of humiliation. *You did the right thing*, she told herself. *You stood your ground. You refused to be a doormat. And what did that get you?*

Canned.

"That doesn't look good."

She straightened and turned, finding Peter standing just outside the open sliders to the deck.

"Oh! Peter. I didn't know you were here." She'd been in such a fog, she'd driven right past his parked car.

"Sorry, I didn't mean to startle you." He came a few steps closer, setting a bottle of water on the counter, regarding her closely. "Are you okay?"

Vivien let out a sharp, humorless laugh and ran a hand through her hair.

"Not really. I just got fired from the Fiona Buckman job. Apparently, I can't take direction. Even though the direction was terrible, ugly, and soul-destroying, and I simply couldn't bring myself to ruin a perfectly good house with it."

Peter winced sympathetically. "Oof. Sounds like you dodged a bullet."

Vivien shook her head and walked to the fridge, reaching for the first bottle of wine she saw. "Is it five o'clock somewhere?"

"Here, actually," Peter said, watching her carefully. "You're better off without her, though. You know that, right? I mean, yeah, this sucks, but you're not the kind of person who can just slap some paint on the walls and call it design. You care too much about your work to be a 'yes' woman for a rich tyrant with no taste."

Vivien sighed, pulling a plastic cup from the cabinet, then grabbing another. She turned to him with a questioning look. "Don't make me drink alone."

He laughed and shook his head. "Eli and I are going to the gym, if he ever gets off a client call."

She nodded and poured a generous glass. "You know, if I were a 'yes' woman I'd still have this client."

"You'll bounce back. You've got too much talent not to. I mean, look at what you've done with this place." He gestured toward the house that had started off with super perfection décor. Now, with all these people and the possibility that they wouldn't sell, it looked like...a home. A beach house for a happy family.

Vivien smiled and raised her glass to him. "Thank you, Peter. It's nice to see you."

He held her gaze with a smile of his own, letting her feel that tiny new connection they were forming.

Peter McCarthy was good in every sense of the word. Disarming and genuine and...yeah, good. So why was she still thinking about the gleam in Danny Sullivan's silver-blue eyes when he asked her on a date?

Vivien took a long sip, letting the crisp wine soothe her frayed nerves before setting the drink down. "Well, looks like I was totally wrong, by the way."

Peter raised an eyebrow. "About?"

She waved a hand in the air. "Danny. The hapless handyman."

"Let me guess—he's not actually a con artist."

"Nope. Turns out he's her younger brother. He's *helping* her, not sleeping with her."

Peter's jaw dropped slightly before he let out a laugh. "Her brother? Now that I did not find out."

Vivien drew back, not following. "Find out...how?"

"I'm a detective, remember? I did a little digging into one Daniel Sullivan, who resides in a house on Four

Prong Lake, a few miles from here. That's when he's not in his Tribeca condo in in New York City. He's a successful hedge fund manager, apparently on the up and up, and I assumed he might be handling Fiona's investments."

Vivien's eyebrows shot up. "He might be, but mostly he's handling her sprinklers and broken outlets because apparently she burns through professional service people like a bonfire on a windy day."

"Like I said, people aren't always what they seem, Viv."

She sipped the wine, thinking about...Danny. The way Danny had looked at her in the driveway, how easy his smile had been, how non-judgmental and even concerned he'd been by her firing. How...charming and handsome.

A hedge fund manager. *Eesh.*

"Anyway," Peter said, grabbing his water bottle. "I was going to fill you in on all that, but as you walked in, I could see something was wrong."

Vivien sighed and waved him off. "I'm okay. Really."

Peter gave her a long look. "Good, because I think your day might be about to get worse. Or better. Not sure yet."

"What? Why?"

He gestured toward a thick white envelope on the dining room table. "Since Eli was on the phone, I answered the door, and it was a courier. I, uh, think those are from a lawyer."

Her stomach flipped. "My divorce papers."

"It's never easy," he said softly. "I know."

"Thank you." She walked to the table, staring at her name on the front of the package.

She reached for it with slightly shaky hands, sliding her finger under the flap and pulling out the stack of crisp, neatly typed pages.

Ryan had signed everywhere. Every dotted line, every finalization, every piece of their life together.

The only thing missing was her signature.

Peter came closer, watching her carefully. "How do you feel?"

Vivien exhaled, sitting down heavily in a chair. "Like I just lost my marriage and my first big job in the same day."

"That's rough, Viv."

Vivien traced a finger along the edge of the papers. "But also..." She bit her lip, looking up at him. "Like it's a good thing, a new season, as they say. I didn't want this, you know. I didn't ask for a divorce, but now that it's done, I'm okay with it. Really."

Peter leaned on the back of the chair across from her. "Then that's all that matters."

Vivien took a deep breath. "I'll sign it later."

"Hey, Pete, sorry about that." Eli's voice came from the back office and in a second, he walked in, dressed like Peter for a workout. "Oh, hi, Viv. What's that?"

She let the stack of papers hit the table with a thud. "The end of an era, big brother."

His expression softened and he came right to her, pulling her up and into a hug. "Oh, Viv. I'm sorry."

"No, don't be." She eased back and smiled at him, then at Peter, knowing she had tears in her eyes but also knowing they understood. "It hurts to fail at something that big, but I know there are good men in this world—great ones, even—like the two in this room."

They made some kind of self-deprecating joke, but she didn't hear it. Instead, she took her wine glass and backed away, leaving the stack of papers for later.

"I'm going to go upstairs for a while. I need...space. Thank you both for being so understanding."

Holding her wine, she slipped her bag on her shoulder and walked up the stairs slowly, her heart heavy.

Just as she got to her room, her phone hummed with a text. Setting down the wine on the dresser, she fished out her phone and frowned at the screen, which said she had a text from an unknown number.

Now what? Could this day get any worse? Bracing, she tapped the screen.

Fiona will re-hire you, but I'd make her work for it if I were you. Oh, the mirror is gorgeous...and so are you.

Oh, my. She certainly wasn't expecting *that*.

Chapter Twenty-one

Eli

Eli walked out from his office on the main floor and froze at the controlled chaos that gripped the Summer House.

How had he not heard this racket? Well, he'd been on a conference call with a headset on for the last two hours going over final drafting changes with a very particular client building an office complex in Savannah.

The lengthy discussions over front elevations melted from his brain as he tried to process this flurry of silk and satin, flowers and music, and many women—some he knew, some he didn't. They were all buzzing about like honeybees building a comb.

This, he remembered, was the "forty-eight-hour event prep day" Tessa and Lacey were coordinating. He hoped it would be nearly finished by the time he got back from picking up Kate at the airport.

Tessa was clearly in charge, giving orders, whispering to Lacey, and orchestrating the madness like a symphony conductor.

The salon owner he'd met earlier, Akari, draped gowns over the back of the sofa while someone he assumed was her assistant unzipped each bag lovingly.

A few unfamiliar models walked around in bridal gowns, their skirts fanning out as they moved. Nolie flitted through the chaos, her excitement tangible, clasping her hands and exclaiming over lace details and embroidery.

Even Aunt Pittypat was in the midst of it, yipping from her perch on the couch, her tiny paws twitching in anticipation of being scooped up and adored.

Vivien and Crista were elbows deep, too, helping lay out the men's clothes Eli, Jonah, and Peter had been fitted for.

He glanced at his watch, impatient for his phone alarm to let him know it was time to leave for the airport.

"Do you want to try on your shoes?" Vivien asked him, holding black dress shoes that looked like medieval torture devices.

"Not particularly. I'm an eleven. I'll wear anything."

"These run tight."

"I'm sure they do. I'll make it work, Viv. Can I borrow your SUV to get Kate and the crew? I don't want to stuff them into my truck."

"Of course." She held up the shoes. "Put one on."

"Lacey, I need all the veils!" Tessa called out.

"And we have tiaras," Akari added.

"Ooh, tiaras!" Nolie scampered closer. "Is that like a crown? I love crowns."

Eli took a step backwards, the impact of all this femininity too much for him. "I'm, uh, going up to talk to Jonah," he said, pointing to the garage.

"Chicken," Vivien muttered.

He laughed and threaded his way through mountains of silk to the kitchen to escape, grabbing Vivien's keys from the entry table on his way out.

In the garage, he took the steps up to the sanctuary of the apartment, and almost immediately felt the change. The space smelled of wood shavings and fresh paint, the remnants of their latest project—finishing the baseboards.

The kitchenette wasn't done yet, but they could finish that in May. He'd hoped to have furniture in before Kate, Jo Ellen, and the kids came, but it didn't quite happen. They'd figured out the sleeping arrangements, though. Kate would bunk with Tessa, Jo Ellen would go upstairs in what used to be Kate's room, and the kids were on air mattresses downstairs.

It would be like camping. It would be like old times on the property. For Eli, with Kate in his arms again, it would be like heaven.

He meandered through the living and kitchen area, toward one of the bedrooms, surprised not to hear a sound. Jonah usually played music while he painted, but it was silent.

Was he even up here?

Eli stuck his head in one of the bedrooms, blinking at the sight of his son huddled over in a corner.

He sat with his head between his legs. His shoulders were hunched over as he stared at the floor, a half-empty bottle of Gatorade dangling from his fingers. His long hair, usually tousled in an effortless way, was a mess like he'd been running his hands through it for hours.

When he looked up, sunlight cut across his features, highlighting the tension in his jaw, and red-rimmed eyes.

"What's going on?" Eli asked.

"Nothing." The word was gruff, whispered, and definitely not true. Something was most certainly going on.

Eli crouched in front of him, but Jonah's gaze didn't connect.

Didn't matter. Eli knew that pained expression, with agony in his eyes and tears ready any minute. He'd seen it for years after Melissa died, every day—hollow, aching, lost.

He considered making conversation about what was going on downstairs or the progress on the trim or the fact that he had to leave soon to get Kate.

No. Now was not the time to avoid the subject.

He dropped onto the floor. "C'mon. Talk to me."

Jonah exhaled sharply, rubbing his palm against his knee. "Where do I start? First of all, Carly doesn't believe in me."

Eli stilled. "What?"

Jonah let out a bitter laugh, shaking his head. "She thinks the culinary program is a long shot. That I'm wasting my time." His grip tightened on the bottle. "Maybe she's right."

Eli's chest ached at the words. "If she loves you, she believes in you."

Jonah let out a sharp breath, his eyes flickering up to meet Eli's. "I don't have a good track record, and I don't blame her for doubting me. You know, after all this, I'm not sure if she loves me. How's that for sinking into the depths of self-doubt?"

The last words were mumbled and choked like they were competing with a sob he really didn't want to give in to.

"Holy hell, I miss her so bad," he added, swiping at a tear.

Somehow, he wasn't sure how, Eli knew he wasn't talking about Carly. The woman he missed was his mother.

"She was, like, my secret weapon, you know?" he rasped, confirming Eli's guess. "Like I could do anything when she was alive. Now I just drown in second guesses and insecurity."

Eli stifled a grunt, not sure what to say to that admission.

"I could take on the world when she was in my corner," Jonah went on. "And, man, she lived in that corner. She always, always believed in me. No matter what. She said, 'You were made for more, Jonah.' She never said what 'more' was, but she sure made me believe I was made for it."

Eli closed his eyes, easily hearing his long-departed wife's voice. Always strong, always happy, always... invincible.

Until she wasn't.

"She was good like that," Eli said. "She was a professional cheerleader for the people she loved."

"How'd you do it?" Jonah asked, looking hard at him.

"How'd you start a business and...succeed? I mean... without her?"

Eli considered all the ways to answer that, and wondered which would be the most helpful. The truth was he believed in God, who'd gotten him through every dark night and lonely day. His Father in Heaven had guided, protected, and inspired Eli.

But he expected Jonah would roll his eyes at that, not receptive at all to Eli's testimony of faith right now.

"I knew it was what she wanted," he said simply. "She'd have been furious if I gave up. And I do believe I'll see her again. I *know* that. So next time I hold your mother, I do not want her to give me that look."

Jonah puffed out a breath and it turned into a soft laugh. "I know that look. Nothing worse than disappointing Melissa Lawson."

Eli looked at him. "Then you can't give up this dream, Jonah."

He closed his eyes and dropped his head back hard enough that it thudded against the wall. "If I go to the interview tomorrow, I'll break my streak." He glanced at Eli from under his lashes. "Fifteen years. I've never missed it. Not once."

"And to think I didn't even know you were in Atlanta the past four years."

"I didn't want to see you," Jonah said, then held up his hand. "Don't take that the wrong... No, never mind. Take it any way you want. Things were rough between us, Dad, and I knew I'd disappointed you by quitting school. But I had to see her. On this day, the last time I ever hugged her."

He was quiet for a moment, his gaze distant as he remembered.

"I left for school that morning and she knew I had a Calc I exam, and she also knew I hated that teacher with a white hot fury and was really worried about the test. But she was so encouraging, so sure I'd nail it. She made me promise her I'd get an A." He winced. "I did, but I never got to tell her."

Eli could feel his heart drop so hard, it practically hit the garage floor.

"Anyway..." Jonah blew out another loud exhale. "I go for me. It's like a dose of confidence and hope and all the things she gave me. I go sit by that grave and...you don't want to know."

Part of him did, but part of him really didn't. "Listen. Kate and the kids are getting in today, tomorrow you do the interviews, and, hey, you can miss that fashion show on Saturday. Go then."

"It's not the same. The date..."

"Doesn't matter."

"It does. I'm superstitious."

Eli snorted. "If you're going to believe in something you can't see, touch, or understand, I have a much better option for you."

"No, thanks."

Leaning in, Eli forced Jonah to look up and lock eyes. "She would not want you to miss the interviews."

"Don't." Jonah's voice was sharp, his posture stiffening. "You don't get to tell me what Mom would or wouldn't want. I knew her as well as you did. You had a life before her—I never knew one day without her."

Eli pressed his lips together, his hands clenching into fists against his knees. He wanted to argue. He wanted to shake Jonah and make him see what he saw—that Melissa wouldn't want him stuck, wouldn't want his grief to dictate his future.

But he also knew what it felt like to be told how to grieve. It wouldn't help.

His phone buzzed in his pocket, but he ignored the alarm reminding him to leave for the airport.

He looked back at Jonah, at the storm brewing behind his eyes. He didn't want to leave. Not now. Not when his son was unraveling in front of him.

"That's your Kate reminder," Jonah said. "Go pick them up."

"I don't want to leave you."

"Go, Dad. I'm fine. I want to be alone anyway. I'm fine. You don't want them all to pile into an Uber."

Eli stood slowly, hesitating before he reached out, gripping Jonah's shoulder. A firm, steady squeeze. "This isn't over," he said, voice low. "We'll talk more."

Jonah didn't look up, but after a long pause, he gave the barest nod.

"Kate can help you," Eli added. "She'll blow in here and want to cook dinner and—"

"I'll just disappoint her, too."

No one was going to get through to him right now. Maybe together, he and Kate would, later tonight.

Eli exhaled and turned for the door, his chest tight. As he stepped back into the hallway, he felt the weight of the unfinished business settle deep in his bones.

THE MOMENT he saw Kate's smile, Eli's heart lifted from the dark place it had been since he left Jonah. The woman walking next to her as they exited the small airport security area smiled at him, too, and he instantly recognized Jo Ellen Wylie.

He likely wouldn't have known her on the street, since she was thirty years older than the last time he saw her. However, standing next to Kate, it was like those years disappeared and he was looking at "Aunt Jo Ellen" once again.

Now, instead of her long, dark hair, she had soft waves of silver, still thick enough to fall to her shoulders. While her face was etched with the lines and age expected on a woman closer to eighty than seventy, she carried herself with an effortless grace he remembered well.

She didn't need help walking, but he could see her sort of lean into Kate, as if she liked knowing her daughter was next to her.

He recognized Kate's kids from the many pictures she'd shown him last month. Matt, a lanky teenage boy with a mop of dark hair, loped behind them, reminding Eli of when he was fifteen and the growth and changes in his own body surprised him daily.

And seventeen-year-old Emma strode next to him with confidence, her shiny strawberry blond hair swinging from a long ponytail as she elbowed her younger brother to tell him to pay attention to where he was going.

His gaze shifted back to Kate, who hustled a little faster as if she couldn't wait to reach him, mirroring exactly what he was feeling.

Five feet apart, they hesitated for a split second, then both laughed softly as they came together for a hug.

"Hi," she whispered in his ear, the single syllable somehow the perfect greeting.

"Hi, back." He added a squeeze and drew back, smiling into her eyes and wishing he could swoop her up and kiss her, but not with the audience.

He had no idea what she'd told them about the budding relationship, and didn't even know exactly what this enigmatic woman in his arms was feeling at that moment.

There'd be time for a kiss soon enough.

Turning, she gestured toward her mother. "You two remember each other?"

"Jo Ellen." Eli came closer and gave her a light hug. "Been a few decades."

She laughed softly and patted his back. "So good to see you again," she said. "I always thought you were the nicest boy."

"Just the nicest old man now," he said on a laugh, easing away to greet the kids. "Emma? Matt? I'm Eli

Lawson. Hope you two Ithaca natives are up for a few beach days this weekend."

Emma shook his hand, giving him a warm smile that looked very much like her mother's. "I haven't seen the sun since 2021," she deadpanned.

Laughing, Eli reached his hand to Matt, who popped his wired headphones and shook his hand. "I actually don't think I own shorts. I don't believe in them."

Eli laughed. "You'll change your mind."

They all had carry-on only, so Eli took Jo Ellen's bag and they headed back to the parking lot, with Kate chatting about his beautiful design for the Summer House. He let the compliments roll off him, more grateful for her presence than anything.

"So how are things at the beach?" she asked him as they reached Vivien's SUV.

"Sheer chaos," he told her, then shared with all of them the madness of event preparation.

All the way back to Gulf Shore Drive, Emma peppered him with questions, her keen intelligence— another thing she'd inherited from her mother—on full display.

Matt was quiet, though he seemed to perk up at the sight of the Gulf. Jo Ellen, next to him in the passenger seat, got more and more slack-jawed as they drove over the Destin bridge toward town.

"Oh, my," she said on a sigh of mixed emotions. "I remember when this section was nothing but pepper trees and scrub oaks."

Eli nodded. "You'll hardly recognize some parts of

Destin. But the white sand? The turquoise water? That never changes. You'll remember it from all those years when we spent summers here."

Jo Ellen turned to him, shifting her attention from the scenery to the driver. "I understand Maggie is out of the country."

And we're going right there, he thought.

"She's in the Netherlands. Well, she might be in France now. She went with her gardening club on a spring flower tour."

"She always could grow things," Jo Ellen said softly. "We had an apartment together in college and she practically turned the dining room into a greenhouse."

He slid her a smile, encouraged to hear her talk about her friendship with his mother. He was so used to the very mention of the Wylie name eliciting Maggie's darkest glare.

It certainly seemed like the profound dislike and distrust only went one way. Which, he guessed, made sense if Artie was the one who turned Roger in to the police.

Her comments opened the door for what he had on his mind from the moment she got off the plane.

"I'm so sorry about your husband," he said gently. "I loved Uncle Artie. I have some of my best memories of Destin with him."

She gave him a grateful smile, enough sadness in her eyes that he knew the grief was still raw, even at seven months. Heck, for him, it had been raw at seven years.

And look at Jonah...

"I'm so relieved to hear you say that," she replied, bringing him back to this conversation. "Under the...well, I'm glad. He liked you so much, Eli."

Eli just nodded and navigated traffic, not sure what else could or should be said.

Honestly, he was tired of thinking about the whole subject. If this dark history and mysterious falling out would be the reason he and Kate couldn't pursue a relationship, he'd be furious and disappointed.

Let it be distance. Let it be time. Let it not be God's plan.

But please, please, *please* don't let this thing—whatever it could be—get stomped out by his own mother.

He glanced up into the rearview mirror to look at Kate, curious if he could read her expression and see if she was thinking the same thing. But all he saw was the light in brown eyes that he'd missed so much.

After a second of eye contact in the mirror, she slid her glasses down her nose and winked at him, making him feel...like he was the third teenager in this vehicle.

"Goodness, we had so many adventures and memories here," Jo Ellen said as they passed a few large hotels. "It's quite eerie being back. Bittersweet, in a way."

"It was the best," he agreed, glancing over his shoulder to check on the kids next to Kate. "I think summer in Destin when you're teenagers should be mandatory. You guys up for it?"

"What?" Matt sat straight up. "Can we, Mom?"

Emma gave him a look like he was crazy. "You can. I

just got a job at the Ithaca Yacht Club this summer and I'm not giving that up for anything."

Eli's heart dropped a little, her news dashing his hopes that Kate might spend the summer here. "What are you doing at the Yacht Club, Emma?" he asked.

"Right now, just working the boat rentals, but I'm certified as a lifeguard and hope to get slotted into one of those jobs."

"Lots of lifeguards in Destin," he said. "Plus beaches and bonfires and now we have a boat with the house. Thanks to Tessa, who somehow managed to persuade a client to pay her with a cabin cruiser."

"Of course she did," Matt said on a laugh.

"I can't wait to see Aunt Tessa!" Emma gave a clap. "She's so much fun."

"She's busy," Kate said.

"And she's going to put you in a gown and parade you up and down the boardwalk," Eli added, making the last turn. "Which you will be able to see in less than a mile."

The excitement level rose as they cruised Gulf Shore Drive and the kids—and Jo Ellen—*ooh* and *ahh*ed over the beautiful beachfront homes.

"Holy cow," Matt crooned. "Who gets to live like this?"

"You, at least this weekend," Eli said, stealing another glance at Kate. "And maybe this summer if your mom brings you back."

She narrowed her eyes playfully, but something told him she wasn't opposed to the idea. Buoyed by that thought, he turned into the driveway.

"Welcome to—" His voice caught in his throat when he saw the empty spot that had been home to Jonah's van for the last six or seven weeks.

He *never* drove it. It was basically parked there permanently and...*where did he go?*

"The Summer House," Kate finished for him, staring at the same empty spot, with the same look of surprise.

"This is so cool!" Matt practically threw the door open the second Eli stopped, and before he knew it, they were piling out onto the driveway.

Where was Jonah? If he had to go somewhere, wouldn't he have taken Eli's truck, which was sitting right there? Maybe Tessa needed him to run an urgent errand, and he couldn't find Eli's keys, although he left them on the entry table where everyone left keys in case cars had to be moved.

Maybe he decided to take a drive to escape the chaos of the event planning, and he wanted his van.

Maybe—

Kate stepped up next to him, a question in her eyes.

"Will you take them up and do the introductions?" Eli asked. "I'll bring the bags in, but I need to call him."

"Of course." She swooped into action, letting Eli step away and pull his phone out.

Seeking privacy, he slipped into the entrance to the first floor while Kate took everyone up to the main living level.

Inside, the large gathering room designed as a family hangout space was now home to more dresses, racks, and clothes. But no one was around.

The door to Jonah's room was closed. His heart sinking, Eli knocked once, then pushed it open and let out a sad, low moan.

The bed was unmade, but there were no signs of life. No clothes, no cookbooks, no hints that Jonah Lawson lived here. Because he didn't. He'd taken his meager belongings and left in his van.

Eli just leaned against the wall and let disappointment rock him.

Of course Eli knew where he was, or where he was going. He'd make it by midnight, maybe later, in that dilapidated vehicle. He'd sleep in some parking lot, marching through that massive cemetery at dawn, and he'd...

He'd miss his interviews and the opportunity that more than a few people had worked to help him get. Including Kate.

"Where is he?"

He turned to find her in the doorway, looking dismayed.

"Did you call him?"

"I don't have to," he said, walking into the room and sitting on the edge of the unmade bed. "I know where he is. He's giving up the interviews and the program, even though he knows that will disappointment me and you and the mother of his baby."

She came closer and sat next to him. "Let's call him, Eli. Let's talk to him and get him to turn around."

"He won't answer." He looked at her, aching for their first time together in weeks to be different. Reaching to her cheek, he tucked a stray piece of hair behind her ear. "I missed you," he murmured.

Her breath hitched. "I missed you, too."

And then, before he could talk himself out of it, before he could remind himself of the million complications between them, he closed the space between them and kissed her.

Kate melted into him, her hands resting lightly on his chest as he pulled her closer, deepening the kiss.

For a moment, nothing else existed. Not the stress. Not the worry. Just *her*.

When they finally broke apart, Kate let out a breathless laugh. "Well. That escalated quickly."

Eli chuckled, pressing his forehead against hers. "Tell me you're glad you came."

She curled her fingers into the fabric of his shirt. "I'm *very* glad I came."

Tomorrow was going to be one of the hardest days of the year, but for once he didn't have to face it alone. If only Jonah had waited...

"Eli?" She leaned into him, pressing her lips to his ear. "I have an idea..."

Chapter Twenty-two
Crista

The gates to Crest Lawn Memorial Park groaned open at exactly 8:30 AM, and Jonah wasted no time slipping through. Not that there was a line to get into the home for a thousand dead bodies.

No one else was insane enough to be standing in a graveyard on a miserably wet, sunless Friday morning, but Jonah wasn't just anyone.

He was a Lawson, and somewhere in the generations of architects and control freaks, high-hopers and over-achievers, ran a flair for self-inflicted emotional torture. He got it in spades, apparently.

Which was why he drove all night in that bucket of rusty bolts he called a van and somehow made it to this place that had seen so many tears for literal centuries.

He stopped at the same 7-Eleven he always visited for the specific ingredients he needed, making his special "Mom meal" in the van and stuffing it into a backpack he had over his shoulder.

As he walked, the rain picked up again, driving harder and slowing his steps.

He didn't care, though. He took the long way around

the massive rolling hills, pausing a moment to check out the graves, some of which were dug in the 1800s. Many of which he remembered every single year.

Like Leyton Wiggle—dude's real name—who kicked the bucket on December 14, 1899 and got a primo spot on a hilltop overlooking the Atlanta skyline.

"Hey, Wiggles," he said, as he did every year when he passed. "Still got the best view in the house, man."

He squinted toward the horizon, but the distant skyscrapers of downtown were obstructed by thick fog and rain, which drenched him as he plowed on to the newer section.

He cut over the flat stones, sorry for walking on any graves and all, but this wasn't a day for meandering.

He slowed when he passed the super creepy giant sculpture of two angels and a massive headstone for Letitia Burns, who lived for three days in 1878. *Beloved daughter of John and Ida Burns, and sister of Mathilda.*

He'd seen this over-the-top monument more than a dozen times, but it hit different today. Jeez. A *baby* had died. He'd never really thought about that before. But then, the last time he was here? He never dreamed he'd have one coming in the not-too-distant future.

This time little Letitia was *personal.*

Powering on, his sneakers squelched against the muddy ground, hands shoved deep into his pockets. Rain had turned the grass into a sponge, soaking through the bottoms of his jeans, but he barely felt it.

He sucked in a lungful of the scent of pine needles and wet stone, the kind of smell that stuck in your nose and made you feel like you were breathing in the past. It fit.

This wasn't a choice, he told himself when a tiny, unfamiliar voice whispered in his head that this was a dumb idea.

It was a magnetic pull he couldn't resist any more than he could resist taking his next breath of rain-scented air. This was a ritual he never let himself break, no matter how much it wrecked him.

Because if he skipped it, if he let one year pass without folding in half in front of that headstone, it would mean he was forgetting her. And Jonah couldn't let that happen. Not after fifteen years. Not after spending just as many years without her as he had with her.

Half his life with Mom. Half his life without.

There was no doubt which was the better half.

He came around the big section of the Lafayette family who must have been burying their dead here for six generations. A minute later, he found Mom's headstone without really looking for it.

Honestly, this trip was muscle memory at this point.

The grass had been cut and it looked like recently laid flowers had shriveled next to the simple gray headstone.

Meredith? Probably. She came out here pretty often and made sure it was tidy. Dad did, too. And Aunt Emily, his mother's sister. Others might show up today, if anyone remembered the date.

But no one was around now, not at this hour. It was

why he always came the minute they opened, so he could beat the crowd.

Very slowly, he shook back his soaking wet hair and lowered himself to the ground in front of the stone, finally letting his gaze settle on her name.

Melissa Anne Lawson.

He let out a slow breath and wiped the rain from her name with the sleeve of his jean jacket. It was pointless, but he did it anyway.

"Hey, Mom."

His voice came out rough, barely audible over the soft patter of rain. He crouched, pressing his palms against the damp earth, and stared at the headstone like it might blink back at him. Like it might tell him what the hell he was supposed to do next.

Instead, silence. Just him, the rain, and a growing pit in his stomach.

He reached into his backpack and pulled out the sandwich he'd just made, wrapped in a paper towel.

"Got me a Mrs. Lawson special," he said with a wry smile. "BLT with burnt bacon—no mean feat on that wretched cooktop in my van. Three thick slices of tomato, or, as you called it 'To-maht' with no O." He grinned at the memory of her goofiness. "Got a swipe of mayo mixed with a splash of Tabasco because you knew I liked a little kick on my sammy."

He stared at the wet stone but all he could see was that pretty lady behind the wheel of her SUV. She'd be rushing from work after she finished reporting on some fire or town council meeting, turning her world upside down and backwards so she could pick him up from football practice.

He lifted the sandwich in a half-hearted toast, silently thanking her for caring about him so much.

"Not as good as yours," he said after the first bite. "Remember, you always had one in the car but wouldn't let me eat until I changed my shirt because you 'weren't about to let sweat ruin a perfectly good sandwich.'" He sniffed, rubbing at his nose. "I used to think that was annoying. Now I'd give anything to hear you say it again."

The rain picked up, soaking into his jean jacket, dribbling down the collar of his T-shirt. He pulled out a bottle of lemonade—sadly, not the tart kind she made from scratch—but it was lemonade, and she always had that for him.

He took a swig and set it on the wet earth.

"So, uh. Guess what? I have a kid on the way. Really stinking soon, too." The words felt foreign, like they belonged to someone else. He let out a breath. "A whole entire human that's gonna be looking to me for...whatever kids need." He snorted. "Everything, I guess. I mean, assuming I meet Carly's exacting standards."

He closed his eyes and tried to imagine his mother's face. What would it look like today? Would she have any gray hair or wrinkles? Probably not. She was magic like that. Plus, she was a TV reporter, so she'd have probably done the tricks to keep her looks.

But what would she say? Would her green eyes go wide with shock? Would she make that squeaky noise when something excited her and insist she be called "Gramma Missy" from this day on?

"Anyhoo, can you imagine that? Me, a dad?" He huffed out a laugh, bitter and small. "Yeah, me neither."

He ran a hand through his rain-drenched hair, frustration bubbling under his skin.

"Carly says I have to get my life together if I want to be in the baby's life. And she's right. But I don't know how. I don't know how to be anything but a screw-up." He exhaled sharply, his hands clenching into fists. "I spent the last fifteen years running, and I don't even know what from anymore."

The lump in his throat swelled, tight and unrelenting. He squeezed his eyes shut. "Now I ran again," he admitted. "'Cause wasn't this just the perfect excuse not to go to an interview that could change my life? Not to fail? I can't do it without you, Mom. A chef? Can you imagine? And a kid that's going to be born in a matter of weeks? *What am I gonna do, Mom?*"

The sob escaped, ripping his chest open.

Crap, he was slobbering now, but who cared? Call it rain. Call it pain. Call it a kid who was unfairly cheated out of the best mother in the world.

"I miss you so much," he managed. "I can't even tell you how much. Same today as fifteen years ago. *It never gets better*. It's just a hole, Mom. A fat, empty hole where you should be. I know I'm a man and I should grow up and accept this. But I was a kid, and I feel like everything stopped—*everything*—when you died. I don't know how to start it again."

A gust of wind cut through the cemetery, sending rustling branches and spring leaves around him. Jonah wiped his face, forced himself to breathe.

He couldn't eat anymore, so he stuffed the sandwich and drink back in his bag and swiped his face again, the denim scratching his cheek.

"I'm going back to California," he said gruffly, hearing the defiance in his voice. "I mean, the baby's coming in a coupla weeks. I know she doesn't want me there, but I'll just...try. I know, it's a dumb move, but hey, I'm famous for those."

He shifted on the grass, soaked to the bone now and not caring.

"I'm not going to be a chef! What the heck am I thinking? And now that I've pulled this stunt, I guarantee Dad's done coddling me. And Kate..." He made a face. "Yeah, you don't know about Kate. She's..."

How would she feel if she knew Dad might have found someone? Knowing her? She'd have approved.

"She's pretty cool," he said. "But I'm—"

He heard movement, footsteps, leaves rustling. He swallowed his sentence, dreading the idea of coming face-to-face-with Aunt Emily or, God forbid, Meredith.

After what she did to help him find that Culinary Arts program? Miss Perfection would blast—

"Jonah!"

Swearing under his breath, he stood and peered through the rain at two figures sprinting toward him, drenched and frantic.

"Jonah!"

Kate's voice hit first, breathless and sharp with urgency. Eli was right beside her, his father—always composed, always put together—looking like he had just run through a hurricane. His hair was plastered to his forehead, his jacket dripping.

Jonah sighed, already knowing why they were here. "You didn't have to come looking for me."

"Yes, we did," Eli shot back, his breath coming in heavy puffs. "You have an interview in five hours and forty-five minutes."

"Yeah, I'm going to miss it."

"No, Jonah." Kate's voice cut through his excuse, sharp but not unkind as she ran ahead and reached him first. "*No, you are not.*"

The vehemence took his breath away more than the fact that the two of them had come all the way here to... save him. She was furious and determined and, good God, she reminded him of the woman six feet under where they were standing.

Not in looks, personality, or anything but...mom-ness.

He looked away, almost unable to take the impact of it. "It's dumb to think I even have a chance."

"It's dumber not to try," she shot back.

He let out a shuddering breath as Eli stomped his way closer, taking a moment to look at the gravestone, a shadow of grief darkening his blue eyes before he leveled a hard gaze at Jonah.

"I lost her, too, Jonah." His voice was raw, the words scraping the air between them. "It's the worst thing in the world."

"You don't seem...like you still hurt." It wasn't an accusation or indictment—if anything, Jonah envied the peace his father seemed to have found.

He snorted. "Define hurt, son. I'm sure you've heard that grief is just love that has nowhere to go. I found a place for it." His eyes flicked toward the sky. "I found... other things."

Jonah swallowed hard. Other things like God. Hey, whatever worked, man. He couldn't argue that he was the one screwing up his life and blubbering in the rain and Dad...

Dad had come here, with Kate, on their special long weekend, to get him.

That...wow. That was love.

"What did she say?" his father asked, glancing at the stone again.

Jonah jerked back, not sure if he understood. "What?"

"Your mom. I always get answers when I come here. I can hear her voice, and I can imagine what she said. What did she tell you to do?"

"I didn't...she didn't..." His throat grew thick. "Nothing."

Kate exhaled and wiped some rain from her face, then reached for his arm. "Can I tell you what I would say if you were my son?"

Jonah didn't answer.

"I'd tell you that you are the finest cook I ever saw in the kitchen." She looked up at him, her brown eyes easy to see since she must have ditched her glasses, and her bangs were plastered to her head. "I'd tell you that when you layer flavors or test a spice or cut a radish, you do it with the flair and touch of a great chef. And you have an opportunity to learn exactly how to be that chef. You are brilliant, Jonah Lawson. And you were made for great things."

Made for...more. He could hear his mother's voice, echoing exactly what this dear, good woman was saying.

"Is that why you drove three hundred miles overnight in the rain?" He tried to slather the words with attitude, but he knew he sounded petulant and small. "To tell me I cut a mean radish?"

"I came because I believe in you completely." She lifted her chin, undaunted by his tone or the rain. "I have bone-deep faith in you. I would do anything—and so would your father—to help you realize your amazing potential."

It was like...it was like Melissa Lawson herself was speaking from that grass-covered hole in the ground.

Something shifted in his chest.

"I don't know if I can be a dad," he admitted, the words barely audible but it was the truth, and it was at the heart of this matter.

He was scared out of his mind and if he didn't get his life together, like Carly insisted, he wouldn't get to find out what kind of father he'd even be. The whole thing just sucked.

"You don't have to be perfect," she said softly. "You just have to show up. And earn that child's respect by following your dreams and passions and talents. By not letting roadblocks and complications get in the way. I know you can do that, Jonah."

His breath hitched. Could he?

Kate sighed. "Plus, you have a good role model." She glanced at his father and in that one second, in that flash of a look, he saw...love.

She *loved* his father. And there was nothing anyone—including the great and powerful Maggie Lawson—was going to do to stop that.

As if he saw it, too, Dad took a step closer. "Son, if you leave now, you can make that interview. Might break a few speed limits, but—"

"Not in that van," he said. "That is not happening."

"Take my truck." He held out keys. "You can make it."

Something inside him cracked wide open. The years of running, of pushing people away—it all felt so heavy. He let out a breath, unsteady and uncertain and right on the edge of agreeing with them.

"I'll drive with you," Kate said, giving his arm a gentle squeeze. "I'll drive for you. Whatever it takes, but you are going to make that appointment and get into the Culinary Arts program."

For a moment, hope surged. Then he looked down at muddy, wet clothes.

"I'm a mess."

"You can change in the van first," Eli said. "No more excuses. Just try. Just give yourself that chance."

Then, slowly, he nodded.

Kate's smile was small but full of relief. She wrapped him in a quick hug—warm, steady, safe.

As they hustled away, he turned back and took one more look at the gravestone, silently thanking her for whatever hand she'd had in this small miracle.

He heard it in the breeze, rustling the spring buds in the trees. A voice he loved saying words he treasured.

You were made for more, Jonah Lawson.

Maybe he was.

He looked down at Kate and smiled. "Let's run. And let's break some laws."

She laughed and picked up the pace. "And let's win the day!" She sprinted ahead, her wet hair flying.

He turned and looked at Dad, who was grinning ear to ear, staring at Kate like...like...yeah.

These two loved each other. They might not know it yet, but Jonah did. And maybe Mom did, too.

August 2, 1990

Tessa Wylie is the most magical person I have ever known!!! I don't care if that sounds dramatic, it's TRUE. Tonight, she danced at sunset on the beach like she was the coolest person alive. And for the first time in my entire life, I was part of it. For like two whole minutes before my mother RUINED EVERYTHING.

We were all down on the sand after the 'rents took us to a nice dinner at AJ's. Eli brought his BoomBox and of course the absolute best song in the world starts playing—"Vogue." And Tessa was wearing this adorable pink skirt with a white tank top—so cute—and she starts dancing on the sand like she's Madonna herself.

Everybody was clapping and she grabs my hand and says, "Come on, let's Vogue!" right with the song.

I wanted to say no. I DID. Because I know better. I know what my mother thinks about acting silly, about being too loud, too much. But the thing is... I didn't want to stop. Tessa made it look so easy, so fun, like the happiest thing in the whole world. And for those two minutes, I felt like someone else—someone wild and free, someone who didn't hear my mom's voice in her head all the time, warning her to be careful, to be good, to be a perfect Southern lady.

But then it happened. Tessa, being Tessa, got a little too playful. She grabbed a handful of watermelon from the snacks on our blanket and smushed a piece onto my nose. It was funny! It was nothing! But before I could even wipe it away, I felt her presence clouding the happy mood.

And then I heard the dreaded three words: "Vivien Leigh Lawson!"

I FROZE.

Mom was standing right in front of me—how does she do that? How does she just appear when you least expect her? And, whoa, she was mad.

I dropped Tessa's hands so fast it was like they burned me. My heart was THUMPING.

Mom looked right at my white dress, which had a big, sticky, pink stain on the eyelet lace top.

She didn't care that everyone was there. She just spat the words at me. "That is a brand-new dress, Vivien. I just bought that for you. And you let her—"

And then Tessa just jumped right between us and said, "She didn't LET me! I did it!"

Oh my gosh, I thought I would faint right on the sand. WHO INTERRUPTS MAGGIE LAWSON?!

But Tessa keeps going because Mom, of course, was speechless. "It was a joke, Mrs.

Lawson. It's just a little watermelon. It'll wash out." She even rolled her eyes (ROLLED THEM AT MY MOTHER!!!). And then, I swear to God, she said, "It's a dress, not the Declaration of Independence."

I almost choked. My whole body turned to ice. I could feel every single person on that beach holding their breath. No one talks to my mother like that. NO ONE. Not even Dad.

And would Tessa back down in the face of my mother's most terrifying look? (And, whoa, she has a few of those up her sleeve.)

Nope. Not Tessa. She tossed her hair and smiled like she wasn't even a little afraid. "Vivien was having fun," she said. "She looked happy. What's so wrong with that?"

I have never seen my mom so mad. She just breathed in like a dragon about to let out fire and I knew she was holding back the granddaddy of all lectures. The kind that would keep me up crying into my pillow later. But she wouldn't do it in front of everyone. Instead, she just told me to go inside and change.

My stomach dropped. I ran into the house and didn't even dare to stop.

But I heard it. As I reached the door, Tessa's voice, light and fearless as ever: "You should try dancing sometime, Mrs. Lawson. It's fun."

Tessa Wylie has a death wish.

And I kind of love her for it.

Someday, I'm going to pay her back for defending me.

Viv

Chapter Twenty-three

Tessa

Tessa sat on the back deck, cradling a warm mug of coffee in her hands, leaning into the breeze and the calm before the storm. Not a literal storm, thank goodness. No, the April weather had cooperated nicely for the late afternoon wedding fashion event scheduled to start in a few hours.

Downstairs, on the first floor, there were racks of tulle, lace, and satin lined up, with bedrooms and the bathroom assigned for changing. They'd manage the "runway" from that level. Beyond that, along the boardwalk and onto the beach, the rental company was hard at work setting up tents, tables, and chairs. The flowers were delivered, the caterer was on the way, and Akari would arrive right before the models for hours of preparation.

Right now, everything was so under control that Tessa could relax, finally alone with Mom and Kate on the deck.

Jo Ellen sat beside her, holding her own cup of coffee, her eyes soft with nostalgia as she gazed out at the Gulf.

Her mother seemed older than the last time Tessa

had seen her, four or five months ago, and it was clear grief had taken a toll on her. There were shadows around her brown eyes and some deeper frown lines.

She always had amazing hair, but her silvery waves sure could use a decent trim. Tessa picked up her mother's hand and closed it in her own, hating that Mom had age spots and her wedding ring was loose.

"I know, I know. I need a manicure," Jo Ellen said. "I always did pink for your dad. He liked that, but..." Her voice faded out.

"I'll go with you and get one tomorrow," Tessa said. "We can all go. You up for it, Kate?"

She lowered her glasses to give a "get real" look. "I'm a research scientist in a lab. I think the last manicure I had was..." She shook her head. "Not in recent memory. But Emma lives for them, so take her."

"I doubt she'll leave that beach," Tessa said, jutting her chin to the surf where Emma and Matt were testing out boogie boards Eli had bought for their visit. "They didn't get out of the water the entire time you were gone yesterday, which was an eternity."

Kate smiled. "Mission accomplished, though. Jonah slayed his interviews."

Nolie's squeal of laughter floated up from the beach as she ran with Aunt Pittypat through the surf, never more than ten feet from Emma, who she'd attached to the minute they'd arrived. Little fair-weather friend, Tessa thought with a smile.

Crista and Anthony sat side by side on a blanket,

watching their daughter, their heads close in conversation.

Tessa still didn't know what the outcome of Crista's pregnancy test had been, or if she had taken one. But she and Anthony seemed like a nice couple, and he'd been over the moon when Nolie had read for him.

"Destin was always magical, especially in the mornings," Jo Ellen said with a bit of melancholy, pulling Tessa from her thoughts. "One of my favorite things to do here was wake up before anyone else and drink my coffee on the beach."

"I like evenings," Kate said, glancing at the water. "Sunset is so beautiful, and I love walking after dinner. I missed it every day in Ithaca."

Tessa glanced at her mother, finally releasing her hand. "It's funny how the magic never wore off. Coming back here, almost fifty years old now, it's still just as special as it was when I was thirteen."

Jo Ellen sighed, her gaze still locked on the horizon. "I suppose it was the way everything felt...possible here. Like life could be exactly how you wanted it to be, even if just for the summer. There were no pressures, no expectations, just the beach, the house, and all of you running wild, making memories."

Tessa hesitated, her fingers tracing the rim of her mug. So far, the subject of the Wylies' falling out with the Lawson family had been easily avoided, especially with Kate and Eli gone for an extended time in Atlanta.

But before Kate had left, Tessa had a few moments alone with her sister.

During that time, Kate told her that she had gently brought up the question regarding their father's role in Roger Lawson's arrest with their mother. Jo Ellen didn't deny it, didn't confirm it, and asked that the topic be dropped.

But they *couldn't* drop it. For one thing, Tessa had to prove her father would never be so disloyal. And it would hang over their friendship with the Lawsons, which had been progressing just beautifully these past few months. Finally, the dark history could certainly derail Kate and Eli's budding romance.

If she feared that, Kate wasn't saying. Like Jo Ellen, she was determined to just gloss over it, but Tessa couldn't do that. So maybe now was a good time to bring it up.

Tessa took a steadying breath and turned to face her mother. "So, can I ask you something? About Dad?"

Jo Ellen's eyes shuttered. "Your sister already told me he's been accused of tipping the police off to Roger's crimes."

"Well..." Tessa's hands fisted as she stared at her mother. "Did he?"

She just stared straight ahead, silent.

"*Mom.*"

"I can't talk about it."

She and Kate both leaned forward, equally surprised by this statement. "Why not?" They asked in perfect unison.

"Because...I can't." She put her coffee mug on the

table with finality. "I made a promise to my husband, and I will not break it."

"What promise?" Tessa asked, her voice rising in frustration.

Jo Ellen turned to her, a world of pain in her dark eyes. "I promised him many years ago that I wouldn't ask about it, talk about it, or mention it ever again."

Kate shook her head. "And by 'it' do you mean Roger's arrest or Dad's role in the investigation?"

Their mother swallowed, refusing to answer.

"Mom, both men are dead," Tessa said. "And the relationship between the two families is on a course to heal. Why won't you tell us the truth now?"

"Because I don't know it," she said simply.

"What *do* you know?" Kate pressed.

Another sigh and this time, Jo Ellen glanced at the door into the house, as though she wanted to be sure no one was lurking about or listening.

"All I know is that Artie did the right thing. He always did."

Kate dropped back with a huff, but Tessa just got closer. "What was the right thing?" she asked. "Did he turn Roger in to the police or not?"

"I don't know for sure," she said, a soft cry in the words. "He said it was better if I didn't know all the details."

Kate and Tessa shared a silent look, sharing their confusion and frustration.

"Does Maggie know what happened?" Tessa asked.

"She thought she knew," Jo Ellen said. "She made a

lot of assumptions and accusations and, of course, tried to protect her husband, who…who…"

"Who was guilty," Kate said softly. "Everyone knows that, Mom. Even the Lawsons have accepted that their father committed crimes. And they've suffered for it. But do our families have to forever be broken because of that?"

"That's what Artie and Roger wanted."

"What?" Again, the question came out in unison.

"Well, I can't speak for Roger, but Artie was quite clear to me—I was never, under any circumstances, to contact, see, call, or have anything to do with Maggie."

"Even after Roger died?" Kate asked.

"I don't know. We never talked about it again."

"Did Dad know Roger died?" Tessa asked, still rocking with dissatisfaction over these responses.

"He must have," Jo Ellen said. "I found a copy of Roger's obituary in your father's papers, and it was from an Atlanta newspaper, so he had to have known."

"Really?" Kate asked on a gasp. "Why wouldn't he tell us? We didn't find out until two months ago."

"He must have had a really good reason," Jo Ellen said.

"Of course he did," Tessa replied. "But we want to know what that reason was."

"Maybe I do know," Kate said, making them both look at her in shock. "Eli and I spoke with Betty and Frank Cavallari a while back. Do you remember them, Mom?"

Her brows furrowed. "The couple who owned the

deli? Oh, yes, we socialized with them a lot those summers. I loved Betty. She was so funny. I'm glad they're still alive because if I'm seventy-eight, then Betty's nearly eighty-seven now."

"They're both alive and in good health," Kate said. "They live in Santa Rosa Beach."

"Well, that's nice to hear," Jo Ellen said. "But they don't know anything about this."

Kate cocked her head. "They think they do."

Jo Ellen's expression darkened slightly. "Then they're lying."

"Or confused," Kate said, glancing at Tessa with a question in her eyes. The fact was, Betty had told Kate that their father had been in love with Maggie, and Frank had told Eli that Roger had been in love with Jo Ellen.

No one believed either version of that story, but Kate and Tessa had decided not to bring it up with their mother, just in case there was a grain of truth to it. That could hurt...someone.

Kate and Tessa looked hard at each other, both of them thinking the same thing—was it the right time to ask? Did it make any sense? Would it answer any questions?

At the very same moment, they both gave their heads imperceptible shakes, proving that they were still connected, these twins who'd shared a womb. Because they both knew that it wasn't the time, it made no sense, and nothing would be resolved by bringing up that conjecture.

"I do know this," Jo Ellen said, picking up her coffee

cup. "Your father was a man of ethics, of strong morals. He loved us all, and he protected us no matter what."

And that, Tessa knew, was the only truth that mattered. After the conversation with Lacey, she'd been thinking about him even more than usual. How he'd been the only person in the world who could help her, hold her as she cried, and promise that he'd always be there for her, no matter what.

Could that loving, kind man of genuine integrity have torn another family apart? Why would he do that?

"I don't know what his true role was in Roger's arrest," her mother continued. "And, honestly? I don't think Maggie knows, either. I think both men took the truth to the grave, and we need to accept that."

"Can you?" Kate asked.

"Of course—I'm here, aren't I? The real question is, can Maggie forgive and forget? I loved the woman dearly, but those two attributes are not exactly her strong suit."

"Tessa!" Lacey came out to the deck in a rush. "The models are pulling up. Akari will be here in five minutes. Guests arrive in two hours."

Tessa pushed up, giving a wistful smile to her mother and sister. "It's showtime."

"You have blown me away, Tessa Wylie." Akari turned and looked at Tessa with nothing but gratitude glimmering in her dark eyes. "Truly exceeded my highest expectations."

"Thank you," Tessa said with a humbled tip of her head. "But the music for the first set hasn't even started yet, so hang on for the real good stuff."

"The good stuff is that there are well over a hundred people here," Akari exclaimed. "Oh, I see someone I have to talk to." She blew a kiss and floated away, leaving Tessa standing at the edge of the boardwalk runway.

From this perch, she could take in the breathtaking spectacle they had pulled off, and it did indeed exceed expectations. The late afternoon sunlight bathed everything in a dreamlike glow, the polished wooden planks gleaming beneath the cloudless sky.

Guests gathered along the dunes and under the tents, champagne flutes in hand. Ivory fabric draped elegantly from wooden archways, billowing with the breeze, while floral arrangements of white roses, peonies, and eucalyptus added a lush romance to the setting. The entire event looked like something out of a bridal magazine—perfect, seamless, magical.

And, for once, it felt like everything was actually going right.

Behind Tessa, on the first floor of the Summer House, the models lined up, each wearing a stunning bridal or bridesmaid gown, excitement buzzing in the air. The hairstylists adjusted final curls while the makeup artists dabbed last-minute touches of shimmer. The whole operation was a well-oiled machine, and Tessa couldn't help but feel genuine pride in her work.

Her gaze landed on Nolie, standing in her soft pink flower girl dress, dancing on her little Mary Janes in anticipation of how she would pirouette down the board-walk. The layers of tulle fluttered around her, her dark hair spilling on her shoulders under a tiny tiara, her eyes bright with excitement.

Looking at that little angel, Tessa felt an unexpected lump in her throat.

She knew how much this moment meant to Nolie—to feel special, to be part of something dazzling. The real thrill was for Tessa, though. She'd made a permanent change in Nolie's life, and she'd been able to give that child the same kind of love and attention Artie had given her.

"She loves you so much."

Tessa turned at the words, finding Crista next to her, wearing the pale blue bridesmaid dress she would be modeling today.

"That's funny," Tessa said. "I was just thinking the same thing about her."

Crista put a hand on Tessa's arm. "Thank you so much for all you've done for her."

"I got a lot out of it, too," she said, then leaned in with a raised brow. "And, uh, how are you doing?"

Crista gave a slow, knowing smile. "Well, you can be the second person to know that I am—"

Just then, Anthony joined them, slipping a hand around Crista's waist. "You okay, babe? Want to sit down before you walk the aisle?"

"Yes, yes, I'm good. I was just talking to Tessa."

"It's fine," Tessa said, giving her arm a squeeze. "I know what you are."

Crista exhaled a small laugh, but Nolie came running up to all of them so Crista could get a good look at her "high heels and crown."

Anthony inched closer to Tessa. "Nolie can't rave about you enough," he added. "You've made her feel like a star."

Giving him a wink, Tessa crouched down to Nolie's level. "You ready to steal the show, Figsworth?"

Nolie giggled, spinning again. "I was born ready!"

Before Tessa could respond, Jonah emerged from the guys' dressing room—the bathroom—in a tuxedo, looking equal parts jaw-dropping and uncomfortable.

"Dude, you clean up very nice," Tessa said as she stepped closer to him.

The man was clearly unused to wearing anything more formal than a button-down, and even that was rare. Now, stuffed into an expensive tux, he tugged at the collar like it was strangling him.

"Let's get this over with before I die of asphyxiation," he grumbled, but couldn't help smiling as he shook back his locks. He turned to Eli, who was looking sharp in a slate-gray morning suit and tails. "But at least I'm not dressed like the guy on the Monopoly board."

Eli laughed but his smile faltered as the "brides'" dressing room door opened and Kate walked out. She wore a shimmery A-line white gown, looking ethereal and perfect and...holy cow, Tessa thought she might cry.

And Eli looked like he already was.

"You're so beautiful," he sighed, walking toward her with the same expression Tessa had seen on so many grooms during the highly photographed "first look" moments at the weddings she'd coordinated.

Jonah and Tessa shared a quick look, their eyes wide.

"He's a goner," Jonah mumbled. "You better get that woman to move here."

"Operation Kate Relo? I'm on it."

"Oh, look at Aunt Vivien." Jonah's smile grew as he peered over Tessa's shoulder.

She turned to spy her friend rising from the hair and makeup station. She sashayed over in an emerald-green tea-length dress, her freshly done lashes popping wide at Jonah.

"You are a vision, my handsome nephew."

"You clean up nice, too, Aunt Viv."

They joked around with Crista and Anthony joining them, with more *ooh*s and *ahh*s for Nolie.

Tessa felt warmth in her chest watching them all, the moment so light, so effortless. A family moment, and it felt like old times on this beach—two families blended and connected.

"You are too talented to go back to the Ritz," Lacey whispered as she slid an arm around Tessa.

"Good, because I turned the job down."

"You did?" Lacey let out a soft squeal.

"It didn't feel right to go back there and..." Tessa smiled. "Now you know my deepest, darkest secret, and I can't take a chance of you blackmailing me."

Lacey's whole expression changed. "I promise, your secret is safe with me."

"You'll never tell your mother? Or my sister?"

She made an X on her chest. "I promise, Tessa. I will not tell them. Now, if you change your mind and want to find this boy? I would love to help you."

For one second, she considered, then...no. It was a complication she didn't need or want. More than that, deep inside, she loved that human she created too much to upset what she hoped was a wonderful life.

"Let's leave the past in the past."

"Are you sure? You're not curious about him at all?"

"Curious if he got my good looks," Tessa joked, adding a wink. "But I don't think—"

A loud noise brought her to a halt, followed by the sound of a door banging, and marching footsteps.

"Who...what was that?" Lacey asked.

None of the guests were upstairs in the house, only the caterer was on the main floor.

"I better go check," Tessa said.

She took a step away just as she heard someone's sharp intake of breath from somewhere in the crowd that made her skin prickle. She turned instinctively, scanning the models, the dresses, the whole room following her gaze toward the stairs.

"For the love of all that is holy, someone better tell me what's going on in my home."

It was like every molecule of air was suddenly sucked out of the room.

A woman with short silver hair, a tailored lavender pants suit, and a look that would scare the devil stood on the third step.

"Grandma Maggie!" Nolie practically flew through

the stunned crowd, her arms outstretched. "You made it! I knew you would!"

Tessa's whole world seemed to shift on its axis.

"What is she…"

"Oh, my heavens…"

"*Mama?*"

The expressions on Maggie Lawson's adult kids' faces were nothing but dismay, shock, and, yeah, no small amount of fear.

Maggie placed one imperious hand on Nolie's shoulder while her sharp gaze scanned the room and landed directly on Crista. It stayed there for a moment, then shifted to Eli. And after he'd been visually decapitated, she settled on Vivien.

Silent, with Nolie's hand in hers, Maggie came down the last few steps and people parted like the Red Sea, uncertain over the meaning of this new arrival.

But not Tessa. She knew what Maggie Lawson's arrival meant—the end of everything.

"Mom," Eli said with what could only be described as a guilty laugh. "Imagine our surprise."

"I have been imagining just that," she said. "Ever since I called Crista and Nolie answered the phone and told me you were all here."

Nolie beamed up at them, utterly clueless to the dynamic. "Remember when everyone was all crazy with the setting up stuff a couple days ago? I heard Mommy's phone ring and saw it was Grandma Maggie and we had a secret talk." Her eyes glinted as she looked up at her grandmother. "And I told Grandma Maggie that I wanted her here for Miss Tessa's big party and..." She did a precious little dance and tugged on Maggie's arm. "You made it, Grandma!"

"Of course I did, sweetheart. I would never miss this event being held in my home, on my property." She closed her eyes. "And yet it's full of strangers."

"I'm not a stranger, Mags." Jo Ellen's words cut through the crowd.

Maggie turned, looked at her, and all the color drained from her face. "What...you...how..." She sucked in a deep breath.

Jo Ellen blanched, too, reaching out her hand as if she needed support, and Kate snagged her fingers immediately.

"Come on, Mom. Let's take a walk."

As they quickly stepped away, Kate threw a pleading look over her shoulder to Eli. He frowned, obviously torn. After a split second of hesitation, he hustled after Kate and Jo Ellen, showing very clearly where his loyalties lay.

And Tessa decided right then and there she loved him for that.

For what felt like an eternity, no one said a word. Then Maggie leaned down to whisper something to Nolie, who nodded and scampered away as if to do whatever the queen had demanded.

Then Maggie looked right at Tessa and narrowed her sky-blue eyes. "I understand you are in charge of this..." She flipped her fingers. "This."

"I am." Tessa lifted her chin, instantly transported back three and a half decades, on another boardwalk, during another showdown. She'd been terrified then, too, but she had to protect and defend Vivien.

But this time? Well, Maggie did own the house and Tessa was merely...an unwelcome guest.

Maggie took one step closer. "Then it will fall on you to get every single person out of my home, off my property, and out of my sight as fast as humanly possible."

Tessa managed a breath. "I'm sorry, Mrs. Lawson, but—"

"Hold on." Vivien appeared at Tessa's side, her body vibrating so much Tessa could feel it. But all she got from her mother was a withering look of disappointment.

Vivien merely stood straighter under the weight of that look, squaring her shoulders. "Mom," she said through gritted teeth. "I want you to come upstairs with me right now."

Maggie lifted one brow. "After these people—"

"Not after anything," Vivien insisted. "Right now."

Inching back, Maggie gave her a shocked look that probably lasted two seconds but felt like an eternity. Then she pivoted and strode through the room, back up the stairs.

"I got this, Tess," Vivien whispered.

"Are you sure?"

"I am."

"All right, she's all yours. But..." Tessa threw a look at the room. "What about...everything?"

"The show must go on. And it will. Just hold it off for ten minutes and I'll..."

"You'll what?" Tessa challenged.

"I'll...take the hit. After all, I owe you one for the summer we danced."

Tessa smiled and gave her friend's hand a squeeze in solidarity. "Good luck."

But she'd need more than luck with that woman. She'd need a miracle.

Chapter Twenty-four
Vivien

In a way, Vivien had been waiting for this moment her whole life. She couldn't remember a time when she stood up to her mother and won—certainly not on anything this big or important.

But she'd been preparing for it since she arrived in Destin.

She'd faced her ex-husband and come out victorious. She'd confronted her wretched client and lost her job rather than be used. And now, the supreme test was standing in front of her wearing a violet suit and a furious expression.

The sounds of the party outside and the catering crew in the kitchen filled the main living area of the house that Maggie didn't even appear to be interested in seeing.

"All the way up," Vivien said, pointing to the top floor. "It's private."

"I wouldn't need privacy if all these people would leave."

"Mom." She put a light hand on her back. "Please. Upstairs."

With a grunt of sheer disgust, Maggie trudged up the

stairs, still refusing to look at the beautiful home that Eli had designed and Vivien had decorated.

"Where's Crista?" she said as she reached the top. "And Eli?"

"Eli is with Kate and Jo Ellen."

She sniffed furiously.

"Crista is probably with Nolie."

"She better not be mad at that child," Maggie said sharply. "Apparently Nolie is the only member of this entire family who loves me enough to be honest with me."

"We all love you," Vivien said, ushering her toward the reading nook that she'd just furnished with two chairs, a table, and a small bookshelf. The tiny retreat was bathed in sunlight from the upstairs windows, which now seemed unforgiving and too bright.

Vivien had hoped this unexpected sitting area would be used for rest and relaxation. But now it would be used for...confrontation.

"What are you doing here?" Vivien asked as they each took a seat.

"I own this house."

Vivien sighed and held up her hand. "I realize that, Mom, but last I checked, you were supposed to be in Europe until next weekend."

"And when the cat's away, the mice will...play house with the enemy." At Vivien's look, she lifted a shoulder. "I called Crista and Nolie spilled all the beans. And when she mentioned...*Wylies*? What else could I do?"

"The Wylies are not the enemy," she shot back.

"Tell that to your dead father."

The words cut like ice through the sunny area, making Vivien draw back. Not in surprise, but from the sheer force of her anger.

"Mom, he's been gone for thirty years. Artie Wylie passed away seven months ago. Is there any way in heaven or on Earth that you would bury the hatchet with these people?" Vivien heard the plea in her voice, but didn't care. This mattered.

"I can't."

"Why not?"

"Because your father told me not to, for one thing," she said. "And for another? If it weren't for Arthur Wylie and his big fat mouth? Roger could be sitting here next to me. Right here, right now. But he's not and they are and..." She shuddered. "I don't know if I can take that."

"Why don't you try?" Vivien asked softly. "We did."

"You knew you shouldn't have," her mother shot back. "If you didn't fully understand just how bad what you're doing really is, you wouldn't have lied to me."

"We lied because we knew this would be your reaction," Vivien said. "Not because we understand anything. Certainly not because we comprehend *why* we can't be friends with Kate and Tessa. They are wonderful women, Mom. Jo Ellen just got here for the event, so I haven't had a chance to get to know her, but Tessa has taught Nolie to read."

She started to respond but the last word hit and she did a double take. "Excuse me?"

"She did."

"Nolie said something about being a flower girl, not reading."

"Because she didn't even know what Tessa was doing. Tessa has dyslexia, too, and she knew exactly how to help Nolie. And it worked. Nolie's passed the practice test to go to third grade."

Maggie stared at her, clearly not sure how to process this news.

"And Kate?" Vivien continued. "Well, Kate has brought a joy out in Eli that I haven't seen since Melissa died. He's happy and she's...kind of perfect for him."

Her mother inched further away, gaping in disbelief.

"And Kate's also worked side by side with Jonah. She's encouraged him to stay here and apply to a Culinary Arts program at a local college in order to be equipped to be a father. You're about to have a great-grandchild, by the way, and if it weren't for Kate, I'm not sure Jonah would do this or ever know that baby."

Her jaw nearly hit her chest. "Excuse... What... Oh my..."

"And Lacey's finally found her career, working for Tessa, doing event management. She's shining and that's what today is all about."

Maggie visibly rooted for words that weren't coming easily. "Well," she huffed. "Y'all have been busy."

"What we've been is...very happy."

Maggie's gaze was still direct, but Vivien could have sworn there was the slightest thaw in her icy eyes.

"That's...something," Maggie whispered. "Jonah and Lacey and...Nolie. A baby and a job and...she's reading?"

An unexpected tendril of hope curled around Vivien's heart, along with a realization. She was tough on her own kids, yes, but Maggie's weakness was and would always be her grandchildren.

Maybe the way to handle this woman wasn't to fight her fire with more fire. Maybe it was to gently remind her whose happiness was at stake here.

At least Vivien hoped so. She took a deep breath and found the nerve to power on.

"You see, Mom," she said softly, "we chose to reconnect with Kate and Tessa, and it's been so incredibly gratifying. Whatever happened between you and Dad and the Wylies doesn't affect us. We are another generation and we don't want to be saddled with that history."

"You were saddled with it for the thirty years you didn't have a father."

"But that's not their fault," Vivien insisted. "Should they bear the burden of what Artie did? Especially because none of us really know what happened."

Maggie blinked at her, her keen mind processing this information, quiet for a long time.

"I still want everyone to leave," she finally said. "I don't know what's going on here, but—"

"No."

"Pardon me?" The edge was back in her voice.

"You heard me, Mom. You cannot pounce in here and ruin something that's important to a lot of people."

She closed her eyes, the slightest slouch of defeat in her shoulders. But when a dog barked, she sat straight up.

"Pitty? Is that you, Pittypat?"

Instantly, the tiny furball shot up the stairs, yapping with joy. She flew into Maggie's lap, her little pink tongue flipping all over her owner's face, her tiny tail knocking side-to-side with unabashed joy.

"Oh, my baby girl," Maggie said, clutching the dog to her cheek. "Did you miss me so very much?"

"Mom." Vivien refused to let Pittypat derail this. "We are not sending anyone home. For one thing, it would break Nolie in two. For another, you may own the property, but you cannot and will not blow in here and pull rank. This is *our* Summer House now and you are more than welcome. But you will not ruin what we've built."

She looked over the little brown head and locked eyes with Vivien. "You've changed," she said softly.

"Yes." She lifted her chin. "I guess you can blame Destin."

A slow, slight smile lifted her mother's lips. "No blame. Credit. It's a good change."

"Hey, are you up here?" Eli's voice came up the stairwell.

"Yes," Vivien called, a little breathless from the genuine compliment and the sense that she'd not only passed the biggest test, she'd reached a milestone with Maggie. "We're here. Come up."

Her brother came up the stairs two at a time, followed by Crista. They both wore expressions of uncertainty as they walked into the alcove. Eli leaned against the wall and crossed his arms, and Crista folded onto the floor, looking up at Maggie.

"I'm sorry I lied," she said, a hitch in her voice, but no actual tears for once. "I just couldn't miss this opportunity for Nolie. She didn't tell me you called."

"I asked her not to," Maggie said, stroking Pittypat's little head. "Nolie's a good girl."

Crista sighed. "She loves you, Mama. We all do."

Maggie tried to look mad, but right then, she didn't look any more ferocious than the Yorkie in her arms.

"Nolie is going to go to third grade," Crista said. "Because of—"

"I know. Tessa. And I'm thrilled." Maggie looked up at Eli. "And Jonah? A baby? A chef?"

"Yes to all," he said. "You're looking at a grandfather in a matter of weeks."

"Congratulations, Eli. And what is this I hear about Kate?"

He tried not to smile, but couldn't help it. "Whatever you heard, it's deeper and stronger and not going away."

She pressed one hand to her lips as if she had to try not to react, the other clinging to the dog.

"Mom, please." Eli crouched down to look her in the eyes. "Please tell us what happened all those years ago. We need to know so we can...process and move on."

"I can't."

"Can't or won't?" he pressed.

She took a moment to inhale, still petting the dog, looking past all of them in thought. "All I know, and this is the God's honest truth, is that Artie turned Roger in to the police that last week while we were here. Why, how, and what he was thinking is a mystery to me. Doesn't Jo know?"

Jo. Vivien had forgotten that Maggie called her "Jo" and the other woman had used "Mags." No one else on Earth called them that, and for some reason, the fact that they both slipped into their ancient sorority sister nicknames gave her hope.

"She says she doesn't know, either," Eli replied. "She says the truth went to the grave with her husband and, I guess, Dad. And that Artie told her not to contact you for any reason, and not to ask questions."

Letting out a slow breath, Maggie inched back. "Roger promised he'd tell me everything when he got out of prison, but..." She tried to swallow. "As you know, he never did."

"But what was there to tell?" Vivien asked. "What was 'everything'?"

"I don't know," Maggie said. "I swear I don't."

"Then why are you so mad at Jo Ellen?" Eli asked.

"Because Roger died and if he hadn't gone to prison..." She whimpered softly, a little more of her bite gone. "I guess you all win and I'll leave now—"

"No." Crista sat up and put her hand on Maggie's leg. "Mama, I know you're upset with me for lying, but Nolie is going down that boardwalk as the one and only flower girl in ten minutes. She literally helped come up with the idea for this event and she wants you there. She's so happy you've come and truly believes you left Europe for the sole purpose of seeing her do this."

Very slowly, Maggie's expression softened even more.

Her gaze warmed. Her jaw loosened. And she gave in to a slight smile.

"I can't let my granddaughter be disappointed." She put her hands on the armrest to push up as Pittypat bounded to the floor. "Let's cheer her on."

The three of them exchanged surprised and victorious glances as Eli took his mother's hand, helping her to her feet.

"Nolie also mentioned getting you in a grandmother-of-the-bride dress—"

She pointed a finger at him. "Don't push your luck."

As they laughed at that and headed downstairs, Vivien couldn't help but think something in the world had completely shifted...and it was good.

THE GOODNESS CONTINUED as Akari took her place at a speaker's podium under the tent, holding a microphone to welcome the guests and kick off the show. Tessa and Lacey stood at the beach end of the boardwalk, looking proud and a little nervous as the music for the "Mothers of the Brides" collection began the event.

Jo Ellen absolutely sparkled in silver, along with a few other older models, slowing her step as she passed a front-row table where Maggie—and Pittypat—sat. The two women exchanged looks, but from Vivien's perspective at the other end of the boardwalk, it was impossible to interpret what that might mean.

"I'm hopeful," Crista whispered to Vivien.

Vivien turned and touched her sister's cheek, noticing the whole thing had made her pale and even the professional makeup artist didn't fully cover the shadows under her eyes.

"You okay?" she asked. "This has been stressful."

"It's not stress," Crista said. "You're going to be an aunt again."

Vivien gasped just as the music changed, which was the cue for the bridesmaids and groomsmen to partner up and start their walk.

"Crista!" Vivien pressed fisted hands to her lips to keep from letting out a cry of joy.

But then Peter was next to her, offering his arm. "Let's go, gorgeous."

Crista just laughed and gave her a nudge. "We'll talk," she promised. "Go show off that dress, Auntie."

Laughing, Vivien looked up at her partner for the fashion show, not the least bit surprised that Tessa had paired her with Peter. But she was surprised that this no-nonsense detective looked positively swoony in a dark suit with a narrow black tie.

"I'd dance with you at any wedding," she teased, purposely flirting as they stepped onto the wooden planks.

"Dance?" He snorted softly. "Are you all signed, sealed, and divorced now?"

"The deed is done," she said through a smile she gave to the crowd as they walked.

"Then I'll be hoping for our first kiss right here on the sands of Destin."

Laughing softly, she tugged him closer. "I wanted that thirty years ago, Detective."

"It'll be worth the wait."

Still laughing and maybe floating a little, she turned to her left to smile at the crowd like Tessa had instructed, but something—someone—caught her attention at one of the back tables.

Was that...Danny Sullivan? And, whoa, Fiona Buckman?

Fiona sat up a little straighter and gave a nervous smile, adding a little, uncharacteristic wave.

What was *she* doing here?

There was no time to give it much thought as they finished their walk and reached the end of the boardwalk. They stepped off the wood to their waiting areas, the bridesmaids separated from the groomsmen.

She turned back to face the boardwalk as the music dropped and became more playful and all eyes shifted for the one and only Figsworth the Flower Girl.

The music softened after Akari announced her, leading into Tchaikovsky's playful *Waltz of the Flowers* just as Nolie took her first careful step forward.

She looked like a dream with her dark eyes wide and serious and her little shoulders square with solemnity.

"Our favorite flower girl is wearing a delicate confection of tulle and lace," Akari told the crowd from her perch with a microphone. "The pale blush fabric catches the light with each graceful movement, certain to delight every wedding guest." She waited a few beats as the tempo increased, then Akari called out, "Dance for us, Nolie!"

At the expected command, Nolie extended her arms with the grace of a ballerina and pirouetted, tossing petals from her tiny basket and earning cheers and applause from the crowd. She did a few steps from the recital she was missing, but no audience could have been more appreciative.

Next to Vivien, Crista let out a small, choked sound, her hands clasped together at her chest. Anthony stood a few feet away, beaming with pride.

And they were having another! Vivien slipped her arm around her little sister's waist and gave her a squeeze.

Nolie finished her last twirl and reached the end of the runway, her tiny hands lifting her dress as she took a bow at the applause, confident and unafraid.

It was a stark contrast to how she'd been when they arrived in Destin—shy, uncertain, struggling in ways no one had fully understood. And now? Now she looked like she belonged here, like she was shining from the inside out.

Tessa stood off to the side, pride all over her face as she gave Nolie a discreet thumbs-up. But there was nothing discreet about Nolie's response. High on her performance, Nolie rushed into the arms of her teacher, overwhelmed by the moment.

Once again, Crista whimpered with happiness.

Vivien stood on her tiptoes, able to see her mother watching the exchange. Then Maggie's gaze shifted and

Vivien followed it, catching her make long and direct eye contact with Jo Ellen.

What was going through the minds of *Mags* and *Jo?* Could this event lead to...reconciliation between these once best friends? Or was that too much to hope for?

The music faded and the first few notes of Wagner's classic *Bridal Chorus* launched the climax of the show. Everyone turned to enjoy a parade of white, cream, and pink perfection on the bride models.

"We're starting this last group with Lumière's 'Seasoned Bride' collection, with a champagne A-line worn by Dr. Katherine Wylie, a research scientist at Cornell University."

But before she could catch a glimpse of Kate, Vivien felt a warm hand on her shoulder.

"You could have been a bride and a beautiful one at that."

At the words spoken softly in her ear, she turned, drawing in a sharp breath at the sight of Danny Sullivan a few inches away. A whiff of a musky scent and the light touch of his fingers nearly made her sway.

"Oh, hello. I didn't realize you were on the invitation list," she said, letting him guide her away from the group. "You or your, uh, sister."

He rumbled an easy laugh, his silvery eyes sparking with mirth. "Yes, Vivien, she *is* my sister. I still can't believe you thought I was some kind of conman after a widow's bank account."

"Shh." She jabbed his arm, not surprised his biceps

were just as strong as the ones she held only minutes ago. "The brides are coming down the aisle."

He tried to look serious but he still smiled. "I was right, you know."

"About?"

"Fiona. She wants you back. She's here with a bona fide apology and a promise to let you do things your way. Mostly. I'm merely her emissary asking if you will accept these terms and return to work for her."

Vivien inched back. "Really?"

"That is, if you want the business. I could see why you wouldn't."

She glanced in the direction of where Fiona sat, watching them intently. Once again, Fiona gave a slightly pathetic wave.

"I can get her to beg," he said, "if that will seal the deal."

She laughed softly. "No begging necessary. I'll talk to her later."

"Good." He leaned in close to whisper in her ear, even though they could hear each other easily over the music. "I hope that means I'll see you again."

Despite the warm air, chills cascaded down her arms and all she could do was pray he didn't notice he had that effect on her.

"I'm sure you will," she said, trying to sound cool and professional.

He chuckled, making her think she'd failed. "Come and sip champagne with us when the show is over. She really should grovel a little, and it'll be fun to watch. You earned it."

She gazed up at him, wanting to look away, knowing she should cheer for the last bride coming down the aisle...but was unable to look away from those mesmerizing eyes.

"I'll...do that," she said, finally forcing her gaze away only for it to land on Tessa and Lacey, who were intently watching the exchange. "Later," she added, giving his arm a slight nudge. "I better get back to business here. We have to go down the aisle again after the brides are finished."

As she turned back, Lacey was already stepping off the boardwalk and giving her the eye.

"What?" Vivien asked as she got next to her daughter and tried to pretend she was interested in the end of the fashion show.

"Who *was* that?" she asked.

"Hapless Handy. Fiona wants me back."

"We thought so." Lacey grinned. "Tessa said we call him Hedge Fund Hunk now."

Vivien snorted. "Oh, do we?"

Lacey gave a sly smile. "Am I imagining things, Mom, or do you have *two* handsome and eligible men after you right now?"

"I don't know," she said on a laugh. "Maybe I do."

And if she did, well, it wasn't the worst problem to have, was it?

"My oh my, this should be interesting," Lacey said.

Or terrifying. Vivien wasn't sure which.

Chapter Twenty-five

Eli

"And that is the last of it." Tessa walked out to the deck where Eli and Kate sat nestled on the sofa after the guests, vendors, and models had finally left the building. "Except for the lights on the boardwalk."

Eli sat up and looked at the soft string of lights that lined both sides of the elevated path from the house to the beach. "Can we keep them?" he asked. "I love the way they look."

"I thought you'd like them," Tessa said as she dropped onto one of the chairs with an exhausted sigh. "So I took the liberty of telling the lighting company I'd call them when we want them gone and they can bill me if we never send them back."

"Good call," Eli said, settling back next to Kate.

"Where is everyone?" Tessa asked, glancing around the empty deck. "I thought I was missing a party."

"Emma and Matt are taking showers, and Mom went for a walk," Kate reported. "We were going to go with her, but she said she wanted to be alone."

"Has she talked to Maggie?"

"Nobody knows," Eli said. "Crista and Anthony are

putting the flower girl to bed, Jonah just said he had to take a call, and Vivien and Lacey are with Maggie giving a grand tour."

"Ahh." She dropped her head back and sighed. "What a rollercoaster of a day."

"You did a magnificent job, Tess," Kate told her. "Everyone had fun, the vibe was perfect, Akari seemed very happy."

"And Maggie didn't wreck the whole thing," Tessa added, opening one eye to look at Eli. "How exactly did that happen again? Who saved the day?"

"Vivien," he said without a second's hesitation, wanting to give his awesome sister the credit she deserved. "She did the damage control and handled it like a pro."

"Who's a pro?" Jonah practically leaped out onto the deck. "I'll tell you who. This guy! The one who just got accepted in the inaugural Culinary Arts program at Northwest Florida State!"

Kate screamed the loudest, jumping from the sofa to throw her arms around him. "I knew it! I knew you could do it."

He picked her up and swung her, landing her back on her feet just as Eli came in for his congratulatory hug.

"I'm so proud of you, man!" He pounded his son's back and added a squeeze.

"Thanks, Dad." He inched back. "I called Carly and told her, too. But she wasn't too talkative." He made a face. "Early contractions."

"Really?" Kate asked, looking concerned. "I guess she's due any day now."

"She is and I..." He blew out a breath. "I want to be there."

"When do classes start?" Eli asked.

"Summer semester starts June second," he said.

"More than a month," Eli said. "You should go to California tomorrow. Be there for the birth."

Jonah stared at him, ready to argue, but Eli held up a hand to stave it off. "I mean it, son. The apartment is almost done and we can't do anything until the kitchen appliances come and as for the cost? Consider it my gift to my soon-to-be-born grandchild."

Jonah swiped a hand through his hair, tears threatening. "Aw, Dad. That would be..." He choked a little and reached out to hug Eli again. "Thank you."

"But be sure to come back," Eli added, only half joking.

"I will, I promise. I'm not going to miss this program." He added a tight smile. "And maybe Carly and Junior or Juniorette will come with me."

Kate gave a clap. "That would be awesome!"

"What's all the commotion?" Crista asked, joining them with Anthony right behind her.

"We're congratulating Jonah," Kate said.

"You got in?" Crista threw her arms out with joy. "That's so awesome! Chef Jonah!"

He gave her a hug and shook Anthony's hand.

"Hey, since we're celebrating," Jonah said. "Let me

whip up some Summer House G&Ts and get a party going."

"Not for me," Crista said, her smile oddly wide as she put her hand on her stomach and looked at Anthony. "Because we're celebrating, too."

"No way!"

"Get out!"

"Congratulations!"

Once again, a cheer erupted and hugs and handshakes were exchanged.

"But we do have something we wanted to talk to you and Viv about," Crista said, wrapping an arm around Anthony.

"I'm right here," Vivien called, joining them with Lacey. "Mom went for a walk. Did you tell them?" She gave a kiss to Crista. "So happy for you! And, yes, I told Lacey."

As they gathered, Eli stayed standing, glancing down at the boardwalk. With the lights, he could easily see his mother making her way toward the beach.

"She'll be okay," Kate said, coming up next to him and following his gaze.

"If she goes left, she's going to pass Jo Ellen," he said.

"Is that so bad?" Kate asked. "It's a day of change."

He sighed, not so sure if either one of them were ready for a confrontation with no kids around. But then he turned to the group where Crista and Anthony stayed standing, waiting for his attention.

"Here's the thing," Crista said, glancing at her

husband, who nodded and held up his hand to take over the speech.

"This is probably on me and I know I'm the in-law," he said, "but I know and love this family well enough to be honest. Cris and I are hoping that, as a family, we can come up with a different solution for Maggie. We are growing our household and we just…"

"You need privacy again," Vivien said, reaching from her seat to take Crista's hand. "We fully understand."

"I love Mama so much," she said, the Crista tears threatening. "But we're both worried—"

"No need to explain," Eli said. "We stand with you and will do what needs to be done."

"It's not as if she needs any assistance," Vivien said.

"She doesn't," Crista assured her. "But I don't want her to be lonely."

"If we keep this place…" Vivien raised a brow. "She could—"

"Whoa. Whoa." Eli raised his hand, glancing down to the beach. "Hang on. Potential fireworks ahead."

The others came closer until all of them were standing near the railing, watching as Maggie and Jo Ellen neared each other at the end of the boardwalk. They could see both women hesitate and stare.

"Oh, boy," Eli muttered.

"Moment of truth," Vivien said.

"This has to happen." Kate slid her arm around Eli's waist and looked up at him. "Otherwise we don't have a chance."

For a long moment, he just looked at her, rocked by

the fact that she was right...and she wanted that chance as much as he did.

"Hey, they're talking," Crista said in a hushed whisper. "Not screaming at each other."

They all stood stone silent, mesmerized by the sight.

"Should I take a picture?" Tessa asked. "This might never happen again."

"I can't believe it's happening at all," Vivien added.

And then their mothers stunned them all by sitting down on the top step of the boardwalk, facing the water, side by side, and—

"Are they laughing?" Kate asked on a whisper of disbelief.

"No!" Vivien exclaimed. "Maybe just talking."

"Or planning each other's death," Tessa deadpanned.

"I'm definitely making G&Ts," Jonah said. "Whatever is happening, someone's gonna need a drink."

Jonah went into the kitchen but everyone else stayed lined up at the railing, as though watching the best movie, with no sound. It lasted for what seemed like an eternity, but might have been ten minutes.

Ten minutes that Maggie Lawson sat on the white sands of Destin deep in conversation with Jo Ellen Wylie.

What was happening here?

"Oh, oh!" Tessa flicked her hand. "They're getting up. Everyone move or they'll know we're watching."

They all scurried away from the railing, laughing, finding seats to act normal. As if *anything* about this was normal.

Jonah came out with a pitcher and a stack of plastic cups and Vivien turned on the firepit and, in a minute or so, they were all seated and pretending not to be waiting for whatever would happen next.

"Think they made up?" Kate whispered to him.

"I don't know. I just..."

They heard noise on the first level. Women's voices. Footsteps. A sigh of...resignation?

All eight of them exchanged looks, no one daring to speak as they heard the sound of footsteps on the outside stairs and waited.

Finally, the two women walked onto the deck, both of them blinking at the sight of the eight family members sitting in an odd and uncomfortable silence.

They stood side by side, arms crossed, tension stretched like an invisible tug of war rope between them.

"You want to tell them, Mags, or should I?" Jo Ellen's voice was soft, but clear.

Eli felt his whole body straighten and his heart rate kick up. "Tell us...what?"

"We're staying," Maggie announced.

Did she say—

"Maggie has invited me to stay for the summer and I've accepted," Jo Ellen said, not reacting to the soft gasps from around the group.

Maggie nodded and slid a look sideways at Jo Ellen. "I'm staying here, too, which might upset a few apple carts, but, to quote my favorite character in literature, 'Frankly, my dear, I don't give a damn.'"

Staying...here? Eli never saw that coming.

"Does this mean...you've forgiven each other?" he asked.

"No one is forgiving anyone of anything," Maggie said. "All we want are answers. We have no idea who's at fault or what our husbands actually did."

"Or why," Jo Ellen added, sounding like that pained her more than anything.

"We each have small portions of the truth about our history and our husbands," Maggie continued, "and that has us frustrated and furious. We want to know what happened."

"We don't think we'll ever have the whole story if we stay separated," Jo Ellen added. "But here, together, we've agreed to try and recreate the missing pieces of the puzzle."

"So you've reached a truce?" Kate asked, leaning forward with a hopeful smile.

"We've reached a..." Maggie looked at the other woman. "Ceasefire. Nothing more than that until we know the truth."

"How are you going to get the truth?" Vivien asked.

"We aren't entirely sure," Maggie admitted. "But we have some ideas. We've made a promise to each other to be one hundred percent honest and share everything we know and can remember. We'll need help and patience and time."

"And..." Jo Ellen gave a wistful smile. "One more summer in Destin."

. . .

WHAT's next in The Destin Diaries? There will be promises made and promises broken, secrets revealed, romance deepened, and a new character who will hit the beach and change everything! Don't miss **The Summer We Made Promises**, the next book in The Destin Diaries.

Other family saga beach reads by
Hope Holloway and Cecelia Scott

Hope Holloway

Coconut Key
Shellseeker Beach
Seven Sisters

Cecelia Scott

Sweeney House
Young at Heart

~

Collaborations by Hope and Cecelia

Carolina Christmas
The Destin Diaries

~

Visit www.hopeholloway.com and www.ceceliascott.com
for details about all of their books!

About The Authors

Hope Holloway is the author of charming, heartwarming women's fiction featuring unforgettable families and friends, and the emotional challenges they conquer. After more than twenty years in marketing, she launched a new career as an author of beach reads and feel-good fiction. A mother of two adult children, Hope and her husband of thirty years live in Florida. When not writing, she can be found walking the beach with her two rescue dogs, who beg her to include animals in every book. Visit her site at www.hopeholloway.com.

Cecelia Scott is an author of light, bright women's fiction that explores family dynamics, heartfelt romance, and the emotional challenges that women face at all ages and stages of life. Her debut series, Sweeney House, is set on the shores of Cocoa Beach, where she lived for more than twenty years. Her books capture the salt, sand, and spectacular skies of the area and reflect her firm belief that life deserves a happy ending, with enough drama and surprises to keep it interesting. Cece currently resides in north Florida with her husband and beloved kitty. Visit her site at www.ceceliascott.com